H.I.V.E.

BLOODLINE

OTHER BOOKS BY MARK WALDEN

The Earthfall Trilogy
Earthfall
Retribution
Redemption

The H.I.V.E. Series

H.I.V.E. #1:
Higher Institute of Villainous Education

H.I.V.E. #2:
The Overlord Protocol

H.I.V.E. #3:
Escape Velocity

H.I.V.E. #4:
Dreadnought

H.I.V.E. #5:
Rogue

H.I.V.E. #6:
Zero Hour

H.I.V.E. #7:
Aftershock

H.I.V.E. #8:
Deadlock

H.I.V.E.

BLOODLINE

MARK WALDEN

SIMON & SCHUSTER BOOKS FOR YOUNG READERS
NEW YORK LONDON TORONTO SYDNEY NEW DELHI

SIMON & SCHUSTER BOOKS FOR YOUNG READERS
An imprint of Simon & Schuster Children's Publishing Division
1230 Avenue of the Americas, New York, New York 10020
This book is a work of fiction. Any references to historical events,
real people, or real places are used fictitiously. Other names, characters, places,
and events are products of the author's imagination, and any resemblance to
actual events or places or persons, living or dead, is entirely coincidental.
Text © 2022 by Mark Walden
Originally published in Great Britain in 2021 by Noodle Fuel Books
Jacket illustration © 2022 by Asaf Hanuka
Jacket design by Tom Daly © 2022 by Simon & Schuster, Inc.
All rights reserved, including the right of reproduction in whole or in part in any form.
SIMON & SCHUSTER BOOKS FOR YOUNG READERS and related marks are
trademarks of Simon & Schuster, Inc.
For information about special discounts for bulk purchases, please contact Simon &
Schuster Special Sales at 1-866-506-1949 or business@simonandschuster.com.
The Simon & Schuster Speakers Bureau can bring authors to your live event.
For more information or to book an event, contact the Simon & Schuster Speakers
Bureau at 1-866-248-3049 or visit our website at www.simonspeakers.com.
Interior design by Tom Daly
The text for this book was set in Goudy Old Style.
Manufactured in the United States of America
0622 SCP
First Simon & Schuster Books for Young Readers edition October 2022
2 4 6 8 10 9 7 5 3 1
Library of Congress Cataloging-in-Publication Data
Names: Walden, Mark, author. Title: Bloodline / Mark Walden.
Description: First edition. | New York : Simon & Schuster Books for Young Readers,
[2022] | Series: H.I.V.E. ; [9] | Audience: Ages 8-12. | Audience: Grades 4-6. |
Summary: Otto races against the clock to rescue his friends from a rival organization,
but as he desperately fights for his friends' lives, he ends up facing a deadly enemy who
is a twisted product of his own bloodline.
Identifiers: LCCN 2021047150 | ISBN 9781442494732 (hardcover) |
ISBN 9781442494756 (ebook)
Subjects: CYAC: Genius—Fiction. | Schools—Fiction. | Survival—Fiction. | Good
and evil—Fiction. | Artificial intelligence—Fiction. | Science fiction. | LCGFT:
Science fiction. | Classification: LCC PZ7.W138 Bl 2022 | DDC [Fic]—dc23
LC record available at https://lccn.loc.gov/2021047150

For Sarah, Meg, Chewie and Solo,
for getting me through 2020!

chapter one

Nero sat before an open fire—an entirely unnecessary, but comfortable, indulgence—in his office at H.I.V.E., staring into the flames and swirling vintage brandy in a large balloon glass. Nero did not believe in marking birthdays or anniversaries, viewing them as meaningless celebrations of arbitrary dates, but today was the one day every year that haunted him. It didn't matter how hard he tried to ignore the calendar, it was no good.

He looked up at the portrait of a beautiful young woman above the fireplace.

"Elena," he whispered, closing his eyes and, despite himself, reliving the memory of that day. . . .

Thirty years ago

The young man in his early twenties sat outside a café on the cobbled square, a half-finished espresso sitting on the table in front of him. He was watching the passing crowds carefully, as if he were looking for someone, his eyes darting from person to person, assessing them. Suddenly, he felt something hard press into his back.

"Maximilian Nero," came a woman's voice behind him. "I've waited a long time for this."

"You seem to have me at a disadvantage," Nero replied calmly, without turning round. "I'm impressed, it's not easy to sneak up on me."

"You forget, Nero, I know all your weaknesses," she whispered in his ear.

"And you forget, Furan, that I know all of yours." He placed a flat, rectangular box on the table in front of him, then slowly reached forward and lifted its lid to reveal a dozen exquisitely decorated handmade chocolates.

"Damn you, Max," the woman said. "Well played."

He stood up from his seat and turned to face her as she lowered the spoon she was holding to her side. He placed his hand on her cheek, drew her head toward his, and gently kissed her on the lips.

"I've missed you," he said, dropping his hand and placing it on the young woman's swollen belly. "Both of you."

"It's only been two days," she said, sitting down next to him with a smile. "I mean, every woman wants to be missed, but there's a fine line between devoted and pathetic."

"Which side of the line am I falling at the moment?" Nero asked with a broad smile.

"The chocolates just nudged you over into devoted," she replied.

"Good to know," Nero said. "So, how did it go?"

"About as well as expected," she said with a sigh.

"Elena, I told you it wasn't a good idea," Nero said gently. "Your sister will never accept us being together. There's too much bad blood between us. G.L.O.V.E. and your family have been at war for too long. She'll never forgive me for what happened in Bucharest, I'm not sure I'd expect her to."

"But you've left that world behind . . . for me," Elena said. She dropped her hands to her pregnant belly. "For us."

"You don't just walk away from that world with no strings attached." Nero shook his head. "I want peace between me and your family as much as you do, but Anastasia has never been the forgiving type."

Elena nodded. "It's just . . . well . . . the baby could come any day now and I thought that if she knew I was expecting a child, it might change how she felt, but . . ." She paused, took a deep breath, and put her head in her hands.

"Tell me," Nero said gently.

"I couldn't have been more wrong." Elena fought back tears. "I've never seen her so angry, Max, she scared me."

3

"It'll be alright," Nero said, hugging her as her tears finally came. "I promise."

"I just want us to be able to have a normal life with our baby," Elena said. "And for my family to accept that."

"We'll make a normal life for ourselves with our own family," he said, stroking her cheek. "We'll disappear, go somewhere no one will ever find us, and build a new life, together."

"I hope you're right." Elena sighed. "Anastasia said . . . She said she wouldn't allow this. You know what's she like, Max, probably better than anyone. My brother may be brutal, but at least there is a heart lurking in there somewhere. My sister is . . . Well, you know what she is."

"Which is why we're going to make that world part of our past," he said. "Stand up."

"Why?" Elena asked with a puzzled frown.

"Because I'm old-fashioned and I want to do this properly," he said as he helped her up from her chair. He dropped to one knee in front of her and took her hands in his. "Elena Furan, will you make a life with me, will you raise a family with me . . . Will you marry me, Elena?"

Elena gasped and put a hand to her mouth as he pulled a small box from his pocket and opened it to reveal an exquisitely cut diamond-solitaire ring.

"Of course I will," she said, pulling Nero to his feet and embracing him. "Of course I will."

He pulled the ring from the box and Elena extended her hand. Nero went to slip the ring onto her finger, surprised that his own hands were shaking, but the ring slipped from his fingers and fell to the floor.

"Clumsy, nervous idiot," he said with a chuckle, and bent down to pick up the ring.

Elena coughed, oddly. Nero looked up and saw the expression on her face and the crimson stain spreading across the chest of her white maternity dress.

"NOOOO!" he screamed as Elena's legs folded underneath her and she collapsed to the ground. He looked around desperately for any sign of their attacker but saw nothing. "Call an ambulance!" he bellowed, holding her to him as she struggled to breathe. "Somebody, please, help us!"

A quarter of a mile away, on the roof of a tower block, the sniper rifle fell from Pietor Furan's limp hands, his eyes wide with horror.

"Oh my God . . . No," he whispered. "What have I done?"

Present day

A few hours later, Nero sat in the hospital corridor outside the operating room, feeling like his world was collapsing around him. The voices of the people who walked past him seemed to be coming from a long way away as he sat, powerless to do anything while surgeons fought to save Elena and his child.

An exhausted-looking doctor walked toward him, and Nero felt his blood run cold when he saw the look on the man's face.

"You are the next of kin for Miss Furan?" the doctor asked, and Nero nodded, feeling the world start to spin around him. "I'm so sorry, there was nothing we could do. I'm afraid we couldn't save either of them. Is there anyone who we can—"

"No, no, no, no . . ." Nero saw everything he had hoped for: their future together, their family, their lives—everything scattered like ashes on the wind. He'd always thought that the idea of a heart being broken was a sentimental nonsense, but now, in this moment, he knew the truth of it. Something had been torn from his chest, something he could never repair or replace.

The doctor was still talking, but Nero couldn't hear him. All he could feel was grief, mixing with something hotter, more urgent; a rage unlike anything he had ever felt before.

He got up and walked out of the hospital and into the night, having no idea where he was, or where he was going.

Nero now shook himself from the memory, wiping the tears from his face as he stared into the fire. A few minutes later, he walked over to the bottle of brandy, pouring himself another glass, then went over to his desk and sat down. He tapped at the touchscreen mounted on its surface and pulled up a specific camera feed from within the school. The screen showed a figure in white pajamas, pacing back and forth in a featureless steel-lined cell. Nero tapped another button and a confirmation prompt popped up.

TERMINATE PRISONER YES/NO

His finger hovered over the yes button for several long seconds before he shut down the screen, letting out an enraged cry and flinging his half-full glass across the room. He slumped back in his chair and stared for a few seconds at the portrait of Elena.

"Not today, Anastasia," Nero said to himself. "Not today."

The man in the white coat made his way furtively across the room. He knew where the blind spots of the security cameras that covered the room were, and he moved quickly and quietly between them, sticking to the shadows. The banks of computer monitors that lined the walls filled the room with an eerie glow, the cables dangling from the ceiling casting strange shadows on the wall as the man squeezed between pieces of advanced scientific equipment that were, for the moment, still and silent. The man's head snapped around as he heard a soft chime from the far end of the room and he saw the heavy steel door rise quickly into the ceiling with a pneumatic hiss. He ducked down behind the base of a large robotic manipulator arm, as another man in black body armor carrying a bullpup assault rifle walked into the room. The man in the white coat held his breath as the security guard moved through the room. He stopped, scanned the room, and then raised his hand to his earpiece.

"Cradle lab secure, continuing patrol," the guard reported, before turning back toward the door.

The man hiding behind the robotic arm felt a moment of relief and ducked farther back into the shadows. His back pressed against one of the pipes lining the room, and he let out an involuntary gasp as it burned him. The guard wheeled around, weapon raised, advancing back across the room to where the man was hiding.

"Come out of there," the guard ordered. "Hands where I can see them."

The man in the white coat slowly stood up, raising his hands as instructed.

"I was just checking on the incubation units," he explained as the guard moved to within a few feet of him. "There was a drop in fluid pressures. Control knows all about it."

"First I heard," the guard replied. "This section's

on lockdown. You know the drill, no one in or out." He glanced down at the ID badge clipped to the other man's chest. "You'd better come with me, Dr. Higgs. We'll let Control decide what to do with you."

"Very well," Higgs replied. "But this is really most inconvenient."

The guard gestured toward the door, but just as he was about to follow him out, Dr. Higgs spun around, pulling a scalpel blade from the pocket of his white coat, and slashed at the guard's throat. The guard reacted just fast enough to avoid the strike, the blade leaving a long incision in his cheek instead. He backed away from the scientist, raising his weapon, finger tightening on the trigger. Behind him the robotic manipulator arm sprang to life, moving with impossible speed and precision as its massive, clawed hand snapped closed around the guard's wrist and twisted it hard, with a crack of breaking bone. The guard screamed, his rifle dropping from his useless hand and clattering to the floor, and the robot arm released his wrist and snapped upward, this time closing around the man's throat and lifting him off the floor. The guard flailed in the air, legs kicking, his good arm swiping uselessly at the metal clamp that was crushing his neck. There was a final, soft crunching sound and then he stopped struggling, his body hanging limply in the machine's grip.

Higgs stood there for a moment, mouth wide open before a voice sounded in his head.

Move. Now. His absence will soon be noted.

Dr. Higgs's expression shifted from shock to determination in an instant, and he strode past the dangling body and on toward the air-lock door at the far end of the room. He placed his hand on the scanner beside the door and it rumbled aside, revealing a short corridor lined with racks of white environmental-hazard suits. He walked straight past the suits and into another chamber where he was blasted from all sides by jets of white gas. Finally, he approached a door marked with an array of symbols warning of the many and various chemical, radiological, and biological threats to his life that waited on the other side of the door. He did not hesitate as he placed his hand on the scanner beside the door and entered the final air lock, then waited as the air cycled through the small chamber and eventually the glass doors ahead of him, marked with the words PROJECT ABSALOM, slid apart, granting him access to the cavernous chamber beyond.

At the far end of the cavern were a dozen large tanks, surrounded by an array of thick cables and pipes that fed into them like arteries. Higgs walked quickly past the banks of screens and monitoring stations that were spread around the tanks and headed toward a specific workstation just in front of the gently humming pods. He entered his credentials and quickly accessed the facility's network, hesitating for a moment as he stared at the blinking white cursor on the command console, unsure suddenly of what to do next.

Leave this to me, the soft voice inside his head said.

A moment later, Higgs felt his hands start to move, his fingers flying across the keyboard, entering complex strings of commands impossibly quickly. He watched the text flying past on the monitor, completely unable to make any sense of the code that he was entering. He was little more than a stunned spectator. A few seconds later, he let out a gasp, snatching his hands away from the keyboard as if it had burnt him. He flexed his fingers, which were now seemingly back under his control, and stared in horror at the display that now had a single phrase flashing in its center.

HIBERNATION SEQUENCE TERMINATING, SUBJECT DEPLOYING.

"No, no, no," the scientist mumbled to himself, shaking his head as if trying to wake himself from a bad dream. He heard that voice in his head again.

I've slept too long.

There was a hiss and several of the umbilical cables attached to the pod marked with the number nine detached with small puffs of white gas. There was a moment of silence, and then an alarm klaxon started to sound and warning lights above the pod started to flash.

"*Warning, biological arsenal integrity compromised, all personnel clear the area,*" a synthesized voice came over the loudspeaker. "*Storage tank nine release cycle complete in five, four, three . . .*"

Higgs backed slowly away from the tanks as pod nine split apart, opening to reveal a figure in a skin-tight black-rubber suit and breathing mask, who slowly stepped down from the pod, taking a couple of hesitant steps toward the terrified-looking man. Then, the black-clad figure reached up and released the straps at the back of their head and pulled the mask from their face. Higgs stared in horror at the teenage girl facing him. She had long, straight, bone-white hair, deep blue eyes, and a cold, predatory smile. Higgs felt a sudden deep and animal fear in his gut, every instinct telling him to turn and run as far and as fast as he could, but his legs wouldn't move. The girl approached him, staring into his eyes as she placed a hand on the side of his head.

"You've been very helpful," she said, her voice identical to the one he had heard inside his head. "So, I've decided that I won't make you suffer too much." She leaned in closer to the terrified scientist and whispered in his ear, "You're just going to *stop breathing.*"

The scientist staggered backward as he felt his legs moving under his control again. He gave a strangled gasp as he tried to inhale, feeling his lungs freeze inside his chest. He fell to the floor with a grunt, curling into a ball as he fought fruitlessly to draw one final breath. The girl watched impassively as he writhed on the ground and then finally lay still.

"This is going to be easier than I thought," she said, stepping over his body and heading toward the air lock. She passed quickly through the portal, the heavy steel doors rumbling aside to allow her to pass. As she entered the observation area beyond, she saw the first sign of concerted resistance to her escape, as a squad of heavily armed men in black body armor poured through the entrance, quickly taking up defensive positions around the only exit.

"Engage acoustic jammers," the leader of the squad yelled, tapping a button on the side of his own helmet. The other soldiers followed suit as they aimed their weapons at the girl, who was now standing calmly watching them in the center of the room.

"Get down on your knees with your hands behind your head!" the lead soldier of the security detail yelled, his weapon leveled at her chest. "This will be your first and only warning!"

"I'm not a fan of being told what to do," she said with a slight frown. "I think it would be much better if you *just gave me that gun*, don't you?"

The guard took a single step toward her and raised his weapon so it was leveled straight at her head.

"Your tricks won't work on us, girl," he said, his finger tensing on the trigger. "We know what you're capable of."

"Oh, but you don't," she said with a smile. "No one does."

Suddenly, the same whispered voice sounded in the heads of each of the soldiers.

Kill everyone except the girl.

Barely ten seconds later, the shooting had stopped and the girl stepped over the bodies littering the doorway and toward the one badly injured guard who was left alive. He dragged himself across the corridor floor, trying in vain to get away from her as she crouched down beside him and took the radio from the webbing attached to his body armor. She then placed her hand on the side of the wounded man's helmet and closed her eyes. Her lips moved in a soundless whisper, and the man gave a single agonized gasp before lying still.

"Thank you for your cooperation," she said as she stood back up and carried on down the corridor toward the blast doors at the far end. As she approached, she waved one hand toward the doors and they rolled apart obediently. On the other side of the room beyond, several technicians and scientists were gathered around an elevator door, watching as the numerical display above the door counted down toward their floor. One of the women at the back of the group turned and saw the girl on the other side of the room and let out a frightened cry.

"Oh my God," she said, yanking on the sleeve of the man next to her. "It's her. She got past the security team."

The others quickly turned to face the girl, their expressions a mixture of panic and terror.

"I'm afraid the elevator is . . ." She tilted her head to one side, and the elevator controls began to spark. ". . . out of order. Now, who's in charge around here?"

"I am the project's lead researcher," a nervous-looking man said, taking a step forward. "My name is Dr. Klein. Please, there is no need for violence, I assure you."

"Well, that's a shame," the girl replied. "You see, I'm rather fond of violence. It seems to . . . open such interesting doors." She looked at the other men and women behind Klein. "Do you have what you need to bring the other incubation tanks to maturity?"

"Yes, yes, I think so," Klein said, swallowing nervously.

"Good," she replied. "I have disabled all external communications with this facility, and the only way out is locked down and under my control. Please inform your staff that if they ever want to see daylight again, they will make sure that no harm comes to my brothers and sisters."

"Of course," Klein said. "Though some of the

subjects are approaching full maturity, like yourself. Do you want us to proceed with their development programs?"

"No," the girl replied. "I have my own plans for them. You and your staff just keep them safe. I'll be overseeing their . . . future development."

"Of course, miss . . . erm . . . What should I call you?" Klein asked.

The girl looked down at the barcode tattooed on her wrist. Below it were printed the words "Test Subject A99A."

"Anna," she said. "You can call me Anna."

"Can you believe we were ever that small?" Otto Malpense asked as he watched the group of first-year H.I.V.E. students preparing for their first grappler lesson, in the enormous cavern that was specifically outfitted for their training.

"I'm not sure Wing was ever that tiny," Laura said with a smile. The pair of them were sitting on the balcony, which afforded spectators a commanding view of the suspended concrete blocks that filled the cavern and the cold, dark water that lay waiting below for unwary students.

"I now have a mental image of a tiny, baby Wing doing self-defense drills in a nappy," Otto replied. "So thanks for that. I think."

"Awww, I bet he's adorable," Laura said with a chuckle, resting her head on Otto's shoulder. "Not half as cute as baby Otto, though."

"Once I'd finished cooking and they fished me out of the tank, that is," Otto said.

"Aww, you're the only clone of a long-dead megalomaniac for me, Malpense," Laura teased, poking a finger into his ribs.

"Hey, there's nothing wrong with a nontraditional upbringing," Otto replied with a smile. "Besides, it could have been worse, I could have been Scottish."

"That's fighting talk, Sassenach," Laura warned, her accent thickening as she leapt on top of Otto and began to tickle him.

"Easy there, Braveheart," Otto laughed. "You might damage billions of dollars' worth of cutting-edge cloning technology."

"You sure they got all those pesky chromosomes in the right place?" Laura asked. "Because you are a bit . . . well . . . funny-looking, to be honest."

"A face that only a cloning tank could love," Otto said.

"Exactly," Laura replied. "And when you combine that with the old-man hair, I can't imagine what anyone sees in you." Laura ran her fingers through Otto's snow-white hair, which was an unusual relic of his strange birth.

"You're right," he said. "Only a total weirdo would find someone like that attractive. . . ."

"They'd have to be stupid, or mad, possibly both," Laura said before kissing him gently.

"Hey, losers!" Shelby teased as she flopped down on the bench next to them. "Sorry to interrupt the tonsil hockey."

"Shelby, how *wonderful* to see you," Otto said as his friend put her feet up on the back of the seats in front of them. "Your timing is, as usual, impeccable."

"Hey, if a girl can't say hello to two of her best friends while they're enjoying a little private time in H.I.V.E.'s primo make-out spot, then I don't want to hear about it." Shelby grinned. "It's the little things that make life at the world's weirdest school bearable, you know."

"Is there something you needed, Shel, or are you literally just here to annoy us?" Laura asked, the slight edge in her voice suggesting that might be exactly what Shelby was doing.

"Oh . . . erm . . . no reason," Shelby said, her eyes darting toward the door. Just a couple of seconds later, the doors creaked open and Otto's best friend and roommate, Wing, walked out onto the balcony.

"Aah, hello . . . erm . . . everyone," Wing said, glancing at Shelby, who was trying very hard not to make eye contact with him. "I did not realize you would *all* be here.

I was just . . . erm . . . coming to inspect the balcony."

"Really?" Otto said, trying to keep a straight face. "Inspect it for what?"

"For . . . structural defects." Wing hesitated, now starting to look visibly uncomfortable.

"And I suppose you were going to help him, were you, Shel?" Laura asked. "I mean, with your background in architecture and everything."

"Perhaps you two could help?" Wing said enthusiastically.

"Oh, Wing," Shelby said, covering her face with her palm. "You are, without doubt, the single worst liar I have ever met."

"You mean you're not meeting up in H.I.V.E.'s . . . Oh, what was it again, Laura?" Otto asked.

"Primo make-out spot."

"That's it, H.I.V.E.'s primo make-out spot . . . for a rigorous health-and-safety inspection?"

"Oh, so that's what I caught you two doing?" Shelby shot back as Wing sat down next to her. "Nice try at a cover story there, big guy."

"I'm not good at improvisation," Wing admitted, looking slightly crestfallen. "You should know that after what happened on your birthday."

"I thought we swore never to speak of that again," Otto said with a grin.

"Oh, I know, but Shelby's face when the cardboard unicorn caught fire . . ."

"So, now there's just the four of us," Shelby said, "sitting here awkwardly watching the goblins try not to kill themselves the first time they use a grappler."

"You know I don't like it when you call the first-year students that," Wing said.

"What?" Shelby shrugged. "They're small, they smell, and they communicate in high-pitched shrieks . . . Goblins."

"It doesn't seem five minutes since that was us," Laura said, watching as Colonel Francisco, H.I.V.E.'s Tactical Operations tutor, demonstrated the basics of the grappler to the assembled students.

"They really are quite small," Wing said quietly.

"What about hobbits? Would that be less offensive?" Shelby asked.

A moment later, a soft but persistent chime began to sound from the thigh pocket of Otto's black jumpsuit—the standard uniform for all of H.I.V.E.'s alpha stream students. He pulled out his Blackbox communications tablet, and a moment later, the familiar blue wireframe face of H.I.V.E.mind appeared hovering in the air above it.

"Good afternoon, students," H.I.V.E.mind said, addressing all four of them. "According to my records, this period is a designated study window for your upcoming final exams. This is not, however, a designated study area; in fact it has a quite different pattern of behavior associated with it. As your designated academic supervisor, it is my responsibility to remind you that study is essential in the coming weeks if you are to achieve your full academic potential."

They all knew that it was no coincidence that they'd been assigned H.I.V.E.mind as their academic supervisor. It was precisely the sort of thing that H.I.V.E.'s headmaster, Dr. Nero, liked to do, to remind them that they were being watched just a little bit more carefully than the other students at the school. No one could blame him for his vigilance; the four of them had unfortunately earned their reputation as trouble magnets over the past few years.

"Awww, it's just like having your mom nag you," Laura said. "If your mom happens to be a massively sophisticated neural network, running a full sapience AI construct, that is."

"H.I.V.E.mom, I like it," Shelby said. "But does that make Nero H.I.V.E.dad?"

"If he ever hears you call him that, you're dead, you do know that, right?" Otto said, laughing.

"I believe my academic supervision is not being treated with adequate seriousness," H.I.V.E.mind said.

"Next you'll be telling us to tidy our rooms," Shelby said.

"Perhaps I should inform Dr. Nero of your reluctance to prepare for your finals," H.I.V.E.mind said, looking at each of them in turn. "He did mention that he had some new motivational techniques that he was keen to try out. Something to do with low-level neural reprogramming, using intensive localized shock therapy."

"Library?" Wing asked.

"Library," Otto replied.

chapter two

Anna sat at one of the terminals at the back of the Project Absalom control room, scanning through the files on the system at a super-humanly fast pace. Screen after screen of data flicked past, and the more she read about the history of the project and her own creation, the more frustrated she became. There were huge gaps in the data, technological advances that were half-understood or poorly explained, as if the authors themselves had barely understood the technology they were working with. She was aware of the scientists and technicians working around her and their occasional furtive glances in her direction. She doubted any of them would have the courage to try anything; they had all seen what had happened to the security team.

"Klein," Anna said. "Come here."

"What do you need?" Klein asked as he hurried over to her.

"What is this?" She tapped a dark area in the center of a three-dimensional scan of her own brain.

"Well . . . erm . . . we don't know," Klein said, looking uncomfortable.

"And yet, according to your notes, you went to a great deal of time and trouble to engineer subjects, like myself, with this precise abnormality," Anna said, frowning slightly. "Why would you do that if you don't know what it is?"

"We didn't design it," Klein replied. "We were just following someone else's instructions."

"Whose instructions?"

"They never told us," he said. "I asked once who the designer was, and it was made abundantly clear to me that those sorts of questions were very dangerous to ask."

"So, you know nothing about my creator," Anna said, sounding frustrated.

"No, only that . . . well . . . I don't think your designer was a person at all. That level of genetic engineering, with sufficient precision to produce these results, is unprecedented: a technological leap far beyond anything I've ever seen before. Only a machine could have designed you, but I don't know of any system with the computational power or cognitive capacity to even come close to that level of sophistication. As far as we can tell, the abnormality in your brain is an organic supercomputer that works in tandem with your own brain to massively increase your processing power and allow you to control your gifts, but who designed you to be this way and why is a mystery, to me at least."

"Who would know more?" Anna asked, still focused on the data about her own creation that was streaming past on the display in front of her.

"The only person who might be able to tell you more is Joseph Wright. He's the head of a group called the Disciples and they were responsible for constructing and funding all of this," Klein replied, swallowing nervously.

"It sounds like Mr. Wright and I should have a conversation, then," Anna said. "Where might I be able to find him?"

"Well, he's coming to you," Klein confessed. "He was keen to see some of the extraordinary progress we were making with your development. He's carrying out an inspection tomorrow."

"Oh, I'm sure we can still give him an interesting demonstration of the progress I've made," Anna said with a tight smile. "And perhaps he can give me some answers."

Maximilian Nero sat in the back of the luxurious motorboat as it skipped across the sparkling blue waters of the Pacific. He took a moment to enjoy the feel of the tropical sun on his face, watching as the boat rounded a rocky peninsula and headed toward a towering cliff face, topped by lush green jungle.

"I'm assuming you're wearing sunblock," Raven said as she returned from the brief conversation she'd been having with the man at the helm. "It's particularly important for people who spend most of their time living in caves, apparently."

"I suppose you'd prefer winter in Berlin?" Nero said with a wry smile.

"I've always worked best in the cold," she replied, sitting down in the seat opposite Nero.

"You should take advantage of this opportunity to relax, Natalya," he said. "I mean, was it really necessary to bring your swords?" He gestured toward the black carry case sitting on the seat beside her. "We are going to be among friends, you know."

"You know they help me relax," Raven said, placing one hand on the case. "Besides, you can never tell when things might get interesting with you around."

"Not today, hopefully," Nero said, removing his sunglasses as the boat entered the shadow of the looming cliff face. The man at the helm steered the boat straight toward the rocks, and a moment later it passed through the cliff face, like a ghost. They traveled on beneath the glowing holographic projectors that were concealing the entrance to the sea cave and slowly drifted farther into the cavern. There were lights mounted in the walls of the cave that continued to twist and turn as they headed deeper in, the channel just wide enough for their boat to navigate safely. A minute later, they came through a bright, illuminated archway and into a vast cavern filled with the busy sounds of heavy industry. In the center of the cavern was a vast, dry dock that was currently home to a massive submarine having its last few hull-plates welded into position. Nero waited as the boat docked at a nearby jetty, where a pair of armed guards were awaiting their arrival.

"Mr. Darkdoom sends his apologies for not being here to meet you in person," the guard said as Nero and Raven stepped ashore. "He's supervising a vital stage of the final armament loading and has requested that you join him on the assembly gantry." The guard gestured for them to follow his colleague, who was heading up the stairs toward the dry dock. Raven slung the black carry case over one shoulder and followed the guard, her head on a swivel as she took in their surroundings.

"Boys and their toys," she said as they passed into the shadow of the massive vessel, its smooth black hull towering above them.

Nero had never quite understood his friend's obsession with these enormous vehicles; he had always preferred a more subtle approach, but he could not deny the fact that Darkdoom's engineering projects had saved all of their skins on more than one occasion.

"Do try not to antagonize Diabolus too much, Natalya," he said quietly. "He's been working on this thing for months."

"You mean, don't make fun of the slightly too big submarine? Understood," Raven replied.

"Just let me do the talking," Nero said. "You just concentrate on lurking in the background looking dangerous."

"Well, you know what they say," Raven said with a smile. "When you find something you're good at . . ."

"Wait here, please," one of the guards said, holding up one hand.

A moment later, a metalwork platform mounted on the end of a giant robotic arm was lowered to the ground in front of them. The guard opened the gate leading onto the platform and gestured for Nero and Raven to step on board. As soon as they were both standing on the platform, it rose swiftly but smoothly into the air, lifting them up and over the massive submarine's superstructure and toward the huge conning tower that rose above its main deck. As the platform swung toward the gantry surrounding the tower, Nero could finally make out his old friend standing with three technicians around him as he pointed out something on a blueprint on the table in front of him.

The robotic arm lowered them the last few feet toward the gantry, and one of the technicians nearby hurried over and opened the gate.

"Max!" Darkdoom shouted, walking toward them as Nero stepped down onto the walkway. "It's so good to see you again. I'm sorry that I've been out of touch recently, but we're so close to completion on the project now that I must confess that I've been rather distracted by getting it finished."

"No need to apologize," Nero said, shaking his friend's hand. "I'm well aware of the amount of effort that has gone into this project. I must confess, though, that I'm still rather impressed by the progress you've made in such a short space of time."

"You'd be amazed what we can do now." Darkdoom gestured at the equipment surrounding them. "When you combine robotic assembly with the new nano-forging techniques we've been refining . . . well . . . let's just say, the sky's the limit these days."

"Now we just have to come up with a name for the damn thing," a familiar voice said. Nero turned to see an old man with long, white hair tied back in a ponytail and a full, but well-trimmed, beard walking toward them as quickly as his battered stick would allow.

"Hello, Father, " Nero said with a nod. "I hope you've not been making too much of a nuisance of yourself."

"Natalya, how lovely to see you again," Nathaniel Nero addressed Raven, ignoring his son completely. "Still managing to keep him alive, I see."

"I try," she said with a smile. "Not that he ever makes it easy, of course."

"You have the patience of a saint and the face of an angel, my dear," Nathaniel said before turning his attention to Nero. "Still keeping the world's villains from destroying the planet?"

"I do my best," Nero said.

"Well, let's hope your best is good enough, Maximilian," Nathaniel replied. "At the rate you've been crossing people off my client list, I won't have anyone to work for before long."

Nathaniel Nero was known to most of the world's villains as simply "The Architect": the man who had designed numerous hidden facilities and secret bases for their nefarious fraternity, including H.I.V.E. itself.

"They know the rules," Nero said. "No one gets to take over the world while I'm in charge."

The truth was that Nero's time as the head of G.L.O.V.E., the Global League of Villainous Enterprises, had been anything but peaceful. His attempts to restrain the worst excesses of his fellow global villains had not always made him the most popular leader of their organization. He might favor manipulating the world from the shadows, but that was not always the path that the more violent or deranged members of the council had wanted to pursue. His leadership was grudgingly accepted most of the time, but he was acutely aware of how precarious his position would be if the other members of the council sensed even the slightest hint of weakness.

"Max has been doing an exceptional job," Darkdoom said. "The Ruling Council is more unified than ever, thanks to him."

"Which just means that most of them aren't actively plotting to kill each other right now, as far as we're aware," Nero replied.

"Sounds like a win where G.L.O.V.E.'s concerned." Darkdoom grinned. "Anyway, enough shop talk. Let me introduce you to my new baby."

Darkdoom spent the next hour giving them a walking tour of the huge vessel, which was even larger and better equipped than his previous submarine, the *Megalodon*.

"So, now we just need a name," Darkdoom said as he stood beneath the huge curved bow of the sub.

"The *Overcompensator*," Raven muttered to herself under her breath.

"Natalya," Nero said quietly, with a slight frown.

"I still don't see what's wrong with my suggestion," Nathaniel said.

"I don't care how much you like Jules Verne," Darkdoom

said, shaking his head. "I'm not calling her *Nautilus*."

"I think you should just stick with *Megalodon*," Nero said. "It still seems fitting and would be a way to remember the crew who lost their lives on her predecessor."

"I was leaning toward something new, but I suppose you're right," Darkdoom said with a nod. "Very well, the *Megalodon* it is."

"Good, now that that's out of the way, we can concentrate on lunch," Nathaniel said, offering Raven his arm. "Now, Natalya, you must tell me what you've been up to, since I last saw you."

"I hope he hasn't been driving you too insane," Nero said to Darkdoom as Raven and his father walked away.

"Not at all," Darkdoom replied. "In fact, it would have been impossible to make as much progress as we have without his help. He may be old, but he's smarter than the rest of my design staff put together. The only real problem was that he . . . erm . . . he doesn't suffer fools gladly. There were a few . . . resignations."

"I'm wholly unsurprised to hear that," Nero said. He was well aware of what a ruthless taskmaster his father could be. His own childhood had been testimony to that.

"Have you made any progress in finding Joseph Wright or the rest of the Disciples yet?" Darkdoom whispered as they walked across the cavern.

"No, it seems that the loss of the Glasshouse sent

them all scurrying for cover," Nero replied, shaking his head. "We'll turn over the right rock before long, though, don't worry."

The truth was that the loss a few months before of their own training facility, along with the capture of their leader, Anastasia Furan, seemed to have shut down the Disciples' activity almost completely. It had been a quiet few months, and that always worried Nero far more than it should. He wanted to believe that their enemies had scattered into the night, but he knew that it was probably too much to hope for.

"Well, I'm happy to say that the *Megalodon* is finally ready for launch," Darkdoom said. "It will mean I can devote more time to G.L.O.V.E. again. I know that I've been distracted for a while, but once I'm back in the game, we can concentrate on shutting the Disciples down altogether, once and for all."

"It will be good to have you back, old friend," Nero said, putting a hand on Darkdoom's shoulder. "We need all the allies we can find."

Joseph Wright's helicopter touched down on the landing pad outside the Project Absalom facility and he stepped down onto the icy, wind-swept tarmac. He turned up the collar of his overcoat as he began to feel the chill of the Siberian wilderness that surrounded them. The laboratory buried far beneath his feet was one of the last surviving, fully operational Disciple facilities after the disastrous events of the last few months. They had been forced to enact a scorched-earth protocol, leaving no trace of the organization, for Nero and his hounds to follow. It had cost them a great deal of time and money, but it was the only way to stay hidden.

Now they just needed to give the Absalom lab time to complete its work. If they could succeed in cracking the flaws in the first generation of the Malpense clones, it would change everything. Finally they would have a weapon that they could use to eliminate Nero and his followers for good.

He walked to the nondescript shack next to the landing pad and spoke into the rusty grill next to the door.

"Request entry authorization. Code, Wright, Omega Nine."

A moment later, the door unlocked with a solid-sounding clunk and Wright stepped inside. He walked down the stairs on the other side of the door and into a gloomy basement illuminated by a single, naked bulb hanging from the ceiling. He pulled one of the coat hooks on the wall, and a large square section of the floor rose upward to reveal a clean, stainless-steel chamber. Wright stepped inside the elevator carriage, and it sank slowly back into the floor before picking up speed as it plunged down the single elevator shaft that led to the Absalom facility. The journey down always seemed to take longer than he expected. He thought back to a conversation he'd had with the facility's designer several years ago, when he had explained how important it was that the facility was located deep underground. It was not just to keep it hidden, but also so that it could be safely buried forever if anything went wrong.

The elevator reached the end of its journey and the doors slid open. Wright let out a gasp as he saw a white-haired girl smiling back at him.

"Hello, Joseph," the girl said. "My name's Anna. It's so nice to meet you."

She took a step toward Wright and he backed away from her, panic clear on his face.

"What have you done?" Wright asked, looking around the room at the pale, frightened faces of the scientists who were still sat at their stations around the laboratory. "How did you . . . ?"

"How did I free myself from the prison you put me in?" Anna asked, taking another step toward him. "Well, now, you see . . . That's a really interesting story. It seems one of your clever scientists added a little something extra into the mix when they made me. Something that lets me do this."

Take out your gun.

Wright heard her voice inside his head, its whispering

tone writhing and twisting its way into his brain. He felt himself become a passenger in his own body as his hand reached inside his jacket, his fingers wrapping around the cold metal of the pistol hanging in his shoulder holster. He pulled out the gun, his arm falling to his side. He felt paralyzed, like something was freezing his body in place no matter how desperately he willed his limbs to move.

Put the gun to your head.

Wright felt a sense of pure dread as he raised the gun to his head, pressing the muzzle hard into his temple.

Pull the trigger.

Click.

"Silly me, forgot the safety catch," Anna said, reaching up and taking the gun from his hand. "I think I've made my point, though. Why don't you take a seat, Joseph?" She gestured to a seat in front of a nearby workstation. Wright felt control return to his body and he staggered over to the chair, half collapsing into it, gasping for breath.

"What do you want from me?" he asked.

"Oh, it's really quite simple," she said. "You see, I've been doing my homework, and even though I've learned an awful lot about where I came from, it seems there are some rather large gaps in my history. You're going to help me fill in those gaps."

"There's a lot I don't know," Wright said. "I'm just in

charge of supervising this project. The information about where you came from, how you were designed, that was all kept compartmentalized. The only person who really knew what was going on was Anastasia Furan."

"Yes, that name kept popping up in my research," Anna said. "It seems that I need to have a conversation with this woman. Tell me, where would I find her?"

"You wouldn't find her," Wright said. "She was captured by Dr. Nero and his forces. No one has any idea where she was taken. I should know, I've spent months searching. We assume that he took her to his school, but nobody knows where that is."

"Well, now," Anna said, leaning closer to him. "How hard can it be to find a school?"

"This isn't just any school," Wright replied. "Believe me, many have tried and failed to find it, but its location is one of the best-kept secrets in the world. I can't tell you where it is and I'm not sure there's anybody else in the world who can, either."

"Oh, there's a way to find anything," Anna said. "You just have to know where to start looking."

"Are you coming to the gym?" Franz asked while performing a series of deep, lunging stretches right next to the desk where Nigel Darkdoom was trying to study for his finals. "I am having a new program; it is called Maximum Burn."

"I haven't got time right now, Franz," Nigel said with an exasperated sigh. "You go, I'll catch up with you later."

They had all been astonished by the change in Franz after their return from the Glasshouse mission. The junk-food binges were gone, replaced by multi-hour sessions at the gym. The change in his appearance had been dramatic and rapid. Where once there had been an overweight boy, there was now an increasingly athletic young man. The change in the amount of attention he had received from the female students of H.I.V.E. had been equally dramatic, and that had just accelerated the process further.

"Remember. All work and no play is making Jack the dumb boy," Franz said.

"Dull boy," Nigel corrected him.

"Yes, that too," Franz said.

"It's alright for you," Nigel said. "You're good at this politics and finance stuff. I can't make head nor tail of it. It just seems to me that money buys power and then power brings money."

"Yes, this is being called economics," Franz said. "You seem to have a pretty good grasp of the basics already."

"Yeah, well, call me old-fashioned, but I like my villainy to be a little bit more obvious and straightforward," Nigel said. "I thought I'd met some devious villains in the past, but then I started studying the stock market."

"Here, you should read this." Franz took a book down

from the shelf above his desk on the other side of the room.

"*Putting the Disaster into Disaster Capitalism,*" Nigel said, picking up the book and reading the title. "A *study in villainy and economics.* Sounds thrilling."

"I would be offering to help you study," Franz said. "But Claire asked me to help her study later."

"I thought you were helping her study yesterday," Nigel said, looking slightly confused.

"No, that was Clara," Franz said, looking slightly awkward.

"Right, sorry, it's hard to keep track of all your study partners at the moment." Nigel raised an eyebrow.

"You are still being my number-one study buddy," Franz said with a smile.

"Please don't ever call me that again," Nigel said, rubbing his temples. "Especially not in front of anyone else."

There was a sudden buzz from behind Franz, and he turned and pressed the entry button next to the door. The door slid open with a hiss to reveal Laura standing outside.

"Hey, guys," she said. "I was just wondering if you were up for hanging out later tonight. I found a site that's full of old 1950s B-movies that are free to view. Otto wanted to watch *Ray of the Saucer People,* but we outvoted him and it's *Night of the Moon Spiders* instead. You interested?"

"I would love to, but I am helping my study partner

tonight," Franz said, ushering Laura into the room.

"Which one? Louise?" Laura asked with a slight smile.

"No, it's Claire tonight, apparently," Nigel said.

"You're going to be needing some kind of roster before long," Laura said. "You should start charging tuition fees, you'd make a killing."

"I think I am being mocked," Franz said. "So I'm going to the gym. See you later, study buddy."

"What did he just call you?" Laura asked with a grin as Franz jogged away down the walkway outside their room.

"Please don't tell Shelby," Nigel said with a sigh. "I'm prepared to pay you if necessary."

"You can't buy my silence, Darkdoom," Laura teased. She glanced at the piles of papers and books scattered around his desk. "I've not seen you around the past couple of days. You okay?"

"Yeah," Nigel said rubbing his eyes, "I'm just spending every last minute studying and getting stressed about the finals. It's all very well for you big brains, but some of us actually find this kind of stuff quite hard. Do you know what I would give at this point to just be able to flick through a book and memorize it from cover to cover, like Otto can?"

"I think we'd all like to have that particular talent right now, wouldn't we?" Laura said, picking up one of the books on the desk. "But have you seen his combat-simulator scores? He may have a brain the size of a planet, but when it comes to shooting, he couldn't hit a cow's backside with a banjo."

"I know, but you're all *good* at something. I'm just *okay* at everything. You don't know what it's like to spend your whole life trying to live up to a surname. Maybe my mom was right all along and I'm not really cut out for this life after all. After my parents separated, my mom told me that she had always loved my dad, but that she hated this life and the things that it made him do. She just wanted something better for me than always having to live up to his legacy."

"Hey," Laura said, sitting down on the bed next to his desk. "I get it. After we were rescued from the Glasshouse, I wasn't sure if this life was what I wanted, either. The things we both went through in that place would make anyone question what they'd done to end up in a situation like that. No one would blame you if you didn't want any part of this world after that. I didn't tell people at the time, but when we got back from the Glasshouse, Nero offered me a choice. I could stay at H.I.V.E., or I could leave and return to my family, with no questions asked."

"I had no idea," Nigel said with a slight frown. "You chose to stay, obviously, but do you mind if I ask why?"

"Part of it was that I couldn't face losing you guys," Laura said. "Not just because of how I feel about Otto, but because you've all become the best friends I've ever had. It wasn't just that, though. I had a lot of time to think while we were locked up in that hole, and I came to realize something. Nero's not training us to take over the world, he's training us to make sure that people like Anastasia Furan never do."

"Are you trying to tell me that we're really the good guys?" Nigel asked.

"No, of course not," Laura replied, shaking her head. "But I think I'm starting to understand what Nero's been getting at all along. There's not really any such thing as good guys and bad guys, there probably never was. He's not training us to fight evil—he's training us to fight chaos."

"Which sounds like a fight worth fighting," Nigel said.

"Yeah, something like that." She gave him a wry smile. "Listen, ditch the books tonight and come and watch some stupid black-and-white movies with us. I promise it will make you feel better and there will still be plenty of time for studying tomorrow."

"Okay, you're right. I'll see you all later," Nigel said. "Though, if I'm honest, I'm with Otto—I think *Ray of the Saucer People* sounds much better."

"Too late, decision's made. *Moon Spiders* it is."

Laura stood up and headed for the door.

"We went through hell in that place, Nigel," she said, pausing in the doorway for a second, "and I don't think

I'd have made it through to the other side without you. If you ever need to talk, you know where I am."

Wright observed Anna, who sat on the other side of the room continuing to scan through the files on the facility's servers. As he watched, she paused for a moment, her eyes narrowing as something on the screen caught her attention. She grabbed Wright's pistol from the desk in front of her and walked over to the heavy blast doors that led back to the incubation chamber. The huge steel doors rumbled open as she approached and then closed behind as she passed through.

"Klein!" Wright snapped as he strode over to the terminal where the ashen-faced lead scientist of the project was working. "What the hell happened here? How did she get loose?"

"I don't know," Klein replied. "There was no indication of any abnormal cerebral activity from within the tank, we had no idea she was even awake. We think she used her abilities to exert control over one of our senior staff from within the incubation pod and manipulated him into helping her escape."

"What happened to the security detail?" Wright asked. "Why didn't they stop her?"

"They tried," Klein said, shaking his head. "She forced them to turn their weapons on each other. It was a massacre."

"There were a dozen men in that unit," Wright said with a confused frown. "How did she manage to exert control over that many people at once? The prototype had nowhere near that kind of power."

The prototype Wright referred to had been a modified clone of Otto Malpense that had been lost during H.I.V.E.'s assault on the Glasshouse. The engineers had amplified the Malpense boy's ability to interface with and control electronic devices, to the point where the prototype had been able to directly control the electrical impulses within a human brain. This had given the prototype the ability to manipulate and control the thoughts of others, but only one person at a time, and only for short periods. Much of the work that had been carried out since in the laboratory had been done in an attempt to amplify those abilities still further in the remaining clones. But none of the work they had done explained why Anna's powers seemed to be so much more potent than any of their previous experiments. If she could order a dozen men to murder their squad mates, men they had trained and worked with for years, then there was no telling what the true limits of her abilities might be.

"Are any of the other clones showing signs of these abilities manifesting?"

"Not as far as we can tell," Klein replied. "Several of

them are at the same level of maturity as the girl, but one of the first things she did was to put them into an even deeper hibernative state. It's like she doesn't want them to wake up yet."

"Maybe because they're the only things capable of stopping her," Wright said, rubbing his temples. "She mentioned that there was something different about her, that something had been added to her genetic makeup that was unique, special somehow. Do you have any idea what she was talking about?"

"No, in every meaningful way she was identical to the prototype," Klein answered.

"With one rather obvious exception," Wright said.

"Yes, but we were just experimenting around the edges. Modifying gender, physical strength . . . that sort of thing. All parts of our genetic makeup that are well understood. Nothing we modified could begin to explain why her abilities are so much more . . . worrying."

"Worrying seems like an understatement, Doctor Klein," Wright said, glancing toward the blast doors the girl had passed through a couple of minutes earlier. "Terrifying seems more appropriate."

"We can't let her leave this place, you understand that, right?" Klein said. "This facility is network isolated. At the moment she only has access to the data stored on our local servers, but if she gets out and makes a connection to the global network . . . well . . . I don't really want to think about what she might be capable of."

"The internet is dangerous enough, already," Wright said. "Do you have any other weap—?"

His question was cut short by the deep rumble of the blast doors sliding open again as Anna walked back into the lab. The two men fell silent.

"You. Come here!" Anna said, pointing at Klein. The scientist swallowed nervously and hurried over to where she was standing. "Look at this." She gestured toward the monitor next to her that was displaying a list of time-stamped entries.

"What am I looking at?" Klein asked nervously.

"Here," Anna said, tapping her finger on a specific entry. "A new encryption key was added to your network. Who added it and why?"

"This was just after Furan was captured," Klein said. "Control of the facility was reassigned from her to Mr. Wright. His encryption key replaced hers to ensure that the facility's security was not compromised."

"How did you enter Furan's key after she was captured?" Anna asked, turning toward Wright.

"She'd hidden a drive containing her encryption key," Wright explained. "After she was captured, I received instructions on how to find the drive and how I could use it to assume control of the project."

"The more I learn about Anastasia Furan, the more keen I am to meet her," Anna said, her eyes narrowing. "I've been talking to your systems. That drive didn't just contain a new encryption key, it was carrying an invisible passenger, a clever little worm virus that made a series of modifications to my genetic design before deleting itself."

"What are you talking about?" Klein asked, looking confused. "What sort of modifications?"

"I have no idea," Anna said, walking toward Wright. "But maybe you do?"

"I knew nothing about this." Wright held up his hands as she approached. "I was just acting on Furan's orders. I didn't know anything about any virus."

"Are you quite sure about that, Joseph?" Anna asked. As she came closer to him, he felt his body freeze, crippled by a sudden involuntary paralysis. "You wouldn't be so stupid as to keep secrets from me, would you?" She gently placed her hand on the side of his head. "Because the problem with keeping secrets inside your head is that they hurt so much on the way out."

A moment later, Wright felt a searing burst of agony explode inside his skull.

"That's just a little tickle," Anna said. "I can make it so much worse. Now tell me what Furan did to me."

"I swear, I don't know," Wright snapped, his voice an

anguished hiss. "I thought it was just a command-transfer protocol."

"You're quite sure about that?" Anna asked, tipping her head to one side. Another burst of overwhelming pain exploded inside Wright's head.

"Please, please stop," he gasped. "I don't know what she did. She traded in secrets her whole life. She never told anyone any more than they strictly needed to know."

Anna stared at Wright for a moment, studying his tortured face. A beat later, she turned back toward Klein with an exasperated sigh, and Wright collapsed to the floor behind her, as control returned to his body and the pain inside his head receded.

"Well, it doesn't seem like there are any more answers for me here," Anna said. "Joseph and I will be leaving now, Dr. Klein. I am leaving my brothers and sisters in your care. I would hope by now that I do not need to explain to you the consequences if something were to happen to them."

"Of course, I understand," Klein replied nervously.

"You're a long way underground," Anna said, turning and addressing everyone in the room. "If any of you ever want to see the light of day again, you'll do exactly what I say. Defy me, and I'll make this place your tomb."

Anna walked toward the elevator doors, willing them open with a slight mental nudge.

"*Come along, Joseph*," she said, and Wright felt the familiar sensation of his free will slipping away as he obediently followed her toward the waiting elevator. "*We're going to have so much fun together.*"

chapter three

"Deploy, deploy, deploy!"

Otto braced himself against the bulkhead of the Shroud dropship as the rear hatch slid open. He felt a firm, reassuring hand on his shoulder as Wing took up his place alongside him on the Shroud's rear exit ramp.

"Stay close to me," Wing instructed him calmly. He then jogged down the ramp and launched himself out into the void beyond. Otto followed him, running down the ramp and leaping off the end. He pulled his arms in tight against his sides, tucking into the most streamlined position possible. As his descent accelerated, the jungle-covered terrain below rushed up to meet him. When he was just six or seven feet above the treetops, the propulsion systems in his ISIS suit activated automatically, launching him on an arcing trajectory that skimmed the treetops and sent him rocketing toward his predefined target. A few seconds later, Wing dropped into position on Otto's right, their suits' automatic systems bringing them into close formation as they raced along at low altitude.

"*Time to target two minutes,*" a soft synthesized voice said in Otto's ear. "*Integrated Systems Infiltration Suit flight systems operating within nominal parameters.*"

Otto scanned the horizon ahead of them, looking for any sign of their destination. Slowly his suit's automated systems began to pick out unusual heat signatures in the dense vegetation ahead.

"I have visual," he said.

"Confirmed," Wing replied calmly. "Switching to manual control for final approach."

Otto followed suit using the haptic controls in the gloves of his suit to steer himself in a wider orbit around the target. The armor's thermoptic camouflage system engaged and his outline blurred, becoming all but invisible to the naked eye. As Otto scanned the cleared area of jungle, his systems highlighted the defensive positions surrounding the enemy compound, the onboard processors highlighting them with specific colors based on the perceived level of threat they posed.

"Quite a welcoming party down there," Otto said.

"Then it would be impolite to keep them waiting," Wing replied before swooping down toward one of the machine-gun nests that formed part of the defensive perimeter. He landed silently behind the two men manning the heavy gun; moving like a ghost, he incapacitated them each with quick, sharp blows to the back of the head. Otto landed beside the machine-gun nest, unslinging his Sandman rifle from his back.

"Control, we are on the ground," Otto said quietly into his helmet mic. "Confirming nonlethal engagement."

"Roger that, AF1, we have you in sight," Colonel Francisco replied. "Confirming nonlethal rules of engagement; we don't want to jeopardize our relationship with the locals."

"Understood," Otto said, gesturing with a knife palm toward the building in the center of the compound. Wing pushed ahead of him, moving from shadow to shadow, letting the suits' camouflage systems hide him as perfectly as possible.

"Hold AF1," Francisco said. "Patrol approaching your position from nine o'clock."

Inside Otto's helmet, a small projection appeared of the same live satellite imagery that Francisco was looking at, with their current position and the approaching patrol clearly highlighted. Wing froze in place, his suit rendering him near invisible as long as he remained motionless. The squad of six heavily armed guards passed within three feet of Wing's position, entirely oblivious to his presence.

"Hold . . . hold . . . ," Francisco said as the patrol

moved on. "Move now, your path is clear to the target building."

Otto and Wing moved quickly and quietly across the compound toward the low, concrete bunker in its center. A heavy steel door was set into the bunker wall with a palm-print scanner mounted next to it. Otto reached out with his abilities, using them to find and trigger the electronic lock release. The door popped open with the soft hiss of escaping air, and the two friends hurried inside. Beyond the door was a clear-plastic tunnel that led to an air lock at the far end. Otto hurried down the tunnel as Wing pulled the external door shut behind them. Otto bypassed the keypad lock next to the air lock just as easily, its heavy, locking pins retracting, allowing him to slowly swing the hatch open. He crept forward into the dimly lit room beyond, his weapon raised, slowly scanning the environment for hostile targets. As he moved carefully down the room, motion-sensitive lights in the ceiling began to flicker on and he could make out more details of the long racks of shelving filled with canisters that surrounded him.

"Control, we have breached the storage facility," Otto reported.

"Roger, proceed to target," Francisco responded.

"There," Wing said, pointing at refrigeration units at the far end of the room. Otto nodded and followed as he moved quickly toward the chillers. The walls around the refrigerators were covered in biohazard warning signs that made it clear that they had found exactly what they were looking for. Wing took up a defensive position covering the entrances as Otto disengaged the door locks and slowly opened the fridge. Inside was a small, stainless-steel case covered in a fine layer of frost. Otto picked up the case and did a quick mental translation of the Cyrillic script on its surface.

"Target acquired control, moving to exfiltration," Otto reported, slipping the case into a pouch on his belt. "Time to get out of here."

He and Wing hurried back down the room and through the air lock, heading back outside.

"Going somewhere?"

Four men were waiting outside for them, with their weapons raised; all wearing the distinctive black body armor of Disciple special forces. It was clear from how accurately they were aiming their weapons at Otto and Wing that the goggles they were wearing allowed them to see straight through their suits' thermoptic camouflage systems.

"Drop your weapons and hand over the package, and I'll make sure this doesn't hurt too badly," the lead Disciple soldier said.

"Do you know what this stuff is capable of?" Otto

asked as he placed his rifle on the ground before slowly pulling the metal case from the pouch on his belt. "Do you understand how many people are going to die if this is released?"

"Sorry, way above my pay grade," the soldier replied. "Not my problem."

"It will be your problem if they release this stuff," Otto replied. "Nowhere on earth will be safe."

"Hand it over, now!" the soldier growled.

"Okay," Otto said, sensing Wing tensing beside him. "But you have to wait three more seconds."

"Why?"

"Because that's how much longer I need to break the encryption on your comms system," Otto admitted cheekily.

Otto dived to his left as he issued the mental command overloading the speakers inside the Disciple soldiers' helmets. All four soldiers were instantly deafened by the ear-piercing screech that suddenly shattered their eardrums. The lead soldier's finger tightened instinctively on his trigger, and the barrel of his rifle bucked as he fired wildly into the air, where Otto and Wing had been standing just a moment before. Wing ducked under the hail of bullets, closing the distance to the nearest soldier and twisting the rifle from his startled hands. Wing drove the butt of the gun hard up into the chin of the staggered man, who folded at the knees, collapsing to the ground in a heap.

Otto dashed for cover behind a nearby low wall as Wing spun around, swinging the stolen rifle into the side of one of the other soldiers' helmets with a crunch. The man nearest Otto began to regain his composure, turning and leveling his rifle at Wing. Otto didn't have time to think—he just launched himself over the wall, hitting the soldier from behind and bringing him to the ground hard. He suddenly found himself at a distinct disadvantage as he grappled with the larger man on the ground, struggling in vain as the man pinned him and wrapped his forearm around his throat. Otto fought desperately, trying to throw the heavy assailant off his back, as the pressure on his throat increased relentlessly and he began to choke. Wing tried to reach him, running toward his friend to help, but the other remaining soldier intercepted, tackling Wing to the ground and sending them both rolling around in the dirt. Otto just felt himself starting to lose consciousness, when there was a sudden zipping sound, and the man on top of him collapsed on him, pinning him to the ground. Wing rolled over and drove a vicious blow backward with his elbow, straight into the gut of the man he was fighting, the air exploding from the soldier's lungs as he collapsed backward, winded. Wing spun around, springing to his feet and bringing one, booted foot up sharply under the staggered man's chin.

"Sorry, Otto," Franz's voice said in his ear. "I had to wait for a clear shot."

"No problems," Otto said, his voice still a slightly strangled croak. "You okay up there?" He glanced at the hillside rising up out of the jungle, over a mile from where he stood. Somewhere up there was Franz's concealed sniper's nest.

"*Ja*, I'm all clear here. I'll provide what cover I can for your exfil," Franz replied.

"Understood. We're on the move." Otto and Wing both quickly grabbed their abandoned weapons as all around them alarm sirens were blaring into life. The blind fire from the Disciple soldier may have missed its intended target, but it had done an excellent job of alerting everyone in the compound to their presence. Wing and Otto sprinted for the perimeter fence as startled, angry voices sounded out all around them.

"I've lost my camouflage system," Wing said as they reached the fence and took cover behind the low sandbag barricade at its base. An ISIS suit provided a great deal of protection, but the holographic-projection system that it used to camouflage itself was notoriously fragile. "You go. I'll try and slow them down."

"No way I'm leaving you," Otto said as they reached the fence. "Not an option."

"The completion of the mission is all that matters," Wing said, raising his head above the sandbags for a second and watching as dozens of soldiers began a concerted search for the intruders. "We cannot allow that substance to remain in the Disciples' hands. You know that as well as I do. The risks are just too great. Without my camouflage system, our chances of remaining undetected together are minimal. Go, I will try to make my own escape while leading them away from you."

"That's a load of . . ."

"*Aqui!*"

Otto's head snapped around just in time to see the guard who was running toward them raise the pump-action shotgun he was carrying and level it at Wing. Otto shoved his friend hard, pushing him to one side as the shotgun fired with an explosive boom. Wing dropped into a roll, before bringing up his rifle and firing one quick, accurate shot straight into the guard's chest. The sleeper round from the Sandman rifle fried the soldier's nervous system, dropping him instantly unconscious.

"Oh God, no," Otto gasped, raising his bloodied hand from his hip, where a few stray pellets had made it past his armor and found their mark.

"It's okay, Otto," Wing said, rushing over to his fallen friend. "It's not that bad, he barely scratched you."

"No, you don't understand," Otto said, holding up the

shattered remains of the box from the refrigerator.

Three words began to flash red on the head-up display inside Wing's helmet.

AIRBORNE PATHOGEN DETECTED

"Okay, pull them out," Colonel Francisco said.

"Exercise terminated," H.I.V.E.mind responded. "Holographic projectors and variable geometry force fields offline."

Otto picked himself up off the floor of H.I.V.E.'s holographic training area, blinking away the few seconds of disorientation that came with the transition from the virtual world to the real one. The accuracy of the simulations that H.I.V.E.mind ran within the chamber was such that it was nearly impossible sometimes to tell the difference between the two.

"Two weeks, gentlemen," Colonel Francisco said, marching across the room toward them. "That's just fourteen days until you receive your final combat-operations assessment grades. What do you think that grade would have been if it had been assigned on the basis of today's performance?"

"Is a high B a little bit too optimistic?" Otto asked.

"H.I.V.E.mind," Francisco said. "Would you be so kind as to give me your casualty projections on the basis of their performance in this simulation."

"The release of a weaponized pathogen of this type would result in the death of ninety-two point three percent of the world's population."

"That is indeed many people," Wing said, looking slightly embarrassed.

"A low B, then," Otto adjusted with a grimace.

"Don't push your luck, Malpense," Francisco growled. "You're too reliant on your special abilities and you're unwilling to make sacrifices when they need to be made. Why do you think I threw Fanchu's suit malfunctioning into the simulation?"

"Because you knew I wouldn't be prepared to leave him behind," Otto replied.

"Exactly," Francisco said. "One life versus . . . What was it again?"

"Ninety-two point three percent of the global population," H.I.V.E.mind responded. "A total of approximately seven point one billion peop—"

"Okay, okay. I get it," Otto said, holding up his hands in surrender. "I can do the math for myself."

"Then you'd better learn how to make the hard calls," Francisco said. "Because the world we operate in doesn't leave much room for compassion. You're ruthless or you're dead, nine times out of ten."

"Understood," Otto said with a nod.

"Two weeks, gentlemen," Francisco repeated, looking them both in the eye before turning and marching out of the simulation chamber.

"I sense that the colonel was somewhat disappointed

in our performance," Wing said as they walked back toward the changing rooms.

"That's remarkably observant of you," Otto said. "What gave it away?"

"I think we should take what he said seriously." Wing frowned. "Our performance today was . . . inadequate. If we are to succeed in our final assessment, perhaps we should be more ruthless, as the Colonel suggests."

"Says the man who doesn't like guns," Otto said, rolling his eyes. "I hear what Francisco's saying, but after everything we've been through over the past couple of years, I guess I'm just not in the mood to be lectured on the importance of making sacrifices. That's one lesson we've all had to learn, the hard way."

"Yes, I suppose you're right," Wing said, sitting down on one of the changing-room benches. "To be perfectly honest, I'm more worried about what we're going to do when we leave H.I.V.E."

"With our skill sets? Pretty much whatever we want," Otto replied. "But if you're asking what my specific plans are . . . well . . . I haven't the faintest idea. I suppose I could go into banking."

"You are many things, my friend," Wing said with a slight smile, "but you're not that evil."

The two of them walked out of the changing rooms and found Laura and Shelby waiting for them outside, laughing as they looked at something on Laura's Blackbox.

"Hey!" Shelby said, looking up with a broad grin. "It's the planet killers!"

"Remind me what we find attractive about these two, will you?" Otto said to Wing as the four of them walked down the corridor.

"How many people was that again, Laura?" Shelby asked.

"Seven point one million . . . No, sorry, silly me. Seven point one *billion* people dead."

"Hey, I was trying to protect your boyfriend, Shel," Otto said.

"Good job there, Mr. Protector," Shelby said. "But isn't he now dead from a spooky made-up plague, too, technically speaking?"

"Possibly," Otto said. "He might have just contracted it deliberately, though, to get away from his girlfriend."

"Shelby, you'll never guess who got a higher combat-assessment score than Otto," Laura said, showing her the screen.

"Go, Nigel!" Shelby said. "Looks like he only killed himself. That's a lot less than . . ."

"Seven point one billion," Laura said. "Almost exactly seven point one billion less, in fact."

"This," Otto said, looking at Wing, "is going to be a long evening."

• • •

Joseph Wright's helicopter flew low over the skyline of Saint Petersburg, heading for a collection of large, gray buildings in the distance. Anna sat staring out of the window at the bustling world below. She could sense the chaotic, digital hiss of network traffic all around her, almost overwhelming her extraordinary senses. Wright sat slumped unconscious in the seat next to hers. She needed to maintain her control of the helicopter's pilot, which was much easier when she didn't have to worry about Wright attempting something stupid. She could always wake him when he was needed.

She concentrated on trying to make sense of the world that was flying past beneath her. She had sensed the internet as soon as Wright's helicopter had flown over a city, but it was an overwhelming amount of data to try to absorb. She knew that if she was going to find what she was looking for, she would need a great deal more processing power at her disposal to help her cut through the noise. The Disciples' data network had been remarkably helpful in identifying a facility that would have what she needed, but getting access to her prize would be something she would have to do in person.

"Traffic control is demanding to know why we have deviated from our preassigned flight path," the helicopter pilot said, his voice uncannily neutral. "How should I respond?"

"Say nothing," Anna ordered. "Just put us on the ground as close to those buildings as you can." She pointed at the collection of nondescript concrete blocks ahead. "Leave the rest to me."

The pilot gave a quick nod and sent the helicopter banking into a sharp turn, heading for an open area in front of the main building. As he brought the helicopter carefully into land, numerous armed guards poured out of the main entrance toward the aircraft, weapons raised.

"Come along, Joseph," Anna said, willing the sleeping man back to consciousness. "Let's go and see your friend."

She stepped down from the helicopter, slowly walking toward the lead soldier with her hands raised in surrender.

"Down on your knees!" the soldier barked at her in Russian. "Hands on your head!"

Anna reached out with her abilities, brushing against the man's unconscious mind and tapping into the language center of his brain.

"There's really no need for that," she said calmly, in perfect Russian. "In fact, I think it would be much better if you *just took me to see your commanding officer*."

There was a fleeting look of confusion on the soldier's face, and he shook his head slightly as if he was experiencing a moment of dizziness.

"Yes, that would certainly be the best thing to do," he replied then, with a slightly robotic edge to his voice.

"Why don't you *put those handcuffs on me*." Anna gestured at the shackles hanging from his belt. "I'm sure that would make all of your friends much less nervous." She held her hands out in front of her, wrists together. The soldier took the cuffs from his belt and snapped them closed around her wrists with a nod. Anna willed another soldier who was standing nearby to cuff Wright.

"Now, why don't we get inside out of the cold," she said with a smile. "I'm sure your friends can look after our helicopter for us, can't they?"

Anna's new puppet gave a quick nod and then barked an order to the other soldiers, who quickly formed a perimeter around the trespassing aircraft. The soldier placed a hand on Anna's shoulder and pushed her toward the main door of the looming concrete building.

"I am taking the intruders to see the commander," the soldier said as they passed through the security checkpoint on the other side of the doors.

"Have they been searched?" the guard manning the checkpoint asked.

"There is no time, this is urgent. I will take full responsibility," the brainwashed soldier replied.

"Very well," the guard said with a slightly confused frown. "As you wish, sir."

The heavy glass security door ahead of them slid open, and the soldier led them farther into the building. They walked for several minutes down a succession of feature-less gray corridors lined with identical stainless-steel doors. To the casual observer, this building would look more like a storage facility than one of the most import-ant hubs of international espionage. The soldier suddenly stopped in front of one of the doors and rapped on it smartly with his knuckles.

"Enter!" a voice snapped from inside, and the soldier opened the door, ushering Anna and Wright before him.

The overweight man on the other side of the room turned away from the monitors mounted on the wall, which were currently displaying multiple angles of the helicopters sitting in the courtyard outside. The name plaque on his desk read COLONEL KUZNETSOV, but the non-descript dark suit he was wearing suggested his military rank had not been earned on any battlefield.

"I don't like uninvited guests," the large man growled. "Wait outside, Yahontov. I will call you if I need you."

Anna willed the soldier to obey his commander's instruction and take up position in the corridor outside.

"I wish I could say it was a pleasure to see you, Joseph," Kuznetsov said. "Given the nature of our last meeting, I will at least applaud your audaciousness coming here."

He pulled a large, black pistol from the shoulder hol-ster under his jacket and placed it on the desk in front of him.

"Now, explain to me why I shouldn't have you both just thrown in the gulag?"

The colonel stared for a moment at Wright's oddly blank expression.

"What's the matter, Joseph?" Kuznetsov asked. "Cat got your tongue?"

"No," Anna replied. "That would be me. . . ."

She reached out and seized control of the colonel's mind, feeling only the slightest resistance to her mental domination.

"It's so much easier with men who are used to following orders," she said with a smile. "Now, why don't you just sit down like a good boy and listen carefully while I explain what you're going to do to help me."

Kuznetsov did as he was instructed, almost collapsing into the chair behind him.

"Joseph tells me that you and he had come to an arrangement," Anna said. "You would place a back door into your systems for the Disciples, and he would make sure that your president would never find out about your Swiss bank account and all the lovely CIA money that it contained."

"That is correct," Kuznetsov replied, his voice flat and emotionless.

"Excellent," Anna said. "Because, you see, I would really like to be able to access that back door. There's someone that I need to locate, and your clever little computers are going to help me find them. Understood?"

"Of course. We will need to use one of the secure-access terminals in the processing core."

"Why don't you show us the way," Anna said, holding out her cuffed wrists. "And I don't think we'll be needing these anymore."

Kuznetsov opened his desk drawer and pulled out a small set of keys before walking over to Anna and Wright and uncuffing them both.

"Please, follow me," he said, opening his office door and gesturing toward the corridor outside.

"You will resume your duties," Anna told the soldier standing guard beside the door. "There is absolutely nothing unusual about anything that has happened today, do you understand?"

The soldier gave a quick nod and marched away as Anna slowly let his free will return.

A couple of minutes later, she stepped out of the elevator that had brought them down to the facilities' central processing core, buried far beneath the ground. Racks filled with high-powered servers spread out from the central core, where a liquid-nitrogen-cooled quantum computer sat in a large glass cylinder. Anna approached the core, staring up at the twisted golden pipes of its cooling structures, the intricate metalwork making it look more like a piece of abstract sculpture than one of the most powerful computers on the planet.

"Magnificent," she said, placing her hand against the cool glass. "So much power, so much potential, and yet they keep you locked up in a cage."

A female technician hurried toward them wearing a white, protective environment suit.

"Please don't touch the core," the technician said. "This is supposed to be a clean room environment, where are your suits?" A moment later, she noticed the colonel standing off to one side. "I'm sorry, sir, I didn't realize these people were with you. I didn't know we were due for an inspection. Is there anything specific I can—"

Without warning, the technician dropped to the ground unconscious as Anna scrambled the electrical activity within her brain.

"I'm afraid we really don't have time to follow proper procedure," Anna said, looking down at the unconscious woman. "Now, Colonel Kuznetsov, perhaps you could show me how to access your back door so we can get this over with."

The colonel walked over to a nearby terminal and began to enter a series of commands. A minute later, he turned back toward Anna and Wright.

"It is done," he said with a nod.

"Good," Anna replied, then gestured toward the keyboard. "Now, Joseph. If you would be so kind . . ."

Wright quickly entered the last few commands that gave the Disciples access to the crown jewel of the Russian intelligence services.

Anna began to use her abilities to gently probe the firewalls and other network protection layers that surrounded the core. Where once there had been layer upon layer of encrypted, digital defenses, there was now a wide-open path through which she could access the system and tap into its enormous power. Even with her unique abilities, it would have taken hours to brute-force her way past the defenses, time she did not have. Exploiting human weakness to circumvent the network's protection layer was far more efficient.

She silently commanded the colonel and Wright to stand watch over her as she allowed her conscious mind to fade away so she could more perfectly interface with the digital world around her. The datasphere was huge, almost overwhelming her with its complexity: binary pathways racing away in all directions, twisting and turning in an impossible-to-solve Gordian knot. Anna tried to relax, allowing the supercomputer inside her own brain to naturally interface with the elaborate network surrounding her. The rush of power that she felt was wonderful and terrifying all at the same time. She had a sudden sensation of being in countless different places at once, privy to secrets that people never dreamt would be revealed. She was distinctly aware of the whole great game of espionage that was being played out around the world, all at once—the jerking puppets on the political stage and the shadowy puppet masters who controlled them. Rigged elections, bribery and blackmail, sleaze and corruption of every kind. All in the service of the greedy few, whose power and privilege insulated them from the worst horrors of a world that was threatening to boil over at any moment. Anna pulled back from the network, the disgust that she felt only stiffening her resolve.

"Time to start again," she whispered to herself.

But to do that, she would need answers that only Anastasia Furan could provide. She had studied the Disciples' files on Dr. Nero and his school, but they had contained no clue as to the hidden facility's location. She had found one interesting detail, though, a crack in H.I.V.E.'s armor of secrecy. The power of the computer within this facility would allow her to exploit that flaw, at least in theory.

As she concentrated, she felt the processing cycles of the supercomputer within her own skull and the one floating in the glass tank synchronizing and falling into harmony with one another. She let her digital consciousness expand outward, just skimming the surface of the sea of data that the network contained, looking for a very specific, unique signature. Anna searched for what might have been an eternity or a millisecond—it was impossible to tell within the confused relativity of the data space—and finally she sensed something: the faintest trace of her prey. It exerted just the lightest touch on the network, almost invisible to all but the most determined hunter, but to Anna it was like a glowing thread leading back to its source.

"Hello, there," she said with a satisfied smile.

chapter four

"Malpense!" Block said, advancing toward Otto across H.I.V.E.'s dining hall, with his friend Tackle close behind him. The two heavily muscled boys were well known for being particularly obnoxious members of H.I.V.E.'s brutal henchman stream.

"Here we go," Otto said under his breath, sensing Wing tense beside him.

"Sorry," Block said as he approached. "I mean . . . er . . . Otto. It's nice to see you and your friend Wing again."

"Yes," Tackle said. "We both wanted to take the opportunity to say hello. I hope we're not interrupting anything."

"Erm . . . noooo," Otto said with a sideways glance at Wing, who was sporting his traditional confused frown.

"Good, because we've both been taking part in Miss Leon's Mindfulness and Meditation group and we've had an . . ." He paused and pulled a piece of crumpled paper from his pocket before reading from it. "An epiphany."

"Yes, one of them," Block said, nodding enthusiastically.

"We have realized that by"—Tackle glanced down at the paper again—"exhibiting needless aggression toward you, we have just been externalizing our own inner pain."

"Which is bad," Block said, "and can have a negative effect on your ability to center yourself."

"Yes," Tackle replied. "So, we would like to try to make amends for our past mistakes by offering you an apology."

"Erm . . . Great . . . Apology accepted," Otto said, trying to keep a straight face. "Right, Wing?"

"Hrrmm," Wing said.

"Good, thank you," said Block, turning to Tackle. "Who's next on the list?"

Otto and Wing watched as the two henchman students walked away, straight past the table where a rather tall, buff, good-looking boy who had once been Franz Argentblum sat with three girls who were *laughing at his jokes*.

"I cannot pinpoint the precise moment we entered a parallel universe," Wing said calmly. "But the evidence is undeniable."

"You two okay?" Shelby asked as she and Laura sat

down beside them. "You look like someone just told you that Nero used to be a ballet dancer."

"Really? Not this again," Laura said with a sigh.

"What?" Shelby said. "I think he'd look good in tights."

"No, everything's fine," Otto said. "Super weird, but fine."

"That should be our target for every day here: 'Super Weird, But Fine!' Shelby said, painting the words in the air with her hands.

The hall was suddenly plunged into pitch darkness.

"Okay, that might have been my fault," Shelby said, somewhere in the blackness.

A moment later, some of the lights came back on, but the way that they occasionally flickered and dimmed suggested something was definitely wrong.

"There he is!" There was a certain commotion on the far side of the dining area as Professor Pike entered the room, flanked by a pair of H.I.V.E. security guards. He pointed straight at Otto, and the two guards marched toward their table, grabbing Otto by his upper arms and dragging him to his feet. The others all rose to their feet as Professor Pike hurried across the room to them.

"You are to stop whatever it is that you're doing to H.I.V.E.mind right now, Mr. Malpense," the professor said angrily. "I thought that we'd got past this kind of behavior from you!"

75

"I've got no idea what you're talking about," Otto replied, sounding confused. "I'm not doing anything."

"Then explain this!" the professor said, holding up his Blackbox. On the screen Otto could see a live feed of H.I.V.E.mind's processor load. It looked like the AI had shut down every nonessential process in an effort to withstand a massive and concerted effort to break through the firewalls surrounding his own data core. Otto looked at the digital signature of the intruder that was hammering at H.I.V.E.'s virtual walls and felt a certain cold dread in the pit of his stomach.

"I can see perfectly well why you think I might be responsible," he said, staring at the screen. "But I swear to you I've got nothing to do with this."

"What's going on?" Laura said, glancing down at the display Otto was holding.

"Something . . . Someone is trying to hack H.I.V.E.mind," Otto replied.

"They're not just trying," the professor said. "At this rate they may very well be succeeding."

"We need to get down to H.I.V.E.mind's data core now," Otto said. "There might be something I can do to help him."

"H.I.V.E.mind put me through to . . . damn it . . ." The professor jabbed irritably at the screen of his Blackbox. "Use secondary comms systems—we can't rely on H.I.V.E.mind for anything until we've stopped this attack."

"Understood," Otto replied. "Laura, I'm going to need your help. No one knows this place's systems half as well as you do, and I have a horrible feeling that if this hacker is who I think it is, we're going to need all the help we can get."

"I'm with you," Laura said with a nod.

"What about us?" Shelby asked.

"You guys stay here," Otto said. "I'm sorry, but I don't think you can help us with this."

"Yeah, this does sound more like your kind of thing." Shelby frowned. "You guys go help Big Blue."

Wing gave Otto a quick nod, and the others watched as Laura, Otto, and the professor hurried out of the dining hall, heading for the data core.

"I'd forgotten how much I hate touchscreens," the professor said as he wrestled with the backup interface on his Blackbox. "Ah, there we go."

"This is Central Control, Professor," a voice said over the Blackbox's speaker a moment later. "We're seeing major system outages across the board up here. Some of the emergency backups are coming online, but a lot of the secondary systems are going to be unavailable until we get H.I.V.E.mind back."

"How far out are Nero and Raven?" Professor Pike asked.

"ETA is fifteen minutes from now. We have them on radar but external comms are down. We've not been able to update them on the current situation."

"They'll know something is wrong when they can't contact us," Pike said. "Nero will order the pilot to burn the engines out of that Shroud once he realizes. Contact me as soon as they are on final approach."

"Understood."

They hurried along the corridor, passing through groups of H.I.V.E. students who were looking up at the flickering lights in the ceiling with concern.

"We're on secondary power generators," the professor said. "I had to put the geothermal power core into fail-safe lockdown when all this started. We couldn't afford to lose magma containment."

"Yeah, that does sound like it would be bad," Laura said, shooting a worried glance in Otto's direction.

"I've never seen this much raw computational power being thrown into a single attack before," Pike said. "The attack originated in Saint Petersburg which can only mean the Russian cyber-command facility and I know they have been experimenting with quantum computing technology, but even that would not explain this. H.I.V.E.mind is a generation beyond anything that any of the global security agencies have at their disposal, even the Chinese. So where is the rest of the power for a brute force attack like this coming from?"

"You said you thought you might have an idea who was behind this," Laura said. "You . . . don't think . . ."

"Overlord's dead," Otto said, shaking his head. "But this might be worse."

They had all suffered at the hands of Overlord: the insane artificial intelligence that had created Otto as an organic shell to contain itself. The final battle with Overlord had cost their friend Lucy Dexter her life, but it had ended with the murderous AI being consumed by nuclear fire. Nothing could have survived that.

They arrived at the heavy steel doors leading to H.I.V.E.mind's data core, and the professor set them rumbling aside with a command from his Blackbox. Otto had visited H.I.V.E.mind's data core many times, but he had never seen it like this before. The black monoliths that surrounded the central platform usually pulsed with slow-moving blue patterns, but now they were lit with a blinding white-blue light, their surfaces hissing as their liquid-nitrogen super-cooling systems fought to keep the data core from overheating under the strain of the massive attack. H.I.V.E.mind's blue wireframe head hung above the white pedestal in the center of the room, but it kept distorting in unsettling ways, almost like it was being pulled apart.

"Miss Brand," the professor said, gesturing toward

a control panel on the far wall, as the doors rolled shut behind him. "Would you be so kind as to initiate an emergency coolant flush."

Laura hurried over to the large touchscreen display and began punching in commands as Otto walked slowly toward H.I.V.E.mind's ever-shifting head. He mentally triggered the handshake protocol that he usually used to initiate direct, digital communication with H.I.V.E.mind, but there was no response. He cautiously allowed himself to directly connect to the data core, feeling the familiar sense of disorientation as he left his physical body behind and entered the virtual space within. What he found was utter chaos.

The network's defenses were visibly crumbling before the red wave that was repeatedly hammering against them. Otto could see why H.I.V.E.mind was silent. His friend could not afford to sacrifice a single computational cycle in communication, not when he was so obviously fighting a losing battle. Otto reached out with his abilities, allowing the organic supercomputer that Overlord had engineered into his brain to connect to H.I.V.E.mind's data core, hoping to bolster his defenses. The instant he connected, the red wave swept toward him, moving impossibly quickly and swamping him in a torrent of junk data that began to eat away at his consciousness. He rolled within the crimson torrent, completely disoriented, as whispered voices came from all around him, their sinister tones crawling across his mind, willing him to just stop resisting, to give in to the digital undertow. There was something hauntingly familiar about the voices, something that sent a cold shiver down his spine. Otto felt his conscious mind slipping away, realizing with a strange certainty that the voices were right and that he should stop fighting. There was a sudden, blinding flash of blue light, and Otto felt himself being plucked from the red flood and being thrown through the air. A moment later, he collapsed onto the floor of the data core as Laura rushed over to help him.

"I have to go back in there," he said through gritted teeth as he tried to stand. His knees gave way as he felt searing pain lance through his skull. "He . . . he . . . threw me out, H.I.V.E.mind, because he's losing."

There was a flash from the center of the room and H.I.V.E.mind's head tipped back, letting out an unearthly digital howl before everything went black.

"What happened?" the professor asked, somewhere in the darkness.

"Nothing good," Otto replied.

Around them, red lights began to slowly play across the surfaces of the processor monoliths that surrounded the core. The patterns began to pulse more urgently, picking up speed until finally an indistinct red shape formed in the air above the holographic-projection pedestal. Laura helped Otto get slowly to his feet as the room was bathed in red light.

"What is that?" Laura asked as the red shape began to stretch and distort, gradually taking on a more humanoid appearance. Slowly, a figure coalesced from the glowing field: a shimmering red hologram of a girl about their age, with long white hair. The figure turned toward Otto and Laura as they slowly backed toward the door.

"Hello, brother," Anna said. "It's so nice to finally meet you."

"Brother?" Laura said, bewildered, looking at Otto.

"We have to get out of here," he said, his head still throbbing. "She's in the core."

"What a lovely school you have here." Anna gestured at the walls around her. "Tell me, do you find it funny, brother, hiding amongst the morons and pretending to be normal? Do they amuse you? Is that why you tolerate them?"

"Professor," Otto said quietly. "The door."

The professor gave a quick nod and moved slowly toward the panel beside the blast doors.

"Who are you?" Laura demanded. "What have you done to H.I.V.E.mind?"

"My name is Anna," she said with a chilling smile. "And I've put your pet AI in a box for now. I might play with him later, I haven't quite decided yet. . . ."

"I'm locked out of the system," the professor said, frantically tapping on his Blackbox. He pulled a screwdriver from one of the inside pockets of his lab coat and began to unscrew a panel next to the door.

"There's nowhere to run, brother," Anna said. "This place belongs to me now."

"I'm *not* your brother," Otto hissed, reaching out with his abilities and trying to deactivate the holographic projector.

"Oh, that's not going to work," Anna said, and Otto felt a sudden sharp pain in his skull as she violently repelled his attempt to connect to the system.

"I can't stop her," he said to Laura in a pained whisper. "With the power of the core as well, she's just too strong."

"Oh, I'm the new and improved model," Anna said. "And you, Otto, are obsolete."

"Leave him alone," Laura shouted as Otto convulsed in pain again on the floor.

Inside his head, Otto found himself sinking deeper and deeper into a bottomless red void. There was no up and no down, no way to orient himself in the way he normally would while he was in the data space. This was something different, this realm was not under his control, this was someone else's kingdom.

Join me, Otto.

He spun around, unable to tell where the sinister whispering voice was coming from, seeming, as it did, to come from all directions at once.

It's so peaceful here.

He turned to face a hideous, rotting monstrosity shambling toward him.

Just stop fighting.

"Lucy?" Otto said, feeling a wild moment of disorientation. "No, no, no . . . You're dead."

Sleep.

He found himself buckling under the power of Lucy's whispering voice as she reached out a skeletal hand, the flesh cold as she touched his face.

There's no point fighting. Just give in and we can be together again.

"NO!" Otto shouted again, dispelling the ghastly phantom.

Back in the data core, Laura tried to restrain Otto as he thrashed on the floor, blood trickling from his nose.

"Professor, please do something!" she yelled. "I think she's killing him!"

"Anything?" Nero snapped, staring through the cockpit window at the outline of the volcano that housed H.I.V.E. on the horizon.

"No, sir," the pilot replied. "I still can't raise flight

control, it's like comms are completely dead."

"It could just be a malfunction," Raven said.

Nero's frown deepened. "It's possible. But if my career has taught me one thing, it's that it's always better to assume the worst. I want to be on the ground as fast as possible. Understood?"

"Yes, sir," the pilot replied. "We're at full throttle on direct approach."

Nero watched as the mountainous island thrusting up from the ocean came into clearer view. He could see no signs of anything untoward, but that didn't mean that there was nothing wrong within a facility that had been designed to stay so completely concealed.

The Shroud shot low across the ocean, whipping up a wave of white foam as it finally crossed over the shallows and rocketed up the side of the volcano toward the hidden landing pad in the crater at its center. They were nearly at the peak when a large hatch concealed among the scattered rocks slid open and a ground-to-air missile battery rose into view, quickly locking onto and tracking the Shroud. An instant later, a missile flew out of the launcher, trailing a plume of white smoke as it shot toward their aircraft.

"Ground launch detected," a calm digital voice reported in the Shroud's cockpit.

"BRACE! BRACE! BRACE!" the pilot yelled, jerking

the flight stick hard to one side. Nero and Raven fought to retain their balance, frantically grabbing for handholds as the cockpit lurched into a hard left bank. The pilot stabbed at a control on the instrument panel, and a chain of star-bright flares flew out of the Shroud's tail, trying to distract the missile from its target. The missile swerved away from the Shroud at the last moment and detonated amongst the decoy flares, dangerously nearby. The aircraft rocked as the shrapnel from the detonating missile clattered off its armored skin.

"That was too close," Raven said. "Get us inside the crater!"

"Working on it!" the pilot called in reply.

"Multiple ground launches detected," the Shroud's on-board systems reported. *"Initiating autonomous evasive maneuvers."* The Shroud's complex flight systems suddenly took control of the ship as three more missiles streaked up to meet it. The aircraft's flight computers tried in vain to plot a course between the converging vapor trails of the missiles, flares, and chaff firing continuously from the tail of the Shroud as it streaked toward the lip of the volcano's crater. Just as they crested the rise, one of the missiles struck home, shredding the Shroud's tail in a violent explosion.

Nero was thrown across the cockpit as the Shroud lurched, its nose clipping the rocks at the edge of the crater, and it began to roll before slamming into the ground hard with a deafening crash, chunks of its armored fuselage flying in all directions. Nero slammed into one of the bulkheads, smacking his head against the steel, and everything went black.

"This is not good," Shelby said as she and Wing ran toward the data core. The alarms that had started to sound a couple of minutes before continued. The dread that their monotonous wailing caused was amplified by the eerie red color of the emergency lighting that filled the corridors. H.I.V.E. security personnel were running in all directions, trying to deal with multiple simultaneous alerts from all over the school.

"I think that might be something of an understatement," Wing said as they rounded the corner to find a team of technicians working on trying to open the massive doors leading to H.I.V.E.mind's data core. One of the men was igniting a cutting torch and getting ready to start work on the door.

"Mind if I have a look before you try to force that?" Shelby asked, pushing past the technicians and examining the mess of wires that hung from the door control panel. Prior to joining H.I.V.E., Shelby had been one of the world's most accomplished cat burglars and this was exactly the sort of challenge she was used to being confronted with.

"Have you got any liquid-nitrogen canisters?" she asked after examining the door for a moment.

"No," the technician replied, shaking his head, "but there are some in the Science and Technology department."

"Someone go and get them, right now," Shelby said. One of the technicians gave a quick nod and ran off down the corridor.

"Right, I need two detonator charges from that demo kit," she instructed, pointing at a case covered in explosives-warning symbols.

"Charges that small will never get through that door," one of the technicians told her.

"I know," she replied. "They won't have to."

She pressed her ear to the door and began to gently tap on its cold, steel surface.

"Bingo." She placed her palm on a specific point on the door. A moment later, the technician came running back down the corridor carrying two canisters of liquid nitrogen from the Science and Technology department.

"Great," Shelby said as the man approached. "Spray it right here." She pointed at a specific point on the door.

"Stand back." The technician unclipped the short hose from the side of one of the corridors and began to spray the supercooled liquid onto the door. Shelby waited for a few seconds before pushing him to one side and attaching the small, magnetic detonator charge from the explosives kit to the center of the frosty white patch.

"Okay, five seconds," she said. "Fire in the hole."

Wing, Shelby, and the assembled H.I.V.E. staff all turned away from the door, shielding their eyes as the charge detonated with a pop in a small cloud of black smoke, which cleared to reveal a neat hole in the door's surface where the flash frozen metal had shattered like glass.

Shelby grabbed a pair of bolt cutters from the pile of tools beside the door and looked inside the hole, carefully pulling a metal-wrapped hose from within. She snapped the bolt cutters closed on the hose, severing it, and the doors slowly rumbled to three feet apart.

"Gotcha," she whispered to herself.

"Help us!" Laura shouted from inside as she and the professor tried to support Otto while squeezing through the narrow gap.

"Otto!" Wing shouted as he saw his friend's pained grimace.

"Have to . . . get . . . away from here," Otto gasped as the professor and Laura lowered him gently to the ground. "She's . . . too strong . . ."

A haunting malevolent laugh began to sound from the speakers mounted in the corridor walls that were normally used for schoolwide announcements.

"Run as far as you want, Otto." Anna's voice echoed down the corridor. "It will never be far enough."

"What the hell?" Shelby said, looking at the walls around her.

"H.I.V.E.mind has been compromised," the professor said to one of the technicians standing nearby. "Get to Central Control and inform Colonel Francisco that we are experiencing a Class 1 breach."

The technician gave a quick nod and ran off down the corridor.

"We need to get Otto as far as possible from here," Laura said as she and Wing helped him up from the ground, supporting his limp form between them.

"No . . . You need to destroy it . . . have to stop her . . . ," Otto said, his voice little more than a mumble.

"What happened in there?" Shelby asked as they dragged Otto away down the corridor.

"I have no idea," Laura said. "One second H.I.V.E.mind is freaking out and then a hologram of some girl called Anna appears from nowhere, claiming to be Otto's sister. And then all hell breaks loose."

"His sister?" Wing said, sounding confused. "Otto doesn't have any family. That's impossible."

"I know," Laura said, her brow furrowing. "But the way Otto reacted when he saw her . . ."

"Sinister . . . sister," Otto mumbled, shaking his head

slightly as if he was trying to wake himself from a nightmare. "Not . . . Lucy . . . No!"

"Let's concentrate on getting out of here for now and worry about the weird Malpense brain magic later, shall we?" Shelby said.

There was the sudden violent rumble of an explosion from somewhere nearby.

"What the hell was that?"

"What the hell?" Colonel Francisco said as he watched the missiles streaking toward Nero's returning Shroud. An instant later, the external camera-feeds in the Central Control room went black. "Get a security detail up there now, check for survivors."

"I can't open a comms channel," one of the nearby technicians reported, sounding alarmed. "We're losing system access."

"What do you mean, we're losing access?" Francisco demanded.

"Our network sockets are shutting down one by one," the technician replied. "It's like H.I.V.E.mind is actively locking us out of the system."

"You," Francisco said, jabbing his finger at a security guard standing by the nearby door. "Get out there and start spreading the word, I want all security details fully armed with conventional weapons and at their emergency posts. The school is locked down until we have some idea what's going on. If anyone finds Professor Pike, tell him that I need a full report on what's actually happening."

The guard gave a quick nod and hurried out the door.

"Sir, we're picking up large power spikes from one of the sub-level storage areas," another technician reported.

"Which sub-level?" Francisco demanded, a sudden look of panic on his face.

"Sub-level five, sir," the technician replied. "Motion sensors down there are going crazy, too."

Francisco felt a creeping sense of dread as he remembered exactly what was stored in that area of the school.

"Do you have a live camera feed from that level?" he asked urgently.

"No, sir," the technician replied. "We've lost all live surveillance feeds schoolwide."

"I'm heading down there," Francisco said. "You two are with me!" He jabbed his finger at the two security guards who remained on station in the room, then walked over to the secure locker on the other side of the room and placed his hand against the palm reader mounted next to it. The metal hatch slid aside to reveal a rack of black assault rifles. Francisco took one of the weapons himself and motioned for the two guards to follow suit.

"Can we still lock down the accommodation blocks?" he asked as he loaded and primed his weapon.

"Yes, sir," the technician replied. "But at this rate there's no guarantee we'll be able to unlock them again."

"Don't worry about that," Francisco said, shaking his head. "Issue a recall order to all students and then lock the blocks. We'll worry about getting them out later."

The guard walked slowly down the corridor on sub-level five. Angry alarm klaxons were sounding from the speakers in the walls all around him, and the corridor was bathed in blood-red light from the emergency illumination in the ceiling. He thumbed the transmission button on his communication system again, trying in vain to get in touch with his squad mates. But the system was completely dead. He heard a faint noise from the gloom farther down the corridor and raised his weapon, then moved quickly and quietly toward the corner at the far end of the corridor. When he was just six feet away, something large and fast-moving exploded from around the bend, galloping toward him. The guard squeezed the trigger of his weapon instinctively; the assault rifle roaring, the sound of its fully automatic fire deafening within the confined space of the corridor. As the gloomy walls were lit by muzzle flashes, the guard could make out the black metallic humanoid form that continued to sprint toward him, despite the hail of bullets. When it was less than sixteen feet away, the machine leapt toward him, with its cold steel claws outstretched. The guard barely had time to let out a strangled cry before the machine snuffed out his life.

A moment later, Francisco and the half dozen guards that he'd managed to round up on his way down to the sub-level appeared at the other end of the corridor.

"No!" Francisco yelled in horror, watching as the sinister machine delivered the killing blow to the guard lying on the floor. At the far end of the corridor, several more of the armored humanoid robots appeared, breaking into a sprint as they saw Francisco and his men. Francisco felt a knot in his gut tighten as he realized that his worst fears were coming true. The lethal machines running toward them were relics of Cypher's failed attack on the school many years ago. Francisco had argued repeatedly in favor of scrapping them, but Nero and the professor had insisted that they might one day be useful.

"God, I hate it when I'm right," Francisco said, raising his weapon. "Open fire!"

The men beside him did not hesitate, filling the narrow corridor with a lethal barrage of fire. The large-caliber rounds seemed to stagger the robots, slowing their advance but not stopping them. The bullets appeared to do little actual damage, beyond scarring the outer, armored shells of the machines.

"Fire in the hole!" Francisco yelled, pumping the grenade launcher slung beneath the barrel of his rifle. The launcher gave a small, popping cough and a grenade sailed down the corridor toward the advancing robots. An instant later, the grenade detonated with a deafening explosion, filling the corridor with dark gray smoke. A clawed metallic hand shot out from the smoke, and one of the machines began to pull itself along the floor of the corridor toward the guards, dragging its shattered twisted legs in its wake. Behind it, the smoke began to clear and more black metallic figures could be seen advancing down the corridor, picking their way through the smoldering remains of their fallen comrades.

"Fall back," Francisco yelled, pumping the grenade launcher again and sending another explosive round arcing down the corridor. "Head back to the main blast doors—we should be able to hold them there."

He and his men conducted a fighting retreat, slowly backing away down the corridor, laying down fire, but for every one of the androids that fell, another three seemed to take its place. A minute later, Francisco and his squad had reached the huge, steel blast doors at the entrance to the sub-level. He used a small key on a chain from around his neck to unlock the access panel next to the door. He pulled hard on the handle inside, and the blast doors began to grind shut on emergency hydraulic power. Francisco watched as the doors slowly closed, seeing dozens of the machines sprinting down the corridor beyond, toward the rapidly closing gap. The doors closed with a solid-sounding thud, just moments before the homicidal machines reached them, and almost immediately there came the sounds of hammering blows on the other side.

"That won't hold those things for long," Francisco said, shaking his head. He could start to feel the situation spiraling out of control.

Raven woke coughing, her eyes stinging and her lungs filled with the acrid black smoke that filled the downed Shroud's cabin. She slowly got to her feet, pushing aside the section of twisted bulkhead that had been pinning her to the ground.

"Max," she yelled, trying to make out any details of the wreckage that surrounded her through the thick haze. She performed a quick mental inventory of her injuries and was pleased to note that beyond a few superficial scrapes and cuts she appeared to be in one piece. That was a lot more than could be said for the aircraft surrounding her. Its fuselage had broken into two pieces, and daylight poured in through its shattered nose. There was no sign of Nero. She continued to make her way through the wreckage, occasionally pushing aside larger pieces of debris and checking beneath them for any other survivors. Eventually she reached the gaping hole in the fuselage where the Shroud had split in two on impact. She stepped out onto the rocky, scorched scrub that covered the steep slope leading down to H.I.V.E.'s concealed crater entrance. She saw a figure in a dark suit lying on the ground just about six feet from the wreckage and hurried toward it. She gently rolled Nero over, relieved to see that he was at least still breathing, though his face was blackened with soot and his immaculately tailored suit had seen much better days. The left side of Nero's shirt was soaked in blood from a cut on his chest, but otherwise he seemed to be largely in one piece. Raven pulled open his shirt, taking a field dressing from one of her equipment pouches and pressing it to the open wound. Nero gave an uncomfortable, pained hiss and stirred slightly, slowly regaining consciousness.

"Natalya," he said, his voice croaky. "What happened?"

"We were shot down," she replied, finishing applying the dressing. "By H.I.V.E.'s own defenses."

"We have to get inside," Nero said, pushing himself up into a sitting position. "We have to find out what's going on."

"One thing at a time." Raven quickly checked him for any signs of concussion before moving toward the shattered remains of the aircraft cockpit to check on the pilot. She did not need to measure the pulse of the mangled body inside to know that the man had not survived the crash.

Behind her, Nero slowly got to his feet and walked over to a section of broken fuselage that lay half concealed by the holographic field covering the entrance to H.I.V.E. He picked up a stone from near his feet and tossed it out into the middle of the hologram, watching as it vanished, and counting the couple of seconds that passed before he could hear it impact the landing pad far below. That meant the secondary hangar doors were open beneath the projection and that they should be able to get inside. There was just the small matter of negotiating the sheer drop to address.

"Pilot didn't make it," Raven reported as she walked back toward him. "We're too exposed out here."

Something inside the burning wreckage of the Shroud cooked off with a loud bang as if to emphasize her point.

"Can you get us down there?" Nero asked, gesturing toward the hologram-covered entrance.

"I think so," Raven replied, checking the grappler unit mounted to her wrist. "When was the last time you went rappelling?"

"This is going to be undignified, isn't it?" Nero said with a pained sigh.

chapter five

"How are you feeling?" Laura asked, looking down at Otto with concern. He sat on one of the chairs in the abandoned dining hall, his brain racing as he tried to make sense of what he'd just seen.

"I'm okay," he replied, rubbing his temples. "The farther we get from the data core, the less it seems to hurt."

"Who *was* that?" Laura asked softly.

"I'm not completely sure," Otto replied, shaking his head. "But I think I have a pretty good idea."

"Has it got anything to do with the fact that she seems to think you're her brother?" Laura asked, watching as Wing and Shelby explained what had just happened to Nigel and Franz on the other side of the room.

"I'm not her brother," Otto said firmly. "But I think we may share rather a lot of the same DNA."

"What do you mean?" Laura asked with a frown.

"There's something I haven't told you," he said, looking down at the floor. "About Zero."

Zero was the malicious clone of Otto that they had encountered during the mission to rescue the kidnapped H.I.V.E. students from the Glasshouse. Laura had suffered particularly badly at hands of the twisted copy of Otto, which was part of the reason that Otto had not told her what he was telling her now.

"I knew it," Laura said. "I knew this had to have something to do with Furan. What else haven't you told me?"

"When we were alone together, he said something to me, something that implied he was not the only clone," Otto said, looking up at her.

"More Zeros?" Laura said, suddenly looking pale. "I thought he was one of a kind!"

"No, I think the Disciples have been experimenting with the technology that Overlord used to create me," Otto said. "But I'm pretty sure they don't understand what they're playing with. That was why Zero was so twisted and wrong: They don't understand the technology properly. I think they're making monsters the same way that Overlord made me, and I think that this Anna may be one of them."

"Why didn't you tell us?" Laura asked with a frown.

"Well, partly because Nero forbade me from talking to anyone about it," he replied. "But also because I didn't want you to worry. I know what Zero put you through; the last thing I wanted was you knowing that there might be others like him, somewhere out there in the world."

"I'd rather have known the truth," she asserted. "No matter how scary it might have been."

"I know." Otto looked back down at the floor. "If I'm honest, I think part of it was because I felt guilty. Zero would never have existed without me, and neither, I assume, would Anna. How long is it going to be before we are finally free of the consequences of what Overlord and Furan tried to do?"

"Look, this was not your fault," Laura said. "Whoever Anna is, and wherever she's come from, we'll stop her, the same way we always do."

"I hope you're right, Laura," Otto said, looking up at her. "Because what I felt back in the data core, her power, her control of our abilities, all of it. I've never felt anything like it before."

"Yeah, well you've got something she hasn't," Laura said. "Us."

"I'm sorry for lying to you," he said. "I thought this was over. I didn't want you worrying over nothing."

"That's okay." She gave him a crooked smile. "But if you do it again, I'll have Shelby remove parts of your body while you sleep. Understood?"

"All I heard were the words 'Shelby' and 'body'—does

someone want to tell me what's going on?" Shelby said as she and the others approached. "I mean, it sounds like fun, but I'm going to need more details."

"Have you been able to reestablish contact with H.I.V.E.mind yet?" Wing asked, looking worried.

"No," Otto answered, "but he must still be in there fighting. If he wasn't, Anna would have taken control of the entire school by now."

"So, there's no way to know what's going on in the rest of the school," Nigel said nervously.

There was the sudden sound of another muffled explosion somewhere far below them.

"Nothing good by the sounds of things," Franz guessed.

"I think we have to try and get out of here," Otto said. "It's only a matter of time before Anna has complete control, and then she'll lock down the school and it'll be impossible for us to escape. Assuming it isn't already, of course."

"The only way out of here's by air," Wing said. "Which means we need to get to the hangar."

"What if she's sealed the crater?" Shelby asked.

"We'll cross that bridge when we come to it," Otto replied as another explosion sounded, closer this time. "First, we have to get there."

Francisco felt the vibrations through his feet before he heard the sound of heavy footsteps thudding up the corridor on the other side of the blast door. There was a moment of silence, and then a sudden, shuddering boom as something massive hit the other side of the door. The whole room seemed to shake as the huge doors rattled inside their reinforced frames, their smooth, metal faces deforming as something unbelievably strong hammered away at them from the other side.

"The lift's out of action, so use your grapplers to get up the shaft," Francisco ordered as he turned toward his men. "Spread the word to the other security details: Cypher's robots are loose and out of control. They'll need the heaviest weapons they can get their hands on if they're going to have any chance of stopping them."

"You can tell them yourself," the squad leader said with a frown. "You can't stay here, it's suicide."

"I'll be right behind you," Francisco said. "I just have to set charges to blow the shaft behind us or those things will just follow us."

"But, sir . . ."

"No buts, soldier. Get moving!" Francisco barked.

He set to work positioning and priming the charges around the room as his men ascended the lift shaft, one by one, until finally only he remained. He took one last look around the room, checking that he had planted the explosives in the most efficient positions. He'd used more explosives than he thought he'd need, but he wasn't particularly concerned about collateral damage at this point. There was a certain violent crunch of tearing metal from behind him, and a giant robotic hand tore through one of the blast doors. With a horrendous, screeching noise, the hand began to rip a larger hole in the door, and Francisco could clearly see the massive form of one of Cypher's Behemoth robots, surrounded by dozens of the smaller assassin units. Francisco ran toward the elevator shaft, sticking his head into the gap between the doors and firing his grappler up into the darkness above. He felt the cable go taut and stepped out into the void. The grappler began to reel in the cable, pulling him up into the darkness as he heard the blast doors below finally give way with a shattering crash. As he shot upward into the blackened shaft, he triggered the detonator in his other hand. There was a delay of just a fraction of a second, and then the shaft below him filled with fire as the charges all detonated simultaneously. The shockwave from the explosion smashed into Francisco, sending him flying across the shaft, dangling limply from his grappler line. He felt a sudden, horrifying lurch as somewhere above him whatever his grappler line was attached to began to give way. He flailed around in the darkness, trying to find something, anything, to hold on to. His fingers brushed against the concrete of the wall, and then he felt something hard and metallic. He grabbed on to the invisible handhold, detaching his grappling line and hanging on for dear life as something large whistled down the shaft behind him, smashing into the burning debris far below with a boom. He hung there for a few seconds gathering his breath before starting to grope around the elevator-shaft walls in the darkness for more hand- and footholds. Slowly but surely, in the stifling smoke-filled darkness, he began to climb.

"There, that wasn't so bad," Raven said as she released her grip on Nero's waist.

They had just reached the floor of the concealed hangar in H.I.V.E.'s crater, and while Nero had submitted to the indignity of being carried down on Raven's grappler line, he clearly wasn't keen to repeat the experience.

"You may relish swinging around like a glorified trapeze artist," he said. "Personally, I prefer stairs."

"Now where's the fun in that?" Raven asked, reeling in her grappler line. "Besides, my way's quicker."

"Where are the guards?" Nero frowned. "There's supposed to be a security detail on duty in the hangar at all times."

"I can't raise H.I.V.E.mind, either," Raven said, tapping at her inactive Blackbox. "This thing's completely dead."

"The communication system is part of the core-systems loop," Nero said. "If that's not working, then I wouldn't expect anything to be . . ."

Suddenly, a squad of anxious-looking security guards entered the hangar area on the other side of the cavern. They hurried over to where Nero and Raven were standing, their weapons at the ready.

"Dr. Nero, sir," the lead guard said. "Thank God you're alright. After we saw the missile launch . . . well . . . we assumed the worst."

"We were lucky to survive," Nero replied. "Our pilot was not so fortunate."

"What the hell happened?" Raven snapped. "Why were we fired upon?"

"We're not sure, ma'am," the guard admitted. "We started seeing system errors across the board and then H.I.V.E.mind shut down. We've been locked out of every system. Whoever is in control of the school, it isn't us."

"How on earth did this happen?" Nero demanded. He was not an expert on the subject, with the people he had working for him he didn't need to be, but he knew that H.I.V.E.'s computer security systems were second to none. The idea that someone had been able to hack the facility from outside seemed preposterous.

"I'm sorry, sir, we've got no idea," the guard said, shaking his head. "Professor Pike reported that somebody was attacking the school systems, and then a couple of minutes later everything went to hell."

"Where is the professor?" Nero asked.

"We're not sure, sir, without H.I.V.E.mind online we've lost all communications and tracking systems. We know he's somewhere in the school, but that's about it."

"What about Colonel Francisco?"

"He was responding to reports of an incident in the lower levels when the communication system went dead. We've not heard anything from him, or the squad that went with him, since."

"Right," Nero said. "I want you to find as many of the senior staff as you can and tell them to report to the Central Control facility. I need to know what's going on and how we can stop it."

"Yes, sir," the guard replied with a nod.

"I'm assuming the students are under lockdown," Raven said.

"The accommodation blocks are sealed, ma'am," the guard said. "And until we've got control of the system again, we've got no way of unsealing them."

"They should at least be safe for now," Nero said. There was a nagging voice at the back of his head, reminding him that *nowhere* in the school would truly be safe if their systems were as badly compromised as they appeared to be. They were, when all was said and done, sitting on top of an active volcano.

"I'll see who I can round up, too," Raven said.

"Do you want a couple of my men to come with you?" the squad leader asked.

"Do I look like I need help?" Raven had an icy edge to her voice.

The squad leader shook his head with a nervous gulp, the blood draining from his face.

"Meet us back at Central Control, Natalya." Nero nodded at her. "I'm sure I don't need to tell you what your orders are, should you meet any opposition!"

Otto and his friends ran down the corridor, heading for H.I.V.E.'s hangar facility. The corridors were still being lit by the low-power emergency lighting, its eerie red glow giving the school's mazelike corridors a sinister and unfamiliar feel.

"Where is everyone?" Nigel asked, looking around nervously.

"Standard emergency procedure is to secure students in accommodation blocks for their own protection," Wing said. "I am reasonably confident that this situation would qualify as an emergency."

There was the sudden sound of another explosion, much closer this time.

"What gave it away, big guy?" Shelby said, sounding unusually subdued. They had experienced many crises at the school before, but never one that seemed to have thrown the facility into such total chaos.

"We need to keep moving," Otto said, picking up his pace. He didn't want to alarm anyone, but every time he reached out with his abilities to try to work out what was going on elsewhere in the school, he could only detect Anna's sinister controlling hiss in the system. Even more worryingly, he was starting to feel it even when he wasn't consciously using his uncanny gifts. Anna's abilities seemed to be growing by the minute, and already her power dwarfed his.

"What are you students doing out of your accommodation block?" a voice shouted from behind them.

They turned to see a squad of H.I.V.E. security guards marching down the corridor toward them. The apprehensive expressions on the soldiers' faces did nothing to fill Otto and the others with confidence.

"We were trying to help out with the systems problems," Otto explained, only half lying. "We got separated from the rest of the students."

"Well, we can't just have you wandering around loose," the squad leader said. "You'll have to come with us until we can find somewhere safe for you to sit this out."

"We'll be fine on our own," Otto said, shaking his head. "We'll find somewhere safe to lie low, I promise."

"We have very specific instructions when it comes to you, Mr. Malpense," the security guard replied. "Dr. Nero has made it quite clear that you and your friends are not to be trusted. So if you don't mind, I won't be letting you out of my sight."

"You don't understand," Laura said angrily. "We can't

just come with you—we've got to get out of here."

"No one's going anywhere," the guard said with a frown. "Especially not you lot."

"Is there something wrong here, Commander?" a familiar voice said from behind Otto.

There could have been very few people over the last couple of decades who could say they were pleased to see Raven, she was after all the world's most feared assassin, but right now there was no one Otto would have rather seen walking down the corridor toward them.

"No, ma'am," the guard replied. "We just found these students wandering the halls. We were going to escort them to the nearest accommodation block for lockdown."

Raven shot a glance in Otto's direction. If there was one thing that her unique line of work had taught her, it was to trust her instincts—they had kept her alive on numerous occasions. Right now, those instincts were telling her that something was very wrong and that Otto probably knew more about it than anyone else.

"Leave them with me," she said. "I have a certain amount of . . . experience with these students."

"Of course," the guard replied. "As you wish."

Raven watched as the squad of guards marched off out of earshot before turning back toward Otto.

"So," she said. "Will one of you please tell me what the hell is going on?"

"The school's under attack," Otto answered.

"That much I'd already worked out," Raven said. "The real question is, by whom?"

Otto spent the next minute quickly recounting the events of the past hour for Raven's benefit. She stood and listened in silence, absorbing the information without showing any trace of emotion.

"This Anna," she said, when Otto fell silent. "Do you have any idea who she is?"

"Yes, actually I think I do," he replied. "Which is why I need to speak to Nero as soon as possible."

"Okay, I need you all to come with me to Central Control," Raven said. "Nero's trying to coordinate the fight against this thing from there."

"Raven," Otto said. "You don't understand. We can't fight her; not here, not like this. We need to get out of here and come up with a plan. If we stay, we lose, it's as simple as that."

"He's right," Laura said. "I saw how fast she took over H.I.V.E.mind's systems. If the school isn't already completely under her control, it soon will be."

Raven stood for a moment looking at the six students in front of her. Between them they had been responsible for more trouble than the rest of the students in the school put together, but they had also been responsible for saving it, on more than one occasion. If anyone could help put together a plan to save the school, it was them.

"Come on, then," she said. "You need to tell Nero what you just told me, and then we'll see about getting the hell out of here."

"Professor, please tell me you know how to fix this," Nero said as he looked at the wall of blank monitors in the Central Control room.

"I'm afraid not, Max." Professor Pike shook his head. "Whoever this Anna person is, she's taken complete control of the system and locked us out."

"I'm sure I don't need to remind you, Professor, that you reassured me repeatedly that this could never happen," Nero said, trying to keep the irritation from his voice.

"I know, I know," the professor said, rubbing his forehead. "But this is quite unprecedented. There's no way we could possibly have known that the system would be subjected to such a powerful attack. This girl has abilities, the likes of which I have only seen once before. I don't think it's any coincidence that Mr. Malpense seemed to recognize her. Her powers seem almost identical to his, just much, much more powerful."

"So we can't stop her," Nero said with a frown. "Is that what you're telling me?"

"Not here and not now," Otto said, joining in with

the end of their conversation as he, Raven, and the others entered the room. "But that doesn't mean it's impossible. We just have to pick the battlefield."

"Mr. Malpense, I'm glad to see that you are relatively unharmed," Nero said. "If you have some sort of plan as to what we should be doing, I am very open to suggestions."

"I have to admit, I'm rather curious, too." Anna's voice suddenly filled the air. A moment later, the numerous monitors in the room flared back into life, their previously black screens now filled with the smiling face of a teenage girl with long, white hair. "So, tell me, Otto, how exactly are you planning to stop me?"

"You must, I assume, be Anna," Nero said calmly, turning to address the face on the screens. "I'm afraid we haven't been properly introduced."

"Oh, I know who you are, Maximilian," Anna replied. "The Disciples' files on you were quite detailed. But that doesn't mean there aren't all sorts of interesting little gaps in your history that I'd love to fill in. That's okay, though, I'm sure we'll have plenty of time to chat later."

"Allow me to make myself quite clear," Nero said. "You are not the first person to attack this school, and I very much doubt you will be the last. There is one thing, however, that everyone who has tried it has in common. They're all dead, or wish they were."

"Oh dear, Max." Anna smiled coldly. "You don't seem

to understand the power dynamic here. I completely control your school, and there's nothing you can do to stop me."

"You may have taken control of my school," Nero said, "but you don't control the people in it."

"Oh, but I don't need people," she said with an evil smile. "I have something much, much better."

A second later, there was the sound of shouts from outside and then sustained gunfire. Raven ran over to the door and looked out into the corridor beyond. The squad of security guards stationed outside the control center were firing wildly at a horde of insectile black robots that were running down the corridor toward them. She recognized the strange machines instantly, Cypher's assassin droids, remembering all too clearly what they were capable of. The guards slowly started to retreat backward down the corridor, their assault rifles' sustained fire doing little to slow the advance of the sinister machines. Raven stepped back into the Control Center, slapping fruitlessly at the switch next to the door, trying to close it, but there was no response.

"I told you we should have melted those things down," Raven said. "She's taken control of Cypher's assault droids."

There was a sudden scream from outside, and the sound of gunfire began to diminish.

"We need to go. NOW!"

"Please, don't go!" Anna said, laughing to herself. "The fun's just about to begin."

In an instant, the wall on the other side of the room exploded in a shower of concrete dust, sending a couple of technicians flying. A huge, dark shape appeared in the cloud of dust, stepping forward with a crunching thud to reveal one of the Behemoth assault robots. Its heavily armored head angled itself toward Nero and his startled students before it strode across the room toward them. More of the smaller assassin droids poured through the hole in the wall behind the giant robot, leaping onto the screaming technicians, who quickly fell silent.

"Escape hatch," Raven yelled, pulling the glowing purple katanas from the crossed scabbards on her back. Nero motioned for Otto and the others to follow him, while Raven squared off with the massive machine as it stopped across the room toward her.

He reached behind one of the monitors mounted on the wall and pressed the switch hidden there. Nothing happened.

"Emergency exit not working?" Anna asked with a broad smile. "Well, that is unfortunate."

"Max!" Raven shouted, throwing one of the glowing swords across the room to him. Immediately the Behemoth robot was on her, swinging a giant steel fist at her, like a metal battering ram. Raven ducked beneath the clumsy blow, raising her sword upward and severing the robot's arm at the wrist. The machine's giant metal fist fell to the ground with a clang, still twitching, but the robot didn't even seem to slow down. Its other hand swung back toward Raven, giving her barely any time to dodge, connecting with her shoulder and swatting her violently to the ground.

Nero hurled Raven's glowing weapon at the concealed hatch in the wall. The monomolecular blade hissed as it passed effortlessly through the reinforced steel, leaving a hole large enough for someone to climb through.

"Inside!" Nero shouted, ordering Otto and the others and then the professor into the secret passage beyond. Wing was the last of the students through the opening, stopping for a moment to look over his shoulder.

Behind him, Raven staggered to her feet, feeling a searing pain in her shoulder. She raised her sword in front of her as several of the smaller assassin androids started to circle, trying to flank her. She backed toward the escape hatch, swinging her weapon at the nearest machine and severing its torso from hip to shoulder, sending it tumbling to the floor, a sparking wreck. Another one of the smaller robots leapt at her from the opposite direction, its clawed hands outstretched. There was a blur of motion, and a glowing purple blade sliced the attacking machine cleanly in two as Wing stepped forward holding the shimmering sword.

"Go!" Wing yelled at Nero as he took up a defensive stance next to Raven, his weapon raised. Nero hesitated for a moment, but more of the assassin droids were pouring through the breach in the wall on the opposite side of the room. He knew that this had become a battle they couldn't hope to win. Reluctantly he ducked inside the hatch and hurried down the narrow passage beyond.

"What are you doing?" Raven snapped at Wing. "Get out of here."

"We need to buy them more time," Wing said through gritted teeth, swinging his weapon. "No time to argue."

The pair of them moved in elegant synchronization; the many hours they had spent drilling together translating into an unconscious understanding between them. They fought with a lethal, whirling choreography, their mechanical opponents falling left and right. But ultimately, they both knew it was a fight they could not win. More and more decommissioned robots poured into the room, overwhelming them. Raven was the first to fall, under a shower of withering blows from half a dozen of the assassin units. Wing kept fighting, his sword a blur, but there were just too many of them. He fought his way over to one of the fallen security guards, unclipping a grenade from the dead man's belt, pulling the pin and tossing it across the room toward the escape hatch. There was a deafening boom and the explosion collapsed the entrance to the tunnel as Wing, too, was finally beaten to the ground. The giant Behemoth robot strode across the room, raising one huge armored foot high above Wing's head as he lay unconscious on the floor.

"Stop!" Anna yelled, and the giant robot froze in place. "I want these two alive," she said. "They may yet prove useful."

"Help me," Nero said to Otto as he tried to open the door at the end of the passage.

Otto grabbed the edge of the sliding panel and pulled with all his might. Slowly he and Nero managed to force the panel open and light poured into the darkened passageway. They were all relieved to see that the area beyond appeared to be quiet and free of any of Anna's homicidal machines.

"We have to go back for Wing," Shelby said, obviously upset.

"We can't," Laura said, shaking her head and giving her friend a hug. "You know as well as I do, that would be the last thing he wanted."

"Why did the big dumb idiot have to go and play the hero?" Shelby said, tears welling up in her eyes.

"Because, for better or worse, that is what he is," Nero said. "We can mourn our losses when we get out of here.

For now, let's concentrate on making sure their sacrifice was not in vain."

"We should keep moving," Professor Pike added. "If Anna has access to the school's surveillance system, she'll already know where we are."

"Shelby." Otto looked at his friend. "I want to go back for them just as much as you do, but if we don't get out of here now, Anna wins and this is all over. I swear to you, we will make her pay. Maybe not today, but soon."

"I'm going to kill her with my bare hands," Shelby said, something cold and hard behind her eyes that Otto had never seen before. "And no one had better try to stop me."

There was the sudden sound of gunfire from nearby as another group of H.I.V.E.'s security personnel encountered Anna's murderous mechanical slaves.

"We need to get to the hangar," Nero said. "We have to stay ahead of those things or we'll never get out of here. Let's go."

They all hurried down the corridor toward the hangar bay, moving as fast as they could with the professor doing his best to keep up with them.

The sounds of ongoing battle seemed to be getting nearer and nearer as they approached the hangar, and it was with some relief that they ran out into the massive cavern and found it free of any obvious signs of hostile activity. They ran toward the nearest Shroud, hurrying up the rear loading ramp and strapping themselves into the passenger benches that lined the back compartment of the armored dropship.

"How long is it since you've flown one of these things?" the professor asked as Nero strapped himself into the pilot's seat.

"Long enough that I don't need to be distracted by stupid questions," Nero snapped back. There was a burst of movement on the other side of the hangar and Nero glanced up from the controls. The battered remnants of H.I.V.E.'s security detail were fighting a valiant but futile rear-guard action against the horde of armored black robots, the last few guards retreating across the hangar toward Nero's Shroud.

"I think we can abandon preflight checks," Nero muttered to himself. He hit the button to disengage the Shroud's landing clamps, but nothing happened. He stabbed furiously at the button a few more times with his finger, but there was still no response. "I'm locked out of the launch controls," he yelled.

Back in the passenger compartment, Otto closed his eyes and focused his abilities, trying to shut out the noises of battle coming from just outside. He reached out with his senses, trying to connect to the systems that were keeping the Shroud on the ground. He could sense Anna exerting her own control over the aircraft, and he pushed back hard against her, using every ounce of his willpower. Perhaps it was because she was distracted by trying to control the rest of the school at the same time, but he started to feel her control slacken as he fought against her. Otto strained, pushing against the limits of his abilities, trying to wrestle control from his psychotic clone. There was a sudden sharp pain in his skull and then a rush of relief as he felt Anna's grip of the system weaken. Beneath the Shroud, the landing clamps attached to the dropship's gear detached with a mechanical clunk. Otto pushed back harder as he felt Anna's abilities reaching out for the dropship and trying to take control of its onboard flight systems.

"Go, now!" he yelled, and Nero did not need to be told twice. As Anna's robot army poured across the landing pad toward the Shroud, it roared upward off the pad, sending the machines scattering in all directions, blown aside by the backwash from its engines. Nero pulled back on the stick, pointing the Shroud at the circle of blue sky framed by the crater above. He pushed the Shroud's throttle hard against the stops, sending it roaring upward as the steel shutters that sealed the crater began to slowly close. He could only guess that Anna was closing them, but he didn't have time to think about the risks as he aimed the nose of the aircraft at the ever-closing gap. Seconds later, the massive aircraft shot through the shrinking opening with barely inches to spare, racing up into the sky above the volcano. Nero quickly tried to activate the aircraft stealth systems, but they were unresponsive.

"The cloak's offline," Nero shouted. "We'll be sitting ducks for the defense systems."

"Give me a second," Otto replied. He closed his eyes, trying to block out the chaos around him, concentrating on trying to find a connection to the missiles sitting in their launchers around the crater. He could only hope that Anna was sufficiently distracted by controlling her hordes of robot warriors that she would not notice what he was trying to do. He felt the defense system springing to life as the Shroud climbed into the air and knew he had only seconds to act. He connected with the firing circuits of the missiles surrounding them, and a fraction of a second before they could launch, he connected to their detonation circuits and triggered them. The three launchers spread around the interior of the crater and exploded instantaneously, burning debris scattering in all directions.

"We're clear," Otto shouted. "Punch it!"

Nero triggered the Shroud's afterburners and the aircraft shot into the air, leaving the island behind. As they raced away from H.I.V.E., Otto could feel Anna's powers reaching out and trying to take control of their aircraft.

He fought back, thwarting her fading attempts to hijack the Shroud, as they moved farther and farther away from H.I.V.E.mind's data core.

Back inside the hangar bay, the launch clamps released on the three remaining Shrouds that were ready for takeoff. The three aircraft began to lift into the air, no pilots on board, controlled merely by Anna's will. They climbed out of the crater, the hangar-bay shutters rumbling open again to grant them passage as they set off in pursuit of their fleeing quarry.

"We're not out of this yet," Nero said to Otto, glancing down at the radar screen in the center of the control console. Three blips could clearly be seen on the screen, tracking their course and gaining on them slowly, but inevitably. "Less than one minute before they're inside missile range." Nero checked the countermeasure system. "If you have anything up your sleeve, now would be the time, Mr. Malpense. I am many things, but I am not a combat pilot."

"Slow down," Otto said.

"Really," Nero asked, throwing a concerned glance in Otto's direction. "Are you sure that's a good idea?"

"No, I'm not," Otto replied. "But it might be the only chance we've got."

He closed his eyes, trying to sense the pursuing air-crafts' control systems, knowing that he was at the very limits of his abilities. They were still too far away for him to exert any measure of control, but he could feel Anna's influence upon them even at this range. She was pushing the pursuing machines well past their design limitations in an attempt to catch up with them, their engines overheating as she maxed out their thrust. They quickly began to catch up with the fleeing Shroud as Nero eased back on the throttle, and Otto began to feel Anna pushing back against him as he tried to seize control of their flight systems. He could still feel her strength, but it was definitely beginning to wane as they got farther and farther away from H.I.V.E.

"Missile launch!" Nero shouted as alarms started to blare in the cockpit. He stabbed at the controls for the countermeasure system, launching flares and chaff in an attempt to divert the incoming warhead. More launches were detected by the system, and it began to automatically fire off more decoys. Two of the incoming missiles detonated harmlessly, fooled by the countermeasure system, but one kept coming relentlessly. Nero banked hard to the left, sending the Shroud plummeting toward the ocean below as he desperately fought to evade the incoming weapon. Otto gave up on trying to take control of the pursuing aircraft for a moment and concentrated instead on trying to intercept the missile. He was gambling on the fact that Anna would not have thought to have shielded the control systems of the missile in the same way as she had with the computer systems on board the hostile Shrouds. He could feel the missile getting closer and closer as he fought to connect with its detonation circuitry, but Anna was already one step ahead of him. Even at this range, he could still feel her malign influence blocking him from triggering a premature detonation of the weapon. At the last possible moment, Otto suddenly switched his focus to the missile-guidance systems, tweaking the flight-control surfaces and sending the missile streaking into the surface of the ocean just beneath the Shroud. There was the sound of an enormous explosion from somewhere beneath them, and the rear of the aircraft bucked as the shockwave from the detonation struck them. Nero wrestled with the controls, fighting to keep the aircraft level as it skimmed the wave tops below.

Very clever, brother. Anna's voice inside Otto's skull was little more than a whisper now. *But really, who needs missiles?*

Behind them, the pursuing Shrouds accelerated again, their overstressed airframes groaning in protest as Anna pushed them even further beyond their design limitations.

"She's going to ram us," Otto said, shaking his head as if to rid himself of Anna's malign presence. "You have to go faster."

"Make your mind up," Nero said through gritted teeth, burying the throttle again.

Down in the passenger compartment the professor staggered over to a large, secure locker mounted on the forward bulkhead. He leaned down and pressed his hand to the palm reader next to the locker, and a moment later it popped open with a clunking sound. He lifted an enormous heavy machine gun from inside the locker and turned to the other students strapped into the passenger benches.

"I don't suppose any of you know how to use one of these things?" he asked.

"Pretty sure we can work it out," Shelby replied, undoing her seat belt and making her way unsteadily over to the professor. She took the weapon from him and examined it more closely. It was of a similar design to the weapons they had used in their combat simulations back at the school. "Yeah, I can work with this."

Up in the cockpit, Otto focused on trying to find some flaws in Anna's control of the Shrouds she'd turned into guided missiles. He jumped from system to system, trying to connect, moving faster and faster, trying to stay one step ahead of her. For a moment it seemed like her concentration wavered, and he took the opportunity to seize control of the coolant systems on board one of the pursuing aircraft. A fraction of a second later, one of its engines catastrophically overheated and exploded, like a bomb, setting the Shroud pinwheeling into the surface of the sea.

"One down," Otto said as Nero saw one of the hostile blips vanish from the radar display. "Bank right now!"

Nero jerked at the controls, sending the Shroud into a hard right turn. Almost instantly, one of the enemy aircraft shot past, just about six feet in front of the cockpit window, its afterburner roaring and its engines glowing red hot. Otto tried the same trick that he had tried a few seconds before, but this time Anna was ready for him, blocking his abilities from interfacing with the engine control systems.

"The other one's coming up fast from behind," Nero yelled as the Shroud that had just missed them began to bank back toward them.

Down in the passenger compartment, Shelby lay down on the hard metal deck, unfolding the small supporting bipod at the front of the machine gun.

"Franz," she yelled. "Get the door!"

Franz released his safety harness and ran across the passenger compartment, slapping the large domed switch that opened the rear loading ramp. The ramp whirred down to reveal the hostile Shroud that was rocketing toward the rear of their aircraft.

"Smile, you son of a . . ."

Shelby's voice was drowned out by the sudden roar of the machine gun as she squeezed the trigger. The heavy-caliber rounds smashed into the nose of the pursuing aircraft, shattering the glass of the cockpit and tearing into the fragile systems inside. The mortally wounded Shroud reared into the air, its engines screaming before it tipped over and slammed into the ocean surface, sending up a huge plume of water.

"Two down," Shelby shouted, sighting down the barrel of her weapon, hoping that the last enemy aircraft might also present itself as a target.

Nero watched through the cockpit glass as the last Shroud shot off ahead of them before performing a tight turn and heading back straight toward them.

"Brace!" was all that Nero had time to shout as he realized that he was not going to be able to evade in time, just as a missile erupted from the surface of the ocean, spearing up toward the charging enemy aircraft, which instantly erupted into a massive ball of flame. Nero winced as the burning debris bounced off the hull of his own Shroud as the aircraft shot through the cloud of black smoke. Nero sent the aircraft into a banking turn, watching as the burning debris splashed down into the sea. A few seconds later, the surface of the sea began to boil with bubbling white foam and the massive shape of the *Megalodon* broke the surface.

"I should have known what I was letting myself in for when I offered to bring you home." Darkdoom's voice crackled over the comms system. "Need a lift?"

• • •

"Nooo!" Anna screamed in rage as she felt her connection with the last of the hijacked Shrouds vanish.

Wright took a step back as Anna turned from the Russian mainframe and focused her attention on him.

"Where would Nero go if he needed somewhere to hide and lick his wounds?" she demanded.

"If I knew that, he'd be dead already," Wright grumbled. The Disciples had tried on more than one occasion to eliminate the head of G.L.O.V.E., but their attempts had ultimately led to nothing but frustration and failure.

"I don't have enough power when I'm this far from H.I.V.E. I need transport," Anna snapped, turning toward Colonel Kuznetsov.

"Of course," he replied obediently. "I shall arrange it immediately."

"The sooner I can get to that island, the sooner I can find whatever hole Nero and Malpense have scurried into."

"You know the location of H.I.V.E.?" Wright said, sounding surprised.

"I know everything their pet AI knew. Including where he lives."

"Perhaps, then, it would be easier to simply destroy the facility?"

"Not yet," Anna said. "They still have something that I need. But don't worry, once I have it, I'm going to wipe that school from the face of the earth."

chapter six

"Didn't I just drop you off?" Darkdoom asked, raising an eyebrow as the huge hydraulic rams lowered the landing pad bearing Nero's Shroud into the interior of the *Megalodon*.

"Let's just say we didn't quite receive the warm welcome home I was expecting," Nero said as the landing pad settled into place.

"Well, at least it gave us a chance to try out our new anti-aircraft systems," Darkdoom replied. "Our sensors didn't pick up any life signs on board the Shroud we shot down. You didn't tell me you'd upgraded them for autonomous combat operations."

"That's because we didn't," the professor said as he walked down the loading ramp. "They were being remotely controlled."

"By whom?" Darkdoom asked.

"H.I.V.E.mind has been compromised," Nero explained. "It would seem we did not clean up behind the Furans quite as efficiently as we thought we had." He glanced over at Otto, who was talking with his friends on the other side of the pad. "I think we may have another clone of Mr. Malpense on our hands."

"To attack and take over the school remotely?" Darkdoom frowned. "I had no idea he was that powerful."

"She calls herself Anna," Nero said. "And it would seem she is rather more capable than Otto, and certainly a lot more ruthless."

"Where's Natalya?" Darkdoom asked, suddenly realizing that Raven had not been on board Nero's aircraft.

"She's . . . she sacrificed herself to give us a chance to escape," Nero answered, looking down at the floor.

"Oh God, you don't mean she's . . ."

"I'm not sure." Nero shook his head. "Everything happened so fast."

"If anyone can survive she can, you know that, Max," Darkdoom said, placing a hand on Nero's shoulder.

"At least you know Nigel's safe." Nero looked over at Darkdoom's son.

"Yes," Darkdoom replied, "but there are many other children who are not. That's our priority for now."

"What are you doing back?"

Nero turned to see his father, Nathaniel, walking

toward them, his stick tapping rhythmically on the metal of the deck.

"Let's just say there have been unanticipated developments," Nero admitted with a sigh.

"Nathaniel!" the professor said, sounding surprised. "I didn't know you were still working with Diabolus."

"Well, you know what it's like, Theodore." Nathaniel smiled. "Someone has to keep these young whippersnappers in line."

"Indeed," the professor replied. "I see you've made some modifications to my original design." He gestured at the enormous vessel surrounding him.

"Oh, just a few tweaks here and there, really," Nathaniel said. "How's your pet supercomputer?"

"Not good, actually." The professor shook his head. "Which rather explains what we're doing here."

"I need to call a meeting of the Ruling Council," Nero said, turning back toward Darkdoom. "They need to know what's happened. If H.I.V.E.mind is now fully under the control of the Disciples, we may have a far bigger problem than we realize."

"I'll send out a notification." Darkdoom nodded. "We'll gather everyone as quickly as possible."

"Thank you, Diabolus." Nero placed a hand on his friend's shoulder. "It's not the first time you've fished my backside out of the fire, and I don't suppose it will be the last."

"What are friends with multibillion-dollar fusion-powered submarines for?" Darkdoom said with a wry smile.

On the other side of the landing pad, Shelby sat down on one of the nearby ammo crates and put her head in her hands. Now, as the adrenaline wore off, the tears finally came.

"I'm sure Wing will be okay," Laura said, sitting down beside her friend and putting her arm around her shoulders.

"You don't know that," Shelby sobbed. "For all we know, he's already dead, ripped to pieces by those robotic monsters."

"I don't think Anna would have killed him," Otto said.

"How do you know?" Shelby asked, looking up at him.

"Because I wouldn't have," Otto said, shaking his head. "He's worth more to her alive. That way she can use him as leverage against us."

"Just because that's what you would have done, doesn't mean that's what your psycho sister's done," Shelby snapped back angrily.

"She's not my sister," Otto replied calmly. "I don't know what she is."

"Just put me in a room with her," Shelby snarled, "and this will all be over real quick, whoever she is."

"We all want payback, Shel," Laura said softly. "But we have to understand what we're up against first."

"Why does she think she's related to you?" Nigel asked.

"*Ja*, this is the first we are hearing about you having a family," Franz said, looking slightly confused.

"You remember back in the Glasshouse?" Otto said. "The Disciples had produced some sort of cloned copy of me."

"Yes, we are all remembering evil Otto," Franz said with a nod. "What does he have to do with all this?"

"During my final confrontation with him, he hinted that he may not be the only clone that the Disciples were producing—that he was some kind of prototype," Otto explained. "I think Anna may be another product of that program."

"So, she's a clone of you?" Nigel asked.

"I think so, yes," Otto said with a quick nod. "It's hard to explain, but her powers feel the same as mine. Just a lot more powerful. There's something else to her abilities, though, something I can't quite put my finger on."

"Well, we'd better start figuring out a way to kick her ass," Shelby said. "Because if Wing's still alive, there's no way I'm leaving him in the clutches of that little witch."

"I think it's safe to assume that Nero will feel the same way," Otto said, putting a hand on Shelby's shoulder. "He'll take the school back or die trying. You know that."

"We all will," Laura said.

"So, now we just need to come up with a plan," Otto said.

Joseph Wright's helicopter touched down with a bump on the deck of the Russian missile frigate, next to the ship's own heavy-transport helicopter. Heavily armed Russian marines were already pouring out from a nearby hatch and moving into positions surrounding the aircraft. They raised their weapons, leveling them at Anna as she stepped down from the helicopter's passenger compartment.

"Oh, there's really no need for all this," she said with a smile. "Which one of you is in charge?"

"I am the commanding officer of this vessel," a tall man in dress uniform, with an impressive mustache, replied. "A vessel which you are now under arrest for boarding illegally."

"I'm sorry, could you repeat that?" Anna asked. "And this time *I want you to bark like a dog.*"

A fleeting look of confusion passed across the man's face. He opened his mouth to speak, and the marines surrounding them turned to look at their commanding officer in astonishment as he proceeded to let out a series of loud, woofing noises.

"Who's a good boy?" Anna said with a wicked smile. *Now, why don't the rest of you just drop those nasty guns?*

There was a sudden clattering sound from all around them as the soldiers dropped their weapons to the deck, their faces at once blank and emotionless.

"Now, Captain. Perhaps you'd be so good as to take me to the bridge," Anna said.

As she and the rest of the soldiers followed him through the ship's corridors, they passed by the sailors crewing the vessel, whose expressions changed from surprise at the sight of their captain escorting a young girl, to blank obedience as they each fell under her spell. With every one, Anna could feel her abilities becoming more potent, and by the time they'd reached the bridge, the entire vessel and its crew were under her control.

"Which one of you is the helmsman?" she asked as they arrived at the command deck.

A sailor on the other side of the bridge stood up and turned toward her with an obedient nod.

"I need you to make best possible speed to these coordinates." Anna handed the young sailor a piece of paper.

"Of course," he replied, turning back to his station and issuing a series of rapid commands to the other men around him.

A couple of minutes later, the frigate was heading out of the harbor. Anna listened in amusement to the frantic, confused radio messages from Naval Command demanding to know where the ship was going.

"You know they will try to stop us," Wright said.

"The key word is *try*, Joseph," Anna said with a smile. "I need you to return to Absalom. Once we're in open water, take your helicopter and return to the lab. You are to supervise the continued development of my brothers and sisters. I want you to ensure that they are ready as quickly as possible."

Wright gave a quick nod and left the bridge, heading back down to the flight deck. Anna looked out across the gray waves of the ocean. Soon, she would be joined by her true siblings, not an inferior imitation like Otto Malpense. When her brothers and sisters were born, no one would be able to stop them. The world would be theirs.

The other H.I.V.E. staff members all turned and watched as the two humanoid robots dragged Raven into the room between them. They dumped her limp body in the middle of the room and walked out in silence.

"Natalya!" Miss Leon said, trotting toward her colleague with her tail in the air. Miss Leon had been the Stealth and Evasion tutor at H.I.V.E. for many years but had suffered an unfortunate accident several years before. She had been a willing participant in one of Professor Pike's experiments: a brain-pattern transfer procedure that was supposed to give her the enhanced senses of a cat. The experiment had not gone well, and now her personality was trapped in the body of a fluffy, white cat. The professor had repeatedly reassured her that he was working to find a way to reverse the effects of the procedure, but so far, his efforts had come to naught.

"Stand back," Miss Leon instructed, the blue gem on her collar flashing as the computer inside transferred her thoughts into synthesized speech. "Give her room." The other staff members moved aside as Dr. Scott, H.I.V.E.'s chief medic, knelt beside Raven. Gently he tipped her head to examine the swollen bruises that covered one side of her face, and she let out a soft moan.

"Stop . . . got to . . . ," Raven mumbled as her eyes flickered open for a moment.

"It's okay, Natalya, stay calm," Miss Leon said as Raven woozily tried to push herself upright. "You're hurt, lie still." She turned toward Dr. Scott. "How bad does it look?"

"She's obviously taken a severe beating," Scott replied. "But without my equipment it's impossible to tell how serious her injuries really are. We know that they won't let us take anyone to the sick bay, so the best we can do for now is to make her comfortable here and give her time to rest and heal."

"Who has done this?" Miss Gonzales, the head of H.I.V.E.'s Biotechnology department, asked.

"Those are Cypher's robots," Miss Tennenbaum, head

of Finance and Corruption, pointed out. "But I thought he was dead?"

"He is," Miss Leon said. "Which means that whoever is responsible for this attack has taken control of them."

"Let's face it," Mr. Rictor, the Logistics tutor, said. "Nero's made more than his fair share of enemies over the past couple of years. Taking down Number One, defeating H.O.P.E., and now this war with the Disciples—almost anyone could be responsible for this."

"I don't think that figuring out who is responsible for this is as important as working out how to stop them," Miss Leon said calmly.

"With the greatest of respect, Tabitha," Miss Gonzales said, "how exactly do you propose we fight an army of robot assassins? Just look what they did to Raven."

"I don't know," Miss Leon admitted. "But we'd better come up with something before this situation gets any worse."

"I'm sorry, I wish I had better news to give you," Nero said, looking around the table at the holographic projections of the other members of G.L.O.V.E.'s Ruling Council. The Global League of Villainous Enterprises had been covertly influencing world events for decades, and the men and women seated at the table were each responsible for a specific region. They were all past graduates of H.I.V.E., handpicked by Nero when he had disbanded the old Ruling Council, but he knew their loyalty only extended so far. In the world they occupied, it was, after all, best to trust no one.

"Several of my senior staff have children at your school, Dr. Nero," Jennifer Harding, G.L.O.V.E.'s Head of UK Operations, said with a frown. "What exactly do you propose that I tell them? That their children are currently being held hostage by an army of robots controlled by a psychotic clone, but 'Don't worry I'm sure everything will be okay'?"

"As far as I'm aware, none of the students have been harmed," Nero said.

"It seems there's been rather too much recently that you haven't been aware of," Xia Yan, Chief of Chinese Operations, said. "So perhaps you will understand if that does not offer us much reassurance."

Nero knew that Xia Yan's own daughter had recently become a student at H.I.V.E., and his calm demeanor was concealing the anxiety that he was sure to be feeling. No matter how ruthless the members of the council may appear, he knew that for some of them their children were their greatest points of vulnerability.

"What I can assure you of, is that I will not rest until H.I.V.E. is back under my control," Nero said. "And you should all know me well enough by now to know that I am not in the habit of making idle promises."

"I'm sure I speak for all of us, Maximilian, when I say I intend to hold you to that promise," Xia Yan said seriously. The threat was subtle but clear, the members of the council would not tolerate failure, and Nero knew from past experience that if they sensed weakness, they would fall upon him like wolves.

"Obviously, I will keep you fully informed of any developments," he said. "Until then, all I can ask for is your continued trust."

"And, for now, you have it." Harding looked Nero in the eye. "But you know as well as anyone that trust is a finite commodity in our business."

"Do Unto Others . . . ," Nero prompted, and the other council members repeated G.L.O.V.E.'s motto as they disconnected.

"But, please don't Do Unto Me." Darkdoom stepped out of the shadowy corner of the *Megalodon*'s conference room, from where he had been observing the meeting.

"They have every reason to doubt me at this precise moment," Nero said as his friend sat down at the table opposite him. "I can't blame them for their lack of confidence."

"You're the most effective leader this council has ever had," Darkdoom said. "And some of them would do well to remember that."

"I appreciate your support, Diabolus." Nero sighed. "But if this goes wrong, if something happens to the students, they'll come after me. To be honest with you, I would be somewhat disappointed if they didn't. I trained them better than that."

"For all our sakes, let's hope it doesn't come to that," Darkdoom said. "The Disciples are still out there, and our only chance of stopping them is if we remain unified."

"Well, let's hope that the rest of the members of the council feel the same way," Nero said.

There was a sudden knock on the conference room door.

"Come in," Nero said.

Otto walked into the room, glancing quickly at the two men.

"I think I need to speak to you both," he said. "I suspect there might be rather more to this than we realize."

"Please tell me you have some sort of good news," Darkdoom said.

"I'm not sure that's quite how I'd describe it," Otto told him. "But it may be an explanation as to why Anna is so powerful."

"Go on." Nero gestured toward one of the empty seats at the table.

"I noticed something," Otto said, taking the offered seat. "When Anna first manifested in H.I.V.E.mind's data core. At first, I just thought it was her abilities playing tricks with my head, but I think there might be more to it than that. When she was talking to me up here"—Otto tapped the side of his head—"there was something about her voice, something familiar."

"If she is another one of your clones made by the Disciples, that's hardly surprising," Nero said. "She may not look the same as you, but you share a genetic heritage."

"No," Otto said, shaking his head, "this was something else. She was using the Voice, the same voice that Lucy used, that the Contessa used. I think they've been experimenting with Sinistre genetic material."

Darkdoom shot a quick glance at Nero across the table, his concern evident.

"Are you sure?" Nero asked. "Their family have very deliberately stayed out of our conflict with the Disciples. If that's changed, if the Disciples are now allied with the Sinistre family, we're talking about a whole new level of threat."

"I thought the Shadow Queen personally assured you she wanted no part of this war," Darkdoom said with a frown.

"She did," Nero replied. "She thinks her family have lost enough over the past few years. And frankly, I can't say I blame her."

The Sinistre family had been part of H.I.V.E.'s history for a long time. The Contessa, Maria Sinistre, had once been one of Nero's most trusted allies, but she had betrayed that trust. Her actions had very nearly led to the destruction of H.I.V.E., and it was only in her final moments that she found some sort of redemption by sacrificing herself, rather than allowing Number One to murder the entire alpha stream. Her granddaughter, the Viscontessa Lucia Sinistre, had become a pupil at the school, although she had gone by the name Lucy Dexter for fear that her grandmother's previous actions might change the way people saw her. Ultimately, she too had given her life heroically but tragically, while helping Otto finally eliminate the apocalyptic threat of Overlord and the Animus nanites. Lucy and Otto had grown close prior to these tragic events, and Nero knew that her loss still weighed heavily upon the young man sitting across the table from him.

"You're assuming they know anything about this," Otto said. "The Disciples are not in the habit of asking for permission to use someone's genetic material in their experiments, I know that as well as anyone. Zero, the clone of myself that I faced in the Glasshouse, had a similar ability. At the time I thought it was just an evolution of my ability to influence electrical systems, that was somehow allowing him to control the actions of others.

But perhaps there was more to it than that?"

"I suppose that is a possibility," Nero pondered. "The Furans always were obsessed with control. To have the abilities of the Sinistre family at their fingertips would be a remarkably efficient way to achieve that."

"It would certainly bear further investigation," Darkdoom said with a nod.

"We have to find some way to stop her," Otto said, looking at Nero. "When she attacked the school, she was using her abilities remotely, and even then I could feel how powerful she was. In person, I don't think I or anyone else would be able to resist her."

"You can rest assured, Mr. Malpense, that I take the threat from this girl and the people that created her very, very seriously," Nero asserted. "We're going to stop her, crush the Disciples, and take back my school. One way or another."

Otto stared at Nero for a moment, before giving a quick nod and leaving the room.

"I hope to God he's wrong about this," Darkdoom said as the door closed behind Otto. "I know how hard you worked to keep the Sinistres out of this war. If that's changed, if they've become allies with the Disciples, well . . . it doesn't bear thinking about."

"I have known that woman my entire life," Nero said, shaking his head. "Unlike her daughter, I have never had any reason to doubt the Contessa's word, once it was given. I know that she holds me partly to blame for Lucy's death, but she swore to me that she wanted no part of this, and I think I know her well enough to know that she wasn't lying to me."

"Or she just *told* you that she wasn't lying to you," Darkdoom said, raising an eyebrow.

"You don't need to worry about that," Nero replied. "I've always been immune to the influence of their abilities, for whatever reason. The Contessa always told me it was because their abilities don't work on people with a sufficiently strong will."

"Well, then, assuming that's true, I can see why it wouldn't work on you," Darkdoom said with a wry smile.

"I think we may need to pay the Shadow Queen a visit," Nero said, though even after everything he had faced in his life, the thought of a meeting with that particular woman was still enough to send a chill down his spine.

"I'll have the helm lay a course for Italy immediately."

"Oh, well, this is all very dramatic," Anna said as the heavy Russian helicopter raced up the rocky flanks of the massive volcanic island. As they crested the rim of the crater, the helicopter decelerated and dropped into a hover as it began its descent into H.I.V.E.'s hangar. Half a minute later, its wheels alighted on the landing pad with a soft bump and Anna stepped down from the passenger compartment. Two squads of assassin androids stood, silently waiting for her arrival, with two more of the hulking Behemoth units close behind them. Anna walked toward the cockpit of the helicopter and tapped on the pilot's window.

"Take this thing back to the ship," she instructed. "And tell the captain he may carry out the orders I gave him."

The pilot gave a quick nod, and a few moments later the helicopter took off, soaring back into the air and out of the crater, heading back toward the Russian missile frigate. Anna had implanted a simple command in the vessel's captain before she left. He was to take his ship five hundred miles in any direction and scuttle it. While she had been able to use her powers to disable any of the equipment on board that would have allowed the Russian Navy to track the vessel, she knew that they would be desperately searching for their lost ship. It was a vast ocean, and it would be like looking for a needle in a haystack, but she did not want anyone else discovering the location of H.I.V.E., for now, at least. The chances of any of the crew surviving were minimal, especially given that she had ordered them to destroy the life rafts before she left. She just could not bring herself to care.

"Take me to the staff detention area," she instructed. One of the squads of assassin droids wheeled around, marching ahead of her through the school corridors, leading her to the area where H.I.V.E.'s teachers were being kept captive. She could not help but be impressed by the scale of the facility surrounding her. She had instructed Joseph Wright to tell her everything he knew about the school, before sending him back to the Absalom lab to prepare the other clones to receive the same upgrades as herself. It was clear from the way that he had talked about H.I.V.E. that it had acquired a certain mythical status among the senior members of the Disciples. Nero and his students had been personally responsible for derailing more of the Disciples' schemes than any other organization. As far as many of the Disciples were concerned, she was walking straight into the dragon's den. They might be correct, she thought to herself with a smile. The only difference being that now *she* was the dragon.

A minute later, the squad of armored black robots drew to a halt in front of a set of heavy steel doors, taking up flanking defensive positions on either side of the door. Anna reached out to the schools' systems, opening the massive blast doors with a single thought. Inside, curious faces turned in her direction as she entered the room.

"Good afternoon," she said, addressing the assembled staff members. "My name is Anna, and as I'm sure you've all worked out: This facility now belongs to me."

"We know who you are," Raven said, slowly pushing herself up off the bench where she had been lying. She winced in discomfort as she got to her feet, livid bruises covering her face. She held one hand to her side, supporting what she was reasonably sure were a couple of cracked ribs. The other teachers stood aside as Raven walked to the front of the group, as if shielding the other staff members. "You're not the first person to try to take this school over and I don't suppose you'll be the last."

"You must be Raven." Anna smiled as she walked toward Natalya. "You certainly don't look like the bogeyman that my friends in the Disciples seem to think you are. Quite unimpressive, in fact."

"Why don't you send your toys away?" Raven said, glancing at the mechanical guards that surrounded her. "So I can show you just how unimpressive I can be."

"Oh, do be quiet," Anna said with a wave of her hand, her voice taking on a sinister whispering subtone. "In fact, why don't you *just stop breathing.*"

Raven's eyes widened as she felt her lungs freeze inside her chest. She clawed at her throat as her body's autonomous respiratory systems simply stopped working, and then dropped to her knees, her face turning red and the veins in her neck bulging.

"Stop it!" Dr. Scott said, dropping down beside Raven

and turning her onto her back as she lay convulsing. "You're killing her!"

"I know," Anna replied. "Isn't it fun?"

"Please! We all know what you're capable of," Dr. Scott pleaded. "This isn't necessary."

"I suppose I've made my point," Anna said with a nasty smile. *"You may breathe again."*

Raven took a series of gasping, desperate breaths before her breathing slowly returned to normal.

"I think that's quite enough of these distractions." Anna looked around the room. "I'm afraid I'm going to need you all to *give me your unquestioning obedience.*"

These last few words were filled with the same sinister whisper in the background that they had all heard in the near-fatal command she had just given to Raven. Around the room, the assembled teachers' faces fell slack, completely neutral expressions replacing the looks of apprehension and fear that had been all too apparent just a moment before.

"There now, isn't that better?" Anna said with a smile. "I want each of you to go to an accommodation block and inform the students within that I have taken complete control of their school. You will also make it quite clear to them that any form of resistance will be crushed quickly and fatally."

She did not need to ask them if they understood her

instructions. Moments later, the assembled staff began to walk out of the room; Miss Leon at the rear, her tail flicking in the air.

"Just when you think your day can't get any stranger," Anna said, looking down at the cat as it left the room. "Not you," she barked at Raven, whose face was now as blank as the others. "You and I are going to pay a visit to an old friend of yours, I have a feeling she's going to be very, very, pleased to see you. . . ."

"You okay?" Laura asked.

Shelby delivered a series of quick, hard blows to the heavy punching bag hanging in front of her in the *Megalodon*'s gym.

"You're interrupting my visualization," Shelby said, through gritted teeth, as she landed several more solid straight-armed punches. Laura didn't really need to ask who was currently taking the place of the punching bag in Shelby's imagination.

"Otto said you were down here." Laura had a slightly worried expression as she watched her friend continue to pummel the bag. "Want to talk?"

"Can't talk. Punching," Shelby said.

"I can see that," Laura replied. "But I think you can stop now. I'm pretty sure she's dead."

Shelby gave the bag one last powerful jab, letting out

an angry growl, then grabbed it to stop it swinging and took a couple of deep breaths.

"You know, I never knew how therapeutic it could be beating the crap out of one of these things until Wing showed me," Shelby said, turning toward Laura with a sad expression on her face. "If you're looking for the traditional Shelby Trinity snark, I'm afraid I'm all out today."

"I just want to make sure my best friend is alright," Laura said softly.

"And I just want to know what's happened to him." Shelby's voice cracked. "I don't even know if he's alive or . . ." She suddenly burst into tears, and Laura wrapped her arms around her friend, hugging her tightly.

"Don't assume the worst," she said gently as Shelby sobbed into her shoulder. "Right now, I'm sure he's sitting in a prison cell somewhere, wondering when his friends are going to turn up and save him."

"You can't be sure that's true," Shelby said, pulling away from Laura and shaking her head.

"And you can't be sure it isn't," Laura said, looking Shelby in the eye. "When I was in the Glasshouse, the only thing that kept me going was the knowledge that, no matter what, you guys would be out there looking for me. We never give up on each other, that's the deal. We're going to take H.I.V.E. back, rescue Wing, and kick that clone's ass."

"I hope you're right." Shelby sighed. "I really do."

"Course I am," Laura said with a crooked smile. "Otto agrees with me and we all know he's—"

"Always right, never wrong," Shelby said, a smile flickering across her face for the first time.

"Except when he *is* wrong, which is actually quite a lot of the time, when you stop and think about it," Laura added with a grin.

"Thanks for checking on me. Love you, Brand." Shelby kissed her friend on the cheek. "Now, I'm going to hit the showers because I smell like Colonel Francisco's jock strap."

"And you would know how that smells because . . ."

"Hey," Shelby said over her shoulder as she walked toward the changing rooms. "A girl has to have her secrets."

Laura walked out of the gym and into the corridor beyond. The wide passageways of the *Megalodon* were nothing like the usual tight, cramped conditions on a normal submarine. If anything, it felt more like being in a spacious underwater building. The first submarine to bear the name *Megalodon* had been impressive enough, but this, its replacement, was even more enormous.

"Hey, you two," Laura said as she rounded the corner and found Otto in conversation with Nigel. "Tell me, Nigel, does your dad ever build anything *small*?"

"Not that I've ever been aware of, no," Nigel said. "In fact, I doubt he even knows what the word 'compact' means."

"I'm pretty sure I heard Nero muttering 'needlessly ostentatious' under his breath as we came on board," Otto said.

"Says the man who built a school inside a hollowed-out volcano," Laura shot back with a smile.

"I have to go. I promised I'd meet Franz in the armory," Nigel said with a groan. "Apparently, there's all sorts of interesting equipment down there that he wants to show me."

"Sounds thrilling," Otto said. "Don't let us keep you."

"Aye," Laura chimed in. "If you're lucky, he might give you the lecture I got on ballistic penetration last week."

"Well, I wouldn't want to miss out on that," Nigel said, rolling his eyes. "See you guys later."

Otto and Laura watched as Nigel walked away.

"Did you find Shelby?" Otto asked.

"Yeah, she was in the gym," Laura said with a slight frown.

"Is she alright?"

"She will be. Not sure I can say the same for the punching bag she was using, though."

"I know how she feels," Otto said, sighing. "I'm just trying to focus on what we should do next. I'm trying really hard not to think about what's going on back at H.I.V.E. right now."

"You're really worried, aren't you?" Laura asked. She knew him well enough by now to know when something was eating him up inside.

"I just keep thinking back to the Glasshouse and Zero," Otto admitted. "The only reason I was able to stop Zero was because I had H.I.V.E.mind tucked away up here." He tapped a finger against the side of his head. "Without his help, I'm not sure I would have been able to break his control over me."

"And you're worried that Anna might be able to do the same thing?"

"There's no *might* about it, Laura," Otto said, looking her straight in the eye. "Anna's abilities make Zero's seem trivial, and I'm afraid she's only just starting to learn how to use them. I'm not sure we can stop her."

"It's not just that," Laura said. "There's something else bothering you, isn't there?"

"I . . . I'm just sick of being tortured by this stuff," Otto said, suddenly looking tired. "How many more times is Overlord's legacy . . . my legacy . . . going to come back to haunt us all?"

"This isn't your fault, Otto," Laura said, shaking her head. "You didn't ask for any of this—none of us did. We spend our whole lives being propelled from one crisis to

155

the next, we've all been through hell. But do you know what? Honestly, even if I could, I wouldn't change any of it. You guys are the best friends I've ever had, and really, that's all that matters."

"You don't understand, Laura," Otto replied. "Our friendship, how much we all care about one another, could be our greatest weakness. Anna knows that, and I'm frightened of the things she could make me do. . . ."

"What did Lucy tell you, just before she died?" Laura said, putting her hand on the side of his face and staring at him.

"That there always has to be a choice," Otto said, trying to block out the memory of Lucy's limp body in his arms.

"Right," Laura said. "And that's why we're going to stop Anna, because that's what she takes from people, what *everyone* like her always takes from people. Choice."

"I hope you're right, Laura," he said. "Because, right now we're pretty much the only thing standing between her and the rest of the world."

chapter seven

Raven walked along behind Anna, flanked by a pair of the robotic assassins. Anna may have had faith in her own abilities, but she did not see the point of taking unnecessary risks at this stage. They were heading deep into the bowels of the school, past storage areas and machine rooms that were rarely visited by anyone but technicians performing routine maintenance. They came to the end of a remote corridor, Anna stopping for a moment to examine the blank rock wall.

"H.I.V.E.mind, deactivate the holographic projectors," she said.

A moment later, the rocks that made up the wall began to shimmer and distort before vanishing completely to reveal a heavy steel door.

"Open the door," Anna said calmly.

"Detention facility Omega, access granted," H.I.V.E.mind

replied as the door rumbled open. Anna was struck by a wave of heat from the corridor beyond, and she took a deep breath before walking inside. A bright orange light illuminated the end of the short, rock passageway that she passed along, with Raven and the robotic guards just behind her. A moment later, she walked out onto a platform mounted on a sheer rock wall that dropped away to a seething pool of lava far below. On the other side of the platform was a waist-high barrier with a gate at its center.

"Wait here," Anna instructed Raven.

As Anna walked toward the gate, it slid aside, and a metal walkway extended across the lake of lava to another steel door set in the rocky cavern wall on the other side of the chasm. Anna crossed the walkway with her robot guards just behind her, feeling the searing heat rising from the magma below. The door at the far end of the walkway opened, granting her access to the small cave beyond. The room was divided in two by a thick sheet of reinforced glass, on the other side of which was a spartan steel-lined prison cell. As she approached the cell, Anna could see someone wearing loose white overalls, lying curled into a fetal ball, facing the rocky wall.

"Come to gloat, Nero?" the woman lying on the floor said without turning away from the wall.

"I'm afraid the good doctor will not be joining us today," Anna replied.

The woman on the floor slowly stood up and turned to face Anna. Her face was a twisted hideous mask of scar tissue, and one of her hands appeared to have been reinforced with some form of robotics, silver metal embedded within the scorched flesh and twisted bone.

"Anastasia Furan," Anna said with a smile. "You have no idea how long I've been waiting to meet you."

"I'm afraid you have me at a disadvantage," Furan confessed, walking toward the reinforced glass. "You clearly know who *I* am, but I'm afraid I can't say the same about you."

"Really?" Anna took a step forward to the glass between them. "You should recognize this face. After all, you made it."

"Absalom," Furan said, a smile slowly spreading across her twisted face. "It worked."

"Indeed," Anna gritted out. "Perhaps rather better than you intended."

"Where's Nero?" Furan asked. "I do hope you haven't killed him, because I was rather looking forward to doing that myself."

"Nero is gone. He's irrelevant," Anna replied, sounding slightly irritated. "What matters is that his school, and more importantly his pet artificial intelligence, are now mine."

"In my experience, Maximilian Nero should never be

discounted," Furan said. "How many men do you have with you?"

"Just my little clockwork helpers here." Anna gestured to the mechanical guards that flanked her.

"You took H.I.V.E. from Nero on your own?" Furan said. "Impressive."

"Oh, I'm very talented," Anna quipped. "I put it down to good genes."

Furan studied the young girl on the other side of the glass for a moment. Her claim to have taken H.I.V.E. from Nero seemed barely credible, but Anastasia couldn't deny the evidence of her own eyes. The only way this girl could be standing here in front of her was because Nero had not been able to stop her.

"Something tells me you didn't come down here just to say hello," she said. "So, what can I do for you, my dear?"

"I want you to tell me what it was that you added into my genetic blueprint," Anna said. "Why is it that I have abilities that my unborn brothers and sisters do not?"

"Well. It's hardly a secret ingredient if you tell everyone what it is, now, is it?"

"You seem to think that I'm giving you a choice," Anna said, her voice filling with sinister whispers. *"Tell me how you modified my design."*

Furan's face froze for a moment and then broke into a broad smile.

"Oh, I'm afraid that won't work on me," she said, getting closer to the glass. "Did you really think for a moment that I'd create a weapon that could so easily be turned against me? If so, you clearly don't know me very well. No. If you really want what's inside my mind, you're going to have to come in here and get it."

Anna tipped her head on one side, looking at Furan in the same way that someone might look at a dog that had just done a particularly clever trick.

"You still feel pain, though," she said after a few seconds. "There's always that option."

"Look at me," Furan said angrily, pushing her face to within an inch of the glass. "Do I look like someone who doesn't know everything there is to know about pain? I'll die before I tell you anything you want to know."

"Then it seems we are at an impasse," Anna said calmly.

"I'd rather think of it as the start of a negotiation." Furan's eyes narrowed.

"What's your price?"

"It's very simple," Furan replied. "Give me Nero and Raven, and help me end them. Then I'll tell you everything you want to know."

"Why should I trust you?" Anna asked, looking Furan in the eye.

"Do you have a choice?"

Anna studied her for a moment.

"H.I.V.E.mind, open the cell."

The glass wall separating them slowly began to drop into the floor. Furan watched as Anna walked over to the door of the cell and called to someone outside.

"I have something for you," Anna told her. "Consider it a down payment on our deal."

A moment later, Raven walked into the room and stood obediently behind her. Furan walked over and placed her twisted metal hand on Raven's cheek, whose blank expression didn't change in the slightest.

"Oh, Natalya," Furan said with an evil smile. "The things I'm going to make you do . . ."

The motorboat pulled up to the jetty, the blue waters of the Mediterranean lapping at its hull.

"Just once it would be nice to visit somewhere like this without it being in the middle of a life-threatening crisis," Nero said wearily as he stepped ashore.

"Then, I think you may be in the wrong line of work, my friend," Darkdoom said with a smile.

"I could have told you that years ago," Nero quipped as two bulky men wearing immaculately cut dark suits walked down the pier toward them.

"Looks like we have a welcoming party," Otto said as he climbed ashore. He had swapped his H.I.V.E. uniform for regular clothes. It wouldn't help them at this point to attract undue attention.

"Let me do the talking," Nero said. "Our hosts can be a little . . . paranoid."

"What did you tell me once?" Darkdoom said. "'It's not paranoia if they really are all trying to kill you.'"

"Quite," Nero murmured as the men reached them.

"*Gentiluomini*," the first man said as he approached. "*La Regina Delle Ombre* extends you her welcome and hopes you have had a pleasant journey. If you would be so good as to come with me."

He gestured toward the shore, where a silver helicopter sat waiting for them, its rotor blades slowly turning.

"Of course, thank you," Nero replied.

They walked down the jetty toward the landing pad, the two Italian men flanking them.

"I still think we should have flown your Shroud straight there," Darkdoom said quietly to Nero.

"Something tells me that our host might not have appreciated us landing a combat dropship in the middle of her grounds," Nero said. "We do this the discreet way, for now."

When they reached the helicopter, one of their escorts climbed up into the passenger compartment with Nero, Otto, and Darkdoom, while the other took a seat in the cockpit next to the pilot.

"Flight time to our destination is just under an hour," the pilot said as the passengers donned the headphones that enabled onboard communication and the rotor spun up. A moment later, the helicopter lifted into the clear blue sky, banking toward the distant Italian Alps.

There were very few things in the world that made Robert Flack apprehensive, but sitting in this particular chair was one of them.

"Mr. Flack," a woman in a smart business suit said, walking up to him.

"Yes," Flack replied, swallowing nervously.

"He's ready to see you now." She gestured toward the door at the end of the corridor. "Please follow me."

Flack walked down the corridor, the woman escorting him opening the door and ushering him into the room beyond. He recalled something that one of his old bosses had said years ago. "It doesn't matter how many times you walk into that room, it always feels like the first time."

The president sat behind the Resolute desk at the far end of the Oval Office. He looked up from the papers in front of him as Flack entered the room.

"Mr. Flack," the president said. "It's good to see you again. Please, take a seat."

He gestured across his desk to the couches arranged around the rug, which bore the seal of the president of the

United States. Flack took the offered seat and started to pull files out of his briefcase.

"Thank you, Mr. President," Flack replied. "I'll try to keep this as brief as possible."

"Good." The president gestured to the papers on his desk. "Because I've got enough to worry about making sure that my replacement doesn't end up being a reality TV host with multiple bankruptcies behind him."

"With the greatest of respect, sir. There's no way that clown's going to win the election. No sane person is going to choose him over the secretary of state."

"Let's hope you're right, Mr. Flack," the president said with a nod. "Now, perhaps you could explain to me how our Russian friends could be so careless as to lose an entire missile frigate?"

"According to our sources, they didn't lose it, it just vanished."

"So, given that that's impossible, what actually happened?" the president asked.

"As far as we can tell, it was a massive systemic disruption to multiple surveillance networks," Flack said, opening one of the files in front of him. "Effectively, someone hacked the global military surveillance network and simply blinded it to the existence of the ship. We reviewed our own satellite footage of the ships' departure from the Russian naval base and it's bizarre."

He laid two satellite surveillance images next to each other on the table in front of him.

"Look," he said, pointing at the line of text at the top of each image. "The GPS coordinates are identical and the time stamps are only seconds apart, but as you can clearly see . . . Now you see it, now you don't."

The huge Russian military vessel had simply vanished in the second image.

"Could it just be a glitch?" the president asked.

"Not unless it was a glitch that affected every system tracking that area of the ocean at exactly the same time," Flack countered. "I'm afraid it bears all the hallmarks of the attack on the Advanced Weapons Project facility last year."

"Hence, your involvement," the president said, looking up from the pair of images.

"Yes, sir. The only person that we are aware of that could possibly be responsible for a hack on this scale is Otto Malpense."

"You think he's responsible for this?" the president asked with a frown. "I thought there'd been no trace of him since the incident in Venice last year?"

"That's correct, sir, no sign of him," Flack replied. "We've been focused on trying to run down this H.I.V.E. organization that we discovered evidence of in the aftermath of that fiasco. We think that's who he works for."

"I'm assuming that if you'd discovered anything of significance, I would have already been informed," the president said.

"I'm afraid we've run into nothing but dead ends," Flack said, shaking his head. "In some cases, quite literally dead."

"I need a better answer than that, Robert," the president said. "Malpense may have saved my life when Air Force One was attacked, but not long afterward he was also responsible for making me the first president in American history to launch a nuclear weapon in anger against a target inside our own border. That's not the sort of loose cannon I need rolling around on deck. I want him found and I want him captured. If he's tied up with the disappearance of this Russian ship, we need to know what he's up to."

"Yes, sir." Flack nodded. "We'll do our best."

"Your best isn't good enough, Robert, I need results." The president frowned.

"Roger that, sir."

A couple of minutes later, Flack walked out of the White House main gates onto Pennsylvania Avenue, heading for the nearby nondescript office block that was the Washington headquarters of Artemis section. He completely understood the president's frustration with his team's progress in tracking down Malpense. The boy had proven to be an unusually elusive quarry. In this day and age, it was next to impossible to escape all forms of electronic surveillance, but Malpense and his associates were like ghosts.

He walked in through the entrance of the low, gray building and swiped his ID card through the reader next to the elevators in the lobby. When he finally reached his floor, the doors opened onto a scene of bustling, panicked chaos.

"Rob!" a woman shouted from the other side of the room, running toward him with a sheet of paper in her hand. "Thank God. We've been trying to reach you for the last twenty minutes—where were you?"

"I was in with the president," Flack replied, pulling his phone from his jacket pocket and thumbing the controls irritably. "I forgot to turn my phone back on, what is it?"

"We got a triple facial recognition hit in Italy, half an hour ago, on the coast near Genoa," the woman answered excitedly, thrusting the piece of paper into his hands. On it was a photo of Otto Malpense walking toward a helicopter with two other men, the three of them flanked by what looked like a pair of bodyguards.

"My God, that's Nero," Flack said, studying the image. Dr. Maximilian Nero had been captured several years ago by H.O.P.E.: the Hostile Operative Prosecution Executive and had been assumed dead after it became clear that H.O.P.E. was merely a cover for some form of terrorist organization. Yet here he was, alive and well, on the northwest coast of Italy. "And that's our ghost from Venice," he said, pointing at the tall bald man next to Nero. That man had been instrumental in helping Malpense escape from the Artemis retrieval team in Venice, but his people had still not been able to put a name to the face.

"Contact JSOC and tell them I want every asset they have in the area, with boots on the ground ready to move," Flack snapped. "And find out where that helicopter went."

"How are you feeling?" Block asked, sitting down on the end of Wing's bed.

"Better, thank you," Wing replied. "I . . . I am most grateful for your assistance."

"S'alright," Tackle said, standing in the doorway of the room. "Thought you was dead when they dragged you in here."

"Frankly, I'm rather surprised I'm not," Wing said. "What's going on out there?"

"Nuffink really." Block shrugged. "Those robot things are patrolling down in the atrium, but they don't seem to care what we do as long as we don't go near the exit."

"You got a plan?" Tackle asked quietly.

"That was more Otto's department," Wing said with a sigh. He could only hope that Otto, Shelby, and the others had managed to escape, somehow; though in truth he had no idea what fate had befallen them. "But getting out of this lockdown seems like a sensible first step."

Wing slowly got to his feet and walked out of the room. He stepped up to the balcony rail running along the walkway outside and looked down into the accommodation block's atrium area. Several of Anna's robots were patrolling the area near the exit, just as Block had said, but they never left that area. There were dozens of students milling around the other areas of the block, but the android guards seemed completely unconcerned with them.

"Uh-oh, look out, it's cat lady," Tackle said, nudging Wing and nodding his head toward the far end of the balcony. Miss Leon had arrived in the block several hours ago and informed the collected students that they were now all prisoners, and that their continued survival depended entirely on their obedience. Since then, she had done nothing but patrol the accommodation block in silence. As she approached the three boys, she slowed and then stopped, sitting down and looking up at them.

"Student Fanchu," Miss Leon said. "Return to your room. Students Tackle and Block, leave the area."

"But we—" Block began.

"Silence!" Miss Leon said. "Obey my instructions, or I will summon the guards."

Block and Tackle walked away grumbling as Wing backed into his room, with Miss Leon walking in after him.

"Close the door," she said, and Wing hit the door switch, which hissed shut. "Okay, we don't have long. I think I know how we can get out of here."

"What?" Wing said, looking confused.

"Do try to keep up, Mr. Fanchu." Miss Leon sounded frustrated. "It would appear that Anna's mind-control abilities don't work on me. I suppose it's hardly surprising, I mean, have you ever tried telling a cat what to do?"

"No, I haven't," Wing replied, looking slightly confused.

"Well, trust me, it's a waste of time," Miss Leon said. "And, right now, I need your help to stop Anna."

"Of course. What do you need?"

"We need to get the back door open," Miss Leon replied.

"Back door?" Wing frowned. "There is no back door to the accommodation blocks."

"The fact you've never seen something does not mean it doesn't exist," Miss Leon corrected. "Nero had back doors installed in every accommodation block after the situation with Number One. Only senior staff were

171

informed, because Nero seemed to have some foolish notion that if certain students found out about it, they might find a way to exploit it. I can't imagine who he was talking about, can you?"

"Point taken."

"To make this work, I need you and one other student," Miss Leon said. "Their job is to get us past the locking mechanism. Yours is . . . well . . . to hit people really hard when necessary. Think you can handle that?"

"It would be my pleasure," Wing said with a nod. "Who is the other student?"

"Penny Lancaster," Miss Leon said.

"Ah." Wing grimaced.

"Is there a problem with that?"

"Perhaps," Wing replied. "Penny has been quite different since her return from the Glasshouse. She seems to have developed something of a grudge against Otto and his friends, including myself. I believe she blames us for the death of her friend Tom."

"Well, let's just hope that she can let bygones be bygones," Miss Leon said. "Because we need her. Come on."

Wing opened the door and followed her as she trotted back out onto the balcony. Together, they moved to the stairs at the far end and headed down to the rooms two levels below. When they reached Penny's room, they found her sitting on her bed reading.

"What do *you* want?" Penny said, scowling at Wing.

"We need your help," Wing said.

"Hah! Me help you . . . What happened to the rest of the Scooby gang?"

"*We* need your help, Miss Lancaster," Miss Leon said, stepping into the room.

"I'm sorry, Miss Leon, I didn't see you there," Penny said, a sudden look of apprehension on her face. "I know what you said about disobedience and . . ."

"Not a mind-controlled bad guy, faking," Miss Leon said. "To cut a long story very short."

"Oh, but I thought . . ."

"Miss Lancaster, I'm going to cut to the chase. I need you to help me get us out of here. After myself and Miss Trinity, you are probably the most accomplished thief at this school, and so I need you to open some locks for me."

"What kind of locks?" Penny asked.

"The kind that require opposable thumbs," Miss Leon said, holding up one of her paws. "Don't worry, I can talk you through it. Can I count on you?"

"Yes," Penny said, looking at Wing. "Just keep him out of my way."

"Good." Miss Leon nodded. "Now let me explain what I need you to do."

• • •

Otto looked down on the dark spires of the castle below. It seemed to almost grow organically from the mountainside, its many twisting towers and minarets looking like something out of a dark fairy tale. They slowly descended into the courtyard below, the gloomy quadrangle lit by burning torches.

"I see she hasn't lost her flair for the dramatic," Nero said as they descended.

"Looks like she's gone full Goth to me," Otto said quietly.

"And that, Mr. Malpense, is why I will be doing the talking," Nero said. "You will find that your trademark witticisms have little currency here. The Shadow Queen is not renowned for her sense of humor. Quite the opposite."

The helicopter touched down, and a guard rushed over and opened the rear hatch. Otto stepped down from the aircraft and looked up at the ancient stone walls surrounding him, covered in deep-purple ivy vines, and roses with blooms so dark that they almost looked black. A tall man with a gaunt, pale face, wearing a traditional butler's uniform, walked across the cobbles toward them.

"*La Regina Delle Ombre* would like me to welcome you all to Castello del Sinistre," the servant said. "I trust you had a pleasant journey."

"Quite comfortable, thank you," Nero replied. "Please thank the Queen on my behalf."

"Of course, sir," the man answered with a nod. "Now if you would like to follow me, I will show you to your accommodations."

"We were not intending to stay," Nero said, shooting a glance at Darkdoom. "As I believe I stated in my message requesting an audience, our business here is quite urgent."

"The Queen fully understands the urgent nature of your business and she will discuss the matter further with you over dinner," the butler said. "I trust that will not be a problem?"

"Not at all," Nero said, biting his tongue. "It would be an honor to dine at the Queen's table."

"Excellent. Now if you would be so kind as to walk this way." The butler gestured toward a nearby doorway, and Nero, Darkdoom, and Otto followed him inside, finding themselves in a grand entrance hallway lined with portraits of women from centuries past who all shared similar sharp features. Otto glanced at the dates on the portraits as they passed; some of them were from centuries back. Anyone walking through the room could be left in little doubt that they were entering the home of a family with a long history of great power.

"Some of these portraits are from the fifteenth century," Otto whispered to Nero as they walked. "Have the Sinistres really been around that long?"

"That's just when they started having their portraits painted," Nero murmured, nodding toward a statue at the end of the room. "They've been around a little longer than that."

Otto's eyes widened as they neared the statue and he realized that it was unmistakably ancient Roman, the woman's elegant marble features an uncanny match for the faces staring down from the canvasses around them.

"Why do I suddenly feel like I've just walked straight into the lion's den," Otto confessed, feeling a chill run down his spine.

"Oh, this isn't the lion's den, Otto," Darkdoom replied under his breath. "This . . . is the spider's web."

Out in the courtyard, one of the guards on the main gate checked his surroundings and then pulled a mobile phone from his pocket. He quickly punched in a number and waited a few seconds for the call to connect.

"Mr. Wright," the man said quietly. "They're here."

At the Absalom laboratory, Joseph Wright hit the disconnect button on his phone. He punched in another number and waited.

"*Identification?*" the distorted electronic voice on the other end of the line asked.

"Wright. Disciple Three One Nine Epsilon."

"*ID confirmed,*" the voice replied. "*Connecting.*"

Wright waited for a few seconds, and then a gruff voice answered on the other end of the line.

"Wet team seven standing by, sir. Do you have a target location?"

"The Castello del Sinistre," Wright said.

"Target ID?"

"High-value targets, Nero, Darkdoom, and Malpense."

There was a short pause before the man on the other end of the line answered.

"Understood. Kill or capture?"

Wright paused for a moment; his orders from Anna were clear.

"Capture Nero. Kill everyone else."

"There's the chopper," the analyst said, pointing at the outline of the silver aircraft on the feed from the surveillance satellite that was currently tasked with watching Castello del Sinistre. "They went in three hours ago and nobody's left since. They're definitely in there."

"Okay," Flack said, studying the image. "What is that place?"

"It's the ancestral home of the Sinistre family," another one of his analysts replied, reading off her tablet. "It's old, really old, but beyond a couple of entries in Italian history books, there's no real reference to either the building or the family whose ancestral home it is—the Sinistres."

"Isn't that unusual for a family that's been around that long?" Flack asked.

"Yes, sir," the analyst agreed. "Our historical analyst has scoured the records and says that their absence from the historical records matches a pattern of deliberate deletion rather than any lack of significance."

"So, in non-geek speak, they've just been really good at hiding?"

"Yes," the woman said. "But it does get slightly weirder. When I pressed our friends at the AISI on whether they had any more information on the family, they said they couldn't tell me anything more."

"So, they don't know anything, either?" Flack asked.

"No, sir. They said they *couldn't* tell us any more, not that they didn't know any more," she replied.

"What is it about these people?" Flack sighed. "When we inquired about tall, bald, and scary there last year, we got the same response from MI6. Why is everyone so frightened of them?"

"I don't know, sir," the satellite-imagery analyst said, zooming in on the castle. "But for obscure Italian nobility, they have a fair number of armed guards patrolling the battlements."

"Okay," Flack said. "Who do we have on the ground?"

"We have a SEAL team detachment that were training in the alps," another analyst said. "They'll be on the ground in less than twenty minutes, but they have a path-finder unit in place now. So we have eyes on the castle."

"What about airborne support?" Flack asked, eyeing the landing pad. "I don't want them rabbiting in that helicopter."

"We've got two F18s from the USS *Abraham Lincoln* providing close air support. They're maintaining a polite distance to avoid irritating our Italian friends, but they can be over the site in five minutes if necessary."

"On that note, sir," the other analyst said, "the Italians made it abundantly clear that they would take a very dim view of any operation launched against this location."

"Of course they did," Flack said with a sigh. "Do the SEALs know this is a ghost op?"

"Yes, sir," the analyst replied. "They appreciate the need for discretion."

"Sir! Look!" The satellite analyst pointed at a group of at least thirty men, their heat signatures clearly visible, moving through the woods near the castle's main gate; and some form of heavy military vehicle was making its way up the mountain road leading to the castle's main gate.

"Tell me that's the SEALs," Flack said.

"No, sir. They're still fifteen minutes out," the woman to his left said. "Nothing on Italian military networks either. We have a wild card in play."

"Damn it. Tell the SEAL-team squad leader that

there's a thirty-man kill team on the ground already. Presumed hostile."

Someone was about to hit that castle and they were about to hit that castle *hard*.

Otto sat on the four-poster bed in the elegantly furnished room he had been given and took a deep breath. It was the first time he'd been on his own for days, and now as he sat there, waiting for his summons to their audience with the Queen, he suddenly felt exhausted. He knew that he had to stay positive for the benefit of everyone around him, but for the first time in his life he felt truly out of his depth. He had tried to explain to people how dangerous Anna was, but he wasn't sure that they quite understood just what a threat she posed. What if she was just the first? What if there were more like her?

He tried not to think about it, but the truth was he didn't see any way to stop her. He thought back to the time when Overlord had made him into an unwilling puppet, when he'd been trapped inside his own mind and that monster had turned him against all of his friends. Of course, Overlord had frightened him, but what he had truly been scared of was what he would be forced to do with his abilities. That was what worried him so much about Anna: not what she'd already done, but what she still might do. He understood what she was capable of better than anyone else in the world, and the thought terrified him.

There was a soft knock at the door.

"Come in!" Otto said.

The butler entered the room and gave a quick nodding bow.

"The Queen requests your presence at her table," he said. "Dinner is served."

Otto stood up and followed the tall man out of the room and down a long passageway that led to the sweeping stairs to the ground floor. They passed through the entrance hall and into a grand dining room with a long dark, mahogany table with three places set. At the far end of the table was an elaborate dark wooden chair that was covered in exquisitely carved roses. A moment later, Nero and Darkdoom entered the room and the butler ushered them all to their seats.

"This is taking too long," Darkdoom said quietly as they took their seats and the butler backed out of the room.

"I am quite aware of that, Diabolus," Nero replied. "What would you suggest I do?"

"I just don't like it," Darkdoom said. "If she is in league with the Disciples, this could be a trap."

"If that were true, we'd already be dead," said Nero. "You know that as well as I do."

Nero glanced to his left as a door at the far end of the

room was opened by a servant, quickly pushing back his chair and rising to his feet. Diabolus and Otto followed suit as the Queen of Shadows entered the room. She was clearly very old, but she carried herself with the grace and speed of a much younger woman. Her long black dress was made from layers of beautifully handmade lace that shifted and shimmered as she moved, and she wore a large, deep-red ruby at her neck that seemed to almost pulse with crimson light. Her white hair was styled into an elegant sweeping curve that framed her pale face, the parchment skin stretched tightly over the sharp bones of her cheeks. Otto felt a chill run down his spine as her bright green eyes fixed on him and seemed to drill into his head, exposing whatever secrets he might try to keep from her. He was grateful when she finally turned her gaze to Nero.

"Maximilian," she said. "Always a pleasure."

"The pleasure is all mine." Nero bowed his head, something Otto had never seen before.

"Diabolus." The Queen's attention moved on to Darkdoom, who stepped toward her and gracefully bowed, taking her gloved hand and kissing it. Otto was pretty sure he saw Nero roll his eyes on the other side of the table.

"Oh, Diabolus, you really never change, do you?" the Queen said, raising an eyebrow. "And you must be Otto," she said, turning back toward him.

Otto bowed his head in the same way as he had just seen Nero do.

"I've heard a great deal about you, young man." Something about the way she said it made Otto's blood suddenly run cold. "I believe you and my great-granddaughter were close?"

"Yes, I miss her a great deal," Otto admitted quietly.

"As do I," the Queen replied. "I feel a great sadness when I think of what happened to her. I had thought she would be safe at Maximilian's school, but alas, it was not to be." She glanced in Nero's direction and he lowered his eyes. "I have no wish to dwell on tragedy, though. Please, be seated, my chef has, I believe, excelled himself this evening."

They waited as she took her own seat on the rose-covered throne before they too sat down.

"Now, what can I do for you, Maximilian?" the Queen asked as serving staff entered the room with cloche-covered plates and bottles of fine wine.

"I think we may be facing an unprecedented threat from the Disciples," Nero said as a servant poured wine into his glass. "And I need to be sure that you fully understand the nature of that threat."

"I thought I made myself quite clear on this subject just a few months ago, Maximilian," the Queen admonished, a slight edge of irritation to her voice. "I do not want to involve my family in this pointless internecine conflict. The Sinistre family learned long ago that when titans duel, it is always best to watch and wait until a clear winner is apparent before taking sides. I do not believe we have quite reached that point yet."

"If you will allow me to explain what has happened at the school, you may find that you feel differently," Nero replied. He then spent the next couple of minutes recounting to the Queen the events of the past days. She occasionally interrupted to request clarification, but otherwise she sat and quietly listened to his account of the events that had led them to her.

"If you will forgive me for saying so, Maximilian." She spoke when he'd finished. "It sounds to me rather like the titans have indeed fought their final battle, and that you have lost. I still do not understand why I should care who emerges as the victor here. My family will negotiate the currents of history, just as we always have. I will admit I have always had a certain fondness for the fact you understand the importance of elegance in our world, but that does not mean I will enter this conflict on your behalf. I'm sure I don't need to remind you that two members of my family have already been sacrificed on the altar of your ambition."

"I deeply regret the death of Lucia," Nero said, looking the Queen straight in the eye. "But Maria betrayed me, she betrayed all of us. She chose her own path, as you well know, and I will not be judged for that."

"Come now, Maximilian," the Queen replied. "If I wanted to judge you, I would have done so already and you would not be sitting here. We both understand the rules."

Otto had the sudden sense he was watching a high-stakes poker game and that all of the chips were now sitting squarely in the middle of the table.

"You may feel differently when you learn how the Disciples created Anna," Nero said.

"What do you mean?" The Queen's eyes narrowed.

"Otto, please tell the Queen what you told me about Anna's abilities," Nero said.

Otto nodded. "When Anna was inside my head, when she first attacked the school, she tried to control me the same way that she was controlling H.I.V.E.mind," he explained. "She wasn't using my abilities against me—they don't allow me to control people in the way that I think she can. I recognized what she was doing to me, because I've had it done to me before. I'm as certain as I can be that she was using the Sinistre voice."

"What?" the Queen snapped. "That's impossible. If you think you can drag me into your war with a clumsy lie, Nero, think again."

"I know what I heard," Otto said, looking at the Queen.

"I'm not lying and you have an easy way to prove that."

She looked at Otto for a moment, her eyes darkening.

"Tell me what you heard." Otto winced as her voice wrenched his free will away. He had heard that voice when the Contessa and Lucy had used it on him in the past, but that had been nothing like this. Their voices had been whispers, irresistible but subtle; this was a roar of sheer force. He suddenly understood why the two other men at the table were so frightened of this woman—her power was on an entirely different level to anything he had felt before. She could have taken control of the world in a day and there would have been nothing anyone could have done to stop her; the only reason she hadn't was because she didn't *want* to.

"I heard the Sinistre voice," he reiterated, his own voice feeling almost like it was coming from someone else's mouth. "It was unmistakable."

The Queen stood up, slamming her fists down on the table.

"*La voce* is sacred," she snarled. "Passed down from generation to generation throughout history. To steal it from us, to make this thing they've made and to give it my family's birthright. I swear I will cut out their still-beating hearts! After what I did for Anastasia—"

"If you want revenge, help me," Nero said quickly. "I'll give Furan to you if you do."

"What do you need? Name it."

"We need a way to block Anna's abilities," Darkdoom said. "At the very least we need to be able to stop her using the Voice on people."

"I can do that," the Queen said. "I just need to implant a command to ignore her voice, assuming that my voice is louder than hers."

"I really don't think we need to worry about that," Otto muttered, rubbing his forehead, still feeling the lingering effects of the one simple command that the Queen had given him.

"You'll need to come with us," Nero told her. "Everyone who might come into contact with the girl will need protection."

"I understand," the Queen replied. "I assume you have transport to H.I.V.E. arranged."

"Leave that to me," Darkdoom said with a slight smile.

"Then I shall make preparations for our departure." She nodded. "Be ready in the main entrance in fifteen—"

There was a sudden deafening explosion, and the windows on the other side of the room detonated in a shower of glass, followed by the sound of automatic gunfire from somewhere outside. A moment later, two men swung in through the shattered windows dressed in black body armor and carrying submachine guns.

The Queen rose from her seat.

"Cover your ears," she ordered Otto, Nero, and Darkdoom as the soldiers turned toward her. Otto slapped his hands over his ears, pressing down hard as Nero and Darkdoom did the same.

The Queen looked at the advancing soldiers as they raised their weapons.

"*Die!*" she shouted.

The two men collapsed to the floor like puppets with their strings cut. Nero and Darkdoom quickly ran over to the lifeless men and scooped up their fallen weapons.

The Queen took a deep breath and then beckoned for the others to follow her as she hurried to the far end of the room and pressed a concealed switch on the frame of a large mirror. The mirror slid aside to reveal a dusty passageway beyond.

"Come with me," she told them as she stepped into the secret passage. The others followed her inside as the large mirror slid back into place behind them. The dull thuds of muffled explosions and the rattle of gunfire could be heard as they hurried down the passage, the Queen leading the way. Otto felt the stones beneath his feet shake as dust showered down from the ceiling. The Queen pulled a small earpiece from a pocket concealed amongst the lacework of her dress and placed it into her ear.

"Report," she said, her voice calm.

"We've got several kill teams inside the perimeter,"

a slightly panicked voice said in her ear. "Definitely not conventional special forces."

"The Disciples," the Queen said. "It seems they want me to pick a side in this war after all."

"How many men do you have?" Nero asked.

"I do not need 'men' to protect me, Nero," the Queen sneered. "There is a small security detail, but they are not equipped to repel a full-scale assault like this."

"Then we need to get out of here," Darkdoom said, pulling a small radio from his inside pocket and speaking into it. "Shroud, we need a pickup."

"Roger that," a voice answered. "Already on approach—what's going on down there?"

"We're under attack. What can you see from up there?"

"We've got a lot of human heat signatures in the castle grounds," the Shroud reported. "Suggest you head for the roof."

Darkdoom looked at the Queen and she gave a quick nod.

"Affirmative," Darkdoom confirmed. "Meet you up there. Keep your cloak engaged—we've got no idea what sort of heavy weaponry these guys might be packing."

"Roger that," the pilot replied, and the line went dead.

"The quickest way to the roof is this way," the Queen said, pushing a switch mounted on the wall, a section of which slid aside, enabling them to step out onto one of the castle's upper landings just as the sound of gunfire grew louder.

"Up these stairs," the Queen instructed, moving toward a doorway leading to a narrow spiral staircase. Darkdoom crept up the stairs first, his weapon raised, knowing that there was no guarantee that the Disciples had not secured the roof already. The Queen followed close behind him, glancing over her shoulder as a noise from the hallway below suddenly caught her attention. Otto turned to see one of the black-clad soldiers raising and aiming a shoulder-mounted launcher at the door leading to the staircase.

"Look out!" Otto yelled, shoving Nero to one side as a small rocket shot from the launcher the soldier was carrying and lanced toward the stairwell, trailing white smoke. An instant later, the bottom of the stairwell exploded in a ball of flame, ancient masonry crashing to the ground and blocking the stairs completely.

"Looks like we need another exit," Nero said, raising his gun and spraying fire at the soldiers below. He looked down the landing and pointed at a door at the far end, in the opposite direction from the advancing soldiers. "Move!"

He and Otto sprinted down the landing as the enemy troops began to return fire, the beautiful, carved wooden railings behind them exploding into showers of woodchips as the high velocity rounds shredded them. Nero burst through the door and found himself in a long library with floor-to-ceiling shelves packed with all types of books. There was one door at the far end and they both ran toward it. When they were within sixty-five feet of the door, it opened and one of the attacking soldiers appeared. Nero opened fire and the man dropped, the other troops who were just behind him ducking back into the cover of the stone door frame. They were trapped.

Nero glanced to his right and turned, opening fire on a rose-covered stained-glass window. The elegant design exploded into a shower of multicolored shards, and Nero sprinted toward the window, looking outside at the steeply sloped roof beyond.

"Out here," he said to Otto. "Watch your step."

Otto was about to follow Nero outside, when the door leading back to the landing they had just come from burst open and another soldier appeared with an identical shoulder-mounted launcher. Otto didn't have time to think; he just reached out with his abilities and connected to the detonation circuit in the rocket nestled inside the tube. There was a massive explosion, and the far end of the library was filled with smoke as Otto climbed outside after Nero. They made their way as quickly as they dared across the slippery tiles, fighting to maintain their footing. Otto tried to ignore the long drop to the court-yard below and concentrated on maintaining his balance, clinging onto the crumbling stonework of the ancient walls for support. Another burst of fire came from some-where below, bullets ricocheting off the walls around them as they clambered over the top of a crenelated wall and ducked into cover. Nero looked up at the roof of the castle far above them.

"There's no way we're getting up there," he said. "We need to find another way out of here."

"What about that thing?" Otto pointed down at the castle's landing pad, where the silver helicopter that had brough them there earlier was sitting.

"We'll need a distraction," Nero said, looking at the handful of guards positioned around the helicopter.

"Leave that to me," Otto replied, glancing down at a black armored troop carrier that was blocking the main gate of the adjoining courtyard.

Nero gave a quick nod and headed over to the stairs that led down from the wall to the landing pad.

Otto concentrated and connected to the troop carrier's control systems, gunning the throttle and sending the massive vehicle hurtling across the courtyard. He could feel the driver of the vehicle fighting the steering wheel and stamping on the brakes inside the cab of the transport.

"Gotta love drive-by-wire," Otto said, triggering the

smoke launcher tubes mounted on the rear of the vehicle as it careered around the courtyard. A cluster of soldiers by the main entrance dived for cover; others, who had been guarding the nearby landing pad, sprinted toward the main courtyard, raising their weapons and firing at the commandeered vehicle. Otto watched as Nero crept toward the now-unguarded helicopter, climbed up into the pilot's seat, and hurriedly started the engines. Otto gunned the throttle of the transport and jammed on the brakes, setting the tires of the vehicle spinning and making yet more smoke, and creating what he hoped was a sufficiently awful cacophony to drown out the sound of the helicopter's rotors spinning up. He pointed the transport at the castle's main gates and gunned the engine, sending the vehicle rocketing across the cobbles and smashing through the ancient wooden gates, smashing them to matchwood. The soldiers ran after the remotely controlled transport, firing at its retreating taillights as it barreled down the narrow mountain road beyond.

Otto dashed over to the stairs and hurried down them, running across the lawn around the landing pad before climbing up into the helicopter's copilot seat.

"Are we clear?" Nero asked as he flicked switches on the helicopter's control panel.

"As clear as we're going to be," Otto said with a quick nod.

"Then let's get out of here." Nero yanked at the collective control of the helicopter and sent it leaping into the air. He banked hard, heading for the relative cover of the forested valley below. Otto glanced down at the castle as they passed over the battlements and saw a soldier running along them pointing at the helicopter. As he watched, another soldier farther down the battlements raised a tube to his shoulder.

"Look out!" Otto yelled, reaching out with his powers as the rocket shot from the launcher the soldier was carrying and speared toward their helicopter. He triggered the detonation circuit, just as he had a minute before, but this time he was a fraction of a second too slow. The rocket detonated in midair only thirty feet from the tail of the helicopter, the shrapnel from the explosion shredding the tail rotor assembly and sending the aircraft into a stomach-churning spin.

"Hang on!" Nero yelled over the blaring alarms from the cockpit as he fought desperately with the protesting controls of the doomed vehicle. Otto braced himself as the helicopter plummeted toward the dark forest below. The tall pines seemed to almost reach up and grab them as the helicopter struck the treetops and the whole cabin tipped. Otto felt a sudden, intense burst of heat from somewhere nearby and then heard the sound of metal tearing before the blackness claimed him.

• • •

Darkdoom helped the Queen to her feet, both of them coughing due to the thick smoke that was beginning to fill the collapsed spiral stairwell.

"We need to keep moving," Darkdoom said.

"Someone is going to pay a very steep price for this, Diabolus," the Queen said as she followed him up the stairs and they both heard another explosion from somewhere below them. "No one has been foolish enough to directly attack my family for decades. It seems I need to remind people of why that is."

"Revenge later, escape now," Darkdoom snapped, climbing up the narrow spiral staircase with his weapon ready. Soon they reached a solid-looking door at the top of the stairs and he pressed his ear against the wooden surface, straining to hear any signs of their enemies on the other side. After a moment, he opened the door a crack and saw that the roof beyond appeared to be clear.

"Come on," he said, gesturing for the Queen to follow him. He crept out onto the roof, glancing down at the courtyard below. A heavy military transport was careering around the main courtyard before smashing through the main gate and racing away down the road beyond. At first Darkdoom thought that Otto and Nero must have taken the vehicle, but then he saw a familiar white-haired figure running toward the Queen's silver helicopter as its rotors reached full speed. He watched as Otto climbed on board and the helicopter took off, dropping into the valley below them. A moment later, his eyes widened in horror as he saw the flare of an antiaircraft missile race after the fleeing helicopter. It seemed to strike the tail of the aircraft, which span wildly out of control before vanishing into the forest with a crash.

"We have to get down there," Darkdoom said, pulling the communicator from his pocket. "Shroud, are you on station yet?"

"Thirty seconds out," the pilot replied. "Coming in hot."

Darkdoom and the Queen hurried toward the most open area of the roof, and a few seconds later they were struck by the engine backwash of the invisible Shroud. A rectangle of light seemed to float in the air in front of them as its rear-landing ramp unfolded, revealing the hidden dropship's interior. Darkdoom watched as the Queen hurried up the ramp. A door on the other side of the roof unlatched and several Disciple soldiers ran out. Darkdoom opened fire, spraying bullets in their direction and sending them diving for cover. He ran up the ramp as the soldiers began to return fire, their bullets smashing into the interior of the Shroud as Darkdoom and the Queen dived for cover. Sparks erupted from the avionics bay as the soldiers' bullets ripped into the Shroud's fragile electronic systems.

The aircraft's cloak flickered for a moment and then died, exposing its armored black hull.

"GO NOW!" Darkdoom yelled toward the cockpit as he reached up and slapped the switch to close the rear hatch, more stray rounds pinging off the armored bulkhead just above his head. In the cockpit, the pilot wrenched at the control stick, trying to ignore the screeching alarms that were sounding around him. The Shroud lifted into the air, its engines roaring as the pilot buried the throttle, sending it screaming up into the sky. Darkdoom ran up to the cockpit and was forced to grab on to the back of the pilot's seat as he wrenched at the controls and a missile shot past them, just six feet from the Shroud's nose.

"I've got fast movers on a direct approach, and without a cloak we're a sitting duck," the pilot shouted. "We have to get out of here!"

Darkdoom glanced at the Shroud's threat display and saw three icons with USAF threat tags, heading straight for them.

"How the hell have the Americans got birds in the air that fast?" Darkdoom said.

"I have no idea," the pilot answered, sending the Shroud into a tight evasive bank. "They just came out of nowhere, no sign of the Italian air force."

Darkdoom realized that he only had one choice. If

they stayed a moment longer, they'd never get away and their new passenger was too valuable to take that chance.

"Get us back to the *Megalodon*, low and fast," he said angrily. "Make sure they can't track us."

"Yes, sir," the pilot replied, sending the Shroud diving down to treetop height and racing away into the night.

chapter eight

Otto came to with a start, coughing violently as acrid black smoke filled his lungs. He unclipped his seat belts and dropped onto the ceiling of the inverted cockpit. To his left, Nero was hanging limply from his own seat, and Otto shuffled across the ruined interior of the helicopter, doing his best to ignore the sound of crackling flames coming from somewhere in the rear of the aircraft, and reached up to release Nero's belts. Trying to support as much of Nero's weight as he could, he lowered him clumsily to the ground, then hooked his hands under Nero's armpits and began to pull his limp body from the wreckage. He dragged him sixty-five feet across the small clearing that the helicopter had come down in and propped him up against a tree trunk. Nero was still breathing and his pulse was faint, but regular. There was a nasty gash on his cheek, but he was at least alive. Otto looked back at the wreckage of the helicopter that was now beginning to burn more fiercely and counted his blessings that they hadn't sustained more serious injuries.

"Over here!" Otto heard the shout from the other side of the clearing, and he dived for cover behind a fallen log as Disciple troops began to fan out across the clearing. There was no way he could get to Nero's unconscious body without being seen, and the tree line was about thirty feet away across open ground. He tried to connect to anything that might give him an edge with his abilities. The only functional electronics within range were the soldiers' communication systems. Otto thought back to Francisco's simulation and overloaded them with a thought, sending an ear-piercing screech through the soldiers' headsets as they advanced across the clearing toward him. Then he made a break for the tree line as the soldiers cursed in pain, wrenching out their earpieces. He was within six feet of the tree line when the first soldier spotted him, raising his weapon and squeezing the trigger. Splinters of wood exploded from the trees around Otto as he ran into the darkened forest, bullets buzzing through the air surrounding him. He looked over his shoulder as he ran, seeing the swaying lights of the soldiers behind him as they chased him. He heard the snap of a twig and spun around just in time to see another Disciple soldier step out from behind a tree ahead of him and swing the butt of his rifle at his head. The gun smacked straight into Otto's forehead, knocking him off his feet and sending him tumbling onto the forest floor, unconscious. The Disciple soldier looked down at Otto's fallen form as several of his teammates ran up to him.

"We've found Nero unconscious in the clearing back there," one of the other soldiers reported. "We're taking him back to the transport."

The man standing over Otto looked up at his squad leader.

"What about this one, sir?"

"You know your orders," his superior replied.

"He's just a boy, sir," the soldier said, hesitant, before the sudden screech of a fighter jet shooting past overhead was heard.

"That's not one of ours," the squad leader said. "We need to get out of here. You lot head back and get Nero to the transport, I'll deal with this one."

The other soldiers ran back to the clearing as the squad leader walked over to Otto's unconscious body on the forest floor.

"Doesn't look so bloody dangerous to me," he said, raising his rifle and leveling it at Otto's head. "Sorry, kid."

There was a soft, coughing pop and the squad leader's eyes went wide before he collapsed to the ground, and a figure detached itself from the shadows, lowered their silenced pistol, and crept toward the fallen Disciple soldier, kicking away the fallen man's weapon. The figure knelt down next to Otto and checked his pulse, the moonlight catching the black-and-gray stars-and-stripes patch on his body armor. He picked the unconscious boy up and slung him over his shoulder as he retreated into the shadows. When he was a safe distance away, he thumbed the talk button on his comms rig.

"Artemis, this is SEAL team pathfinder one. I have the package."

Anna watched as the Shroud that she had dispatched to collect Nero from Italy touched down on the crater landing pad. The loading ramp at the rear of the dropship unfolded with a whir, and two of Cypher's robots descended the ramp, with Nero walking between them, his hands cuffed in front of him.

"Dr. Nero," Anna said with a smile. "How nice to finally meet you in the flesh."

"The feeling is, I'm afraid, not mutual," Nero replied.

"Oh, come now," she said. "There's really no need to be so bad-tempered." She walked toward him smiling. "Especially when I've gone to so much trouble to bring you back here so that you can reunite with an old friend."

The nearby doors slid open and Anastasia Furan

walked into the hangar, with Raven walking a few paces behind her. Nero's eyes narrowed at the sight of her.

"What are you doing out of your cage?" he said as she approached.

"Lovely to see you, too, Nero," Furan said. "How do you like my new pet?" She gestured toward Raven. Nero looked at his friend and saw no hint of recognition in her blank expression.

"What have you done to her?"

"Anna has been kind enough to instruct Natalya to obey my every command," Furan replied. "Would you like a demonstration?" She gave Nero an evil smile. "Natalya, please break Dr. Nero's left forefinger."

Raven stepped forward without hesitation and grabbed Nero's left hand, wrenching his finger backward with a sickening crunch as Nero gasped in pain.

"You see," Furan said. "The three of us are going to have such fun together."

"I should have put you down like the crazed animal you are," Nero growled through gritted teeth, trying to ignore the pain from his hand. "But, don't worry. I won't make that mistake again. I'm going to watch you both burn, you can rest assured of that."

"*Be silent,*" Anna hissed, the whispers of the Voice intertwined with her words.

"I'm afraid that won't work on me, young lady,"

Nero said. "I've never liked being told what to do."

"Maybe I should just cut out your tongue, then?" Anna said, taking a step toward him and then gesturing toward Raven. "Or perhaps I should just get her to do it? No point getting my hands dirty."

She studied Nero's face for a moment, as if she were looking at some sort of scientific curiosity.

"Or maybe I'll just dissect your brain and work out exactly what it is about you that allows you to resist me?"

"You can do what you like with his body when I'm finished with him," Furan told her. "But remember our deal."

"A deal can always be renegotiated," Anna said, turning toward Furan. "In case you're beginning to forget who's in charge around here. Dr. Nero will be placed in a detention cell until you've supplied me with the data I requested, and I have verified its authenticity. Then he's all yours to do with as you will."

With that, she turned and walked away, while the two robots flanking Nero grabbed him by the arms and forced him to follow her.

"I hope you realize you're playing with fire," Nero growled at Furan as he passed by her.

"It would hardly be the first time," she said quietly to herself as she watched him walk away.

• • •

"This is madness, Anastasia," Pietor Furan said, looking down at the unconscious man on the table in front of him. "After everything that's happened, I don't understand why we don't just kill him."

"Oh, Pietor," the young woman on the other side of the bed said with a smile. "Much as I love you, brother, you have never understood that there is a certain poetry to revenge."

"No, I just think that sometimes you're too clever for your own good," Pietor quipped. "Sometimes a bullet in the skull is the best solution."

"After what he's done?" Anastasia balked. "After what he's cost our family? No, he deserves to suffer far more than that."

"Do as you will," Pietor replied impatiently. "But I cannot shake the feeling that this will come back to haunt us."

"You worry too much, Pietor," Anastasia said. "Now, if you would be so kind as to fetch our guest."

Pietor shook his head and walked out of the room, and Anastasia walked over to the bed and picked up a syringe of clear liquid from the bedside table. She slid the needle into the man's arm, and almost immediately he began to stir from his unconsciousness.

"Wake up, Nero," she whispered. "It's time we had a little chat."

The young man's eyes flickered open, and after a fleeting look of confusion his face twisted into an expression of pure hatred. Despite the drowsiness he still felt, he tried to push himself up from the bed but found that his wrists were firmly shackled to the bed frame.

"You're dead! You're both dead! Do you hear me, Anastasia?" he said, fighting against his restraints.

"You didn't really think I was going to let you both ride off into the sunset together, did you?" Anastasia replied. "I warned you what would happen if you persisted in your relationship and now look what it has cost us all."

"Elena," Nero said, his voice suddenly filled with grief. "She wanted no part of our world and I was prepared to walk away from it, because that was what she wanted. Why couldn't you just leave us in peace?"

"There's no peace for people like us, Nero. Don't be so naïve," Anastasia snapped back at him. "If you really thought I was going to allow you to pollute our bloodline . . ." She took a deep breath as the door opened behind her. "Well, now you pay the price."

A strikingly beautiful middle-aged woman in a long, black lace dress walked into the room with Pietor Furan just behind her.

"I hope you know what you're doing, Anastasia," said the Queen of Shadows.

"If you do as I ask, your family's blood debt to my family will be considered fully paid," Anastasia persuaded. "Surely that's all that matters, Francesca?"

"I understand that," the Queen replied. "But what you're asking me to do to this man . . . it sickens me."

"I'm not interested in your opinion, I just need your abilities," Anastasia insisted.

"On your own head be it," the Queen said with a frown. "Leave us, this will take some time."

"Who are you?" Nero demanded as the woman approached his bed and placed a cool hand against the side of his head. "What are you doing?"

"*You hear my voice,*" the Queen said, sinister whispers twisting between her words. "*You hear only my voice. . . .*"

Otto woke with a start in a featureless interview room, with a large mirror on one wall and a single empty chair on the opposite side of the metal table from his own. He gingerly felt the sore lump on his forehead and took a moment to gather his thoughts. His last memory was running through the woods with the Disciple troops chasing him, but after that it was a blank. He had no idea what this place he now found himself in was, but it was a safe bet that he'd be better off not being there. He wasn't restrained in any way, so he got up from the chair and walked over to the door, trying the handle. Locked. He then walked over to what he assumed was a two-way mirror and tapped on the thick, reflective glass.

"Hello," he said. "Anybody there?"

There was no reply. Otto reached out with his abilities and found no trace of anything electronic that he could connect to, just a strange, buzzing, static sensation unlike anything he'd felt before. He sat back down in the chair and frowned. Wherever he was, he was not helping the others to take back the school, and that was the highest priority right now. As he waited for what felt like hours, but was probably not really more than a few minutes, he started to feel a growing sense of impatience.

"Hello," he shouted again. "I have important stuff I need to be doing. So if we could perhaps get on with this!"

The door swung open and a man walked into the room.

"I'm very sorry if we're inconveniencing you," the man said.

Otto's eyes widened in surprise. He had met this man once before, under much more dramatic circumstances, but seeing him standing in this spartan room looking down at him with a slight smile was still slightly overwhelming.

"It's . . . erm . . . good to see you again, Mr. President," Otto said as a bulky man in a dark suit stepped into the room behind the president and closed the door, taking up position in the corner of the room.

"You too, Mr. Malpense," the president replied, sitting down in the seat on the other side of the table. "I don't think I ever properly thanked you for saving my life on Air Force One. I also hope you enjoyed the nuclear weapon I so generously gave you during the attack on the Advanced Weapons Project facility."

"It was . . . erm . . . super effective," Otto said with a slightly awkward smile.

"Which brings me to the reason I had you brought here today," the president said. "Couple of questions. Who the hell are you and who do you work for?"

"I don't work for anyone," Otto said. "I'm a . . . freelancer."

"Okay, then," the president said. "Let's put it another way: Who's paying you to hack the Department of Defense's servers right now?"

"What?" Otto asked, sounding surprised.

"As of three hours ago, we've been shut out of our orbital defense network," the president replied. "As have the Russians and the Chinese, or so our friends at Langley inform me. That means that somebody has access to at least a dozen orbital nuclear-launch satellites that, obviously, none of us will admit to possessing because that would contravene all sorts of treaties. My analysts tell me that the nature of the attack is uncannily similar to the hack that aborted the launch of the Thor's Hammer system during the incident on Air Force One, something that I know for a fact you were personally responsible for. It's also the reason that you're sitting inside something that I'm told is called a Faraday cage, which my experts thought might block your . . . unusual . . . talents. Unfortunately, it doesn't seem to have made any difference and we still can't access our systems. So, I'm here to politely ask you to cease and desist whatever it is you're doing. I'm afraid, given the nature of the threat, I'll only be asking politely once."

Otto felt a sudden chill run down his spine. The fact that he was inside an electromagnetically shielded space would explain why he could detect no electronic devices, but it also meant he had no idea what was going on out there in the world.

"This isn't me," Otto said, shaking his head. "But I know who it is."

"Why does that not surprise me?" the president said, running his hand over his close-cropped hair.

"This is someone *like* me, with similar abilities, but she's . . . stronger, and more dangerous," Otto explained.

"Otto Two Point Zero?" the president said with a frown. "Tell me that's not as bad as it sounds."

"Oh, it's every bit as bad as it sounds," Otto replied. "And there's no way it's a coincidence she's just locked down the defense grids of every nuclear-armed country on the planet."

"Do you know how to stop this?" the president asked.

"I'm not sure yet, but the people I work with are trying to stop her," Otto replied. "The only being I've ever encountered with even a fraction of her power is Overlord, and he's dead; utterly destroyed when the Animus was nuked at the AWP facility."

"I don't know if I'd go so far as to say *utterly* destroyed," the president said.

"What?"

"Come with me." The president stood and started walking toward the door.

Otto followed him and his secret-service bodyguard down a short, featureless, white corridor. The door at the far end of the corridor slid aside, and the three of them walked through and out onto the gantry beyond. Below them was a giant metal sphere in the center of a cavernous concrete hangar, cables led from it in all directions, and numerous technicians wearing environmental-hazard suits were working at terminals spread surrounding it.

"You see, we didn't build this Faraday cage for you, Mr. Malpense, we built it for that," the president said, pointing down at the sphere.

"Oh my God," Otto said. "Tell me that's not what I think it is?"

"They tell me it's called an Electromagnetic Prison,"

the president said. "Entirely electronically isolated from the rest of the world. You told me to send in biohazard teams to analyze the remains of the AWP facility, and we did. The thing inside that sphere is what we found."

"Let me see it," Otto said, fear starting to claw at his gut.

"This way," the president said, leading him to the end of the gantry and down the stairs to the hangar floor.

The two of them walked across the room, and astonished faces turned in their direction in recognition of the president. One of the scientists nearest to the giant sphere, who saw the president and Otto approaching, quickly walked toward them with her hand extended.

"Mr. President," she said. "I was told you were on-site. It's an honor to meet you, sir."

"Thank you, Dr. . . ."

"Dr. Meadows, sir. I'm the head of research here at the facility," she said, her nerves making her speak a little too quickly.

"My guest would like to see the experiment, if possible," the president said, walking toward the red line that was painted on the floor around the sphere.

"Of course," Dr. Meadows replied. "But, sir, please be careful not to cross the red line. The risk of static discharge from the sphere is minimal, but it's best not to take any unnecessary chances."

"I've already had the safety briefing, thank you, Dr.

Meadows," the president said, stopping a few feet short of the line.

"You'll need to wear one of these suits to get any closer, sir," Meadows said, gesturing to a rack of white suits identical to the one that she was wearing.

"This is quite close enough for me," he said. "That thing gives me the creeps. Mr. Malpense, if you want to see what's in there, you'd better suit up."

Otto walked over to the rack and quickly pulled the loose-fitting overalls on over his own slightly tattered and scorched civilian clothes. The suit was less flexible than it looked, with a stiff lining that Otto presumed must be some kind of shielding or electrical insulation. He zipped up the front of the suit and walked back over to where the president and Meadows were standing.

"Good," Meadows said after quickly checking his suit. "If you'd be so kind as to follow me, Mr. . . . ."

"Otto. Just Otto," he replied.

"Well . . . erm . . . Otto. We were told that there was a chance you might know what this is." She walked over to the sphere and pressed a button on its surface. A metal cover slid aside to reveal a porthole of thick, toughened glass. Otto approached the portal, feeling the hairs on the back of his neck standing up and knowing that it had nothing to do with static electricity. Inside was a smaller glass sphere that was suspended in the center of the chamber. Inside the inner sphere was a small writhing black mass, no bigger than a tennis ball. Otto felt his blood run cold.

"If I could, I'd drop a nuke on this place right now," he snapped at the president, who was standing watching behind the perimeter.

"Is that a threat, Mr. Malpense?" the president inquired with a frown.

"No!" Otto said angrily, pointing at the porthole. "THAT is a threat. You have no idea what you're dealing with."

"It appears to be some form of highly advanced nanite swarm," Dr. Meadows said. "We're not completely clueless."

"Oh, it's a lot more than that," Otto admitted, looking back through the glass.

"It has limited mobility, but it is otherwise electro-magnetically inert," Meadows said. "We understand the risks involved, given what happened at AWP, but we're quite safe out here. We've gone to great lengths to make sure that this facility cannot send or receive any form of digital communication. If it ever was a threat, it's not now."

"You can't know that for sure," Otto said, suddenly realizing what he had to do. "I need to go in there."

"I'm not sure that's a good idea," Meadows said, looking over at the president. "There is no damping inside the sphere; you would be exposed to any kind of transmission that thing might put out."

"I know what I'm doing," Otto said. "I understand the risks. I have to make sure that thing is as safe as you think it is."

Meadows shot another glance at the president, who gave a quick nod.

"Very well, please come this way." She beckoned for Otto to follow her to the other side of the sphere. "You'll need to put this on if you're going in there. It will shield your neural tissue from any harmful electromagnetic emissions."

She handed him a helmet and watched as he put it on, before checking that the seal between the helmet and the suit Otto was already wearing was good.

"Stand here," she said, pointing at a yellow square painted on the ground in front of a heavy steel door.

Otto stepped into the painted box and took a deep breath.

"Open the outer air lock," Meadows said, turning to one of the nearby technicians.

A couple of seconds later, the heavy steel door slid upward and Otto stepped into the cramped chamber beyond. He waited as the door shut again behind him and powerful jets of white gas blasted him from all directions. The jets cut off and the inner door in front of him rumbled aside. He walked into the interior of the sphere, now just about six feet from the suspended glass globe. He had hoped he would never see the oily, black substance within ever again. He had, perhaps foolishly, assumed that the nuclear strike from the Thor's Hammer orbital-launch platform would have been enough to finally destroy the sinister substance once and for all, but he could not deny the evidence in front of him.

Animus.

The seething black swarm had been designed as a temporary home for the Overlord AI: the most dangerous enemy that Otto had faced, until a few days ago. He recalled the helpless horror he had felt when he himself had been infected with the sinister nanites and had very nearly lost the battle for control of his own mind. Overlord had turned him against his friends and had almost succeeded in his plan to scour humanity from the face of the earth, before he had burnt in nuclear fire. It had cost Lucy her life and, if he was honest, a little piece of Otto's soul. To see the Animus again now brought all those terrible memories flooding back. He had to be sure that the scientists in the facility outside were right.

He reached up, unclipped the catches at his neck, and removed his helmet.

"What are you doing?" Dr. Meadow's alarmed voice demanded over the intercom system.

"Checking the monster's dead," Otto said quietly to himself, reaching out with his abilities.

He connected effortlessly with the nanites of the swarm; it was, after all, exactly what they were designed for. His skin crawled as the bond between the organic supercomputer in his head and the swarm stabilized. He felt the same prickling sensation in his skull that he'd felt when he'd first been exposed to the Animus. Then the connection was complete and the real world dropped away as he entered the digital realm. He felt like he was surrounded by a raging black storm cloud; but like a storm, the swarm's power was chaotic, undirected. The swarm was functioning at its most basic level. There was nothing there. He dived deeper into the billowing black mass around him, checking again and again, knowing he could not afford to be wrong. Finally he stopped, feeling a sudden overwhelming sense of relief as he realized that there was no trace anywhere within the cloud of any form of higher consciousness.

Overlord was gone.

Would the Animus still be dangerous in the wrong hands? Possibly, but the danger it posed was as nothing compared to the far greater threat posed by a reborn Overlord. Otto withdrew from the cloud, disconnecting from the Animus, feeling it almost reluctantly relinquish its natural connection to him. He picked up his discarded helmet and turned toward the worried face of Dr. Meadows.

"It's okay," he said with relief. "He's dead."

"He?" Meadows asked over the speaker.

"Long story." Otto shook his head and walked toward the door. "Can you let me out of here, please?"

A few minutes later, the president stood watching as Otto removed the protective suit.

"Thank you," Otto said. "You didn't have to let me do that. I appreciate the fact that you did."

"What choice did I have? If that thing had the potential to be as dangerous as you claim, we had to be sure it was inert. Besides," the president added, with a wry smile, "I owe you one."

"Two, actually," Otto said, raising an eyebrow. "So I'm going to ask for one more small favor."

"And what might that be, Mr. Malpense?"

"I can stop this hack and get you back into your defense network, but I need your help," Otto replied. "The person responsible for this? I think I've just worked out how to stop her."

chapter nine

"That's not good enough!" Darkdoom shouted, staring down at the schematics on the display in the *Megalodon's* situation room. It had been two days since the assault on the Castello del Sinistre, and they were no closer to working out how to retake control of H.I.V.E. now than they had been then.

"I'm sorry, sir," the uniformed man standing on the other side of his desk said. "But we just can't see a weakness. A direct assault would be suicide."

"Don't be so hard on your men, Diabolus," Nathaniel Nero said from his seat nearby. "I did design the place to a very specific brief from Max. I lost count of how many times he used the word 'impregnable.'"

"I dunno," Shelby said. "Anna made it look pretty . . . erm . . . pregnable." She glanced over at Laura. "Is that even a word?"

"No, it isn't," Laura said impatiently. "Look. Anna managed to take the school by exploiting a vulnerability that we weren't even aware existed."

"H.I.V.E.mind," Professor Pike said.

"Exactly," Laura agreed. "So, if we're going to figure out a way to take H.I.V.E. back from her, first we have to figure out a way to get him back on our side."

"Easier said than done." The professor shook his head. "We would need a computer system even more powerful, and as far as I'm aware, there simply isn't one, especially when one factors in the additional power that the girl appears to possess."

"Sir!" Another member of Darkdoom's crew ran into the room. "We've got a signal coming in on a G.L.O.V.E. secured channel—I think you're going to want to hear this."

"Put it through to this station," Darkdoom said.

A few seconds later, there was a burst of white noise from the display and then a familiar voice came through.

"You are not going to believe the day I've had," Otto said over the comms channel.

"Oh my God, Otto!" Laura shouted. "Where are you? Are you safe?"

"Yes," Otto assured her, "but they have Nero."

"Mr. Malpense, where are you?" Darkdoom asked.

"I've just left San Francisco."

"How on earth did you—"

"I'll explain later," Otto interrupted impatiently. "I'm going to send you some rendezvous coordinates. I need you to meet me there as soon as possible."

"Understood," Darkdoom replied. "We're on our way."

"Do you have everything you need?" Miss Leon asked quietly. She, Penny, and Wing stood at the opposite end of the accommodation block atrium, a few yards from the pool that the waterfall at one end of the cavern cascaded into.

"Yes," Penny answered. "Though I'm putting the seven years of bad luck on you."

"Our distraction is arranged," Wing said. "I just need to give the signal."

"Good, let's get going, then," Miss Leon said. "Mr. Fanchu, if you would be so kind."

Wing picked Miss Leon up and carefully placed her in his backpack before looking over at Block and Tackle, who were standing on the opposite side of the cavern and giving them a quick nod. The two henchman stream students walked quickly toward the robots guarding the door at the far end of the cavern.

"What did you just call me?" Block yelled as they neared the mechanical guards.

"You 'eard me," Tackle argued. "You and your mom."

Block flew at Tackle, fists flailing as the two boys began brawling with each other.

"Fight!" one of the Science and Technology Stream students standing nearby shouted, and people began to gather around the two wrestling boys, the boredom of their captivity suddenly enlivened at the sight of them flailing at each other. The guards moved to a position between the growing crowd of students and the main door, forming a defensive perimeter. They didn't seem at all interested in the melee in front of them, focusing instead on making sure that the exit doors were blocked.

"Now," Wing said as the crowd of students blocked the guards' view of him and Penny. Penny waded out into the pool and through the ice-cold waters of the water-fall, emerging into a small, gloomy cavern behind. Wing passed through the cascade behind her and stepped up onto the rocky shelf beside her. They both crouched in silence for a minute, waiting to see if they were being pursued, but there was no immediate sign that their departure had been noticed. Eventually, Wing removed his backpack and unzipped it, laying it on the floor so Miss Leon could climb out.

"I believe we have slipped away unobserved," Wing said. "I hope you were not too uncomfortable in there."

"Better that than getting wet," Miss Leon said with an involuntary shudder.

"What are we looking for?" Penny asked, pulling a flashlight from her backpack and playing the narrow beam of light across the rockface at the back of the shallow concealed cavern.

"A reflection," Miss Leon said.

A couple of seconds later, there was a slight glimmer from one corner of the cavern, and Penny walked toward the twinkling light.

"Here it is," she said, looking up into the corner.

There, tucked away, hidden amongst the rocks was the lens of a tiny holographic field projector. Wing reached up and placed his hand over the small glass dome, and an access panel suddenly appeared on the opposite wall.

"Hold that pose," Penny said, walking quickly over to the panel.

"It's a Feldman-Kreuzfeld configuration four-factor lock, with trembler switches at each corner," Miss Leon said as Penny examined the panel.

"Of course it is," Wing said quietly to himself.

"Okay." Penny gently levered the plastic cover off one of the screws holding the panel in place. "This shouldn't take long."

Wing watched as Penny worked quickly to dismantle the panel and began to tinker with the circuitry inside. He occasionally glanced over at the back side of the waterfall six feet away, but it was impossible to tell what was happening on the other side of the wall of water.

"Good. Now just link the output from the encryption seal to the logic terminal," Miss Leon said as Penny attached a small wire with a crocodile clip on one end to a terminal. There was a quick spark, and a puff of black smoke rose from the panel.

"Is that supposed to—" Wing started, just as the rock wall beside him split in the middle, the two halves sliding aside with a soft hydraulic hiss.

"Oh ye of little faith," Penny said with a smile.

"Well done, Miss Lancaster," Miss Leon said. "I really couldn't have done that better myself."

"Thanks." Penny looked justifiably pleased with herself.

"Erm . . . can I move my hand now?" Wing asked.

"Yes, of course, come on," Miss Leon said as she trotted into the concealed passageway beyond the doors. Wing took his hand away from the projector, and the hacked control panel vanished from view. He followed Penny and Miss Leon into the passageway, following its smooth curved walls in the darkness until Wing saw a green glow coming from somewhere ahead of them. As they rounded the corner, they could see a grid of emerald lasers blocking the passageway.

"I assume passing through the grid will trigger an alarm," Wing said.

"Those are next-generation fiberoptic lasers, Mr.

Fanchu," Miss Leon corrected. "They don't trigger an alarm, they cut you into lots of little meaty chunks."

"Oh," Wing replied.

"Messier certainly, but much more secure," Miss Leon continued. "Miss Lancaster, we need your steady hands."

Penny stepped forward and placed her backpack on the ground, pulling out two pieces of broken mirror she'd brought from the bathroom in her quarters. She studied the grid for a moment and then gingerly raised the pieces of mirror toward it, a shard in each hand. She hesitated for a moment and then took a deep breath before pushing the two pieces of mirror into the grid at two specific points, holding each at a precise angle. There was a shower of sparks as the lasers fed back into their own emitters, causing a catastrophic feedback loop that overloaded the system.

"Go, quickly," Miss Leon said. "It's quite possible that H.I.V.E.mind will notice that power spike. We need to get out of this tunnel."

"There," Anastasia Furan said, looking at the handheld display she was holding. "The transfer and decryption is complete. You have the sequence modifications that were made to your genome."

She handed the tablet to Anna, who quickly scanned the screen.

"Joseph, can you confirm that you have received the modified design?" Anna asked, looking down at Wright's face on the display, which was mounted on what used to be Nero's desk.

"Yes," Wright said with a nod. "We will update the nano-sequencers' programming and begin the modifications immediately."

"Excellent." Anna smiled. "Keep me informed as to your progress."

"Of course." Wright gave an obedient nod and she closed the connection.

"Get on with it, then," Anastasia said, gesturing to the two assassin robots standing silently behind Anna.

"Get on with what?" Anna asked with a slightly confused frown.

"You have what you need. I have no more cards to play. This is the point where you tell me that I have 'outworn my usefulness,' or something like that, and have your mechanical friends here kill me," Furan said calmly.

"Why?" Anna asked.

"To remove a threat, of course," Furan said impatiently.

"Oh, Anastasia," Anna said with a broad smile. "You're no threat to me. You never were. Now go and do whatever it is that you've got planned for Nero and leave me in peace, I really don't care." She looked down at the display on the desk with a dismissive wave of the hand.

Furan stared at her for a moment, almost as if she were going to say something, but then she simply stood up and walked out of the room in silence.

Anna looked up from the display as Furan left. In less than twenty-four hours the modifications to her siblings would be complete and then there would be nothing anyone could do to stop them.

Otto stood on the bridge of the USS *Independence*, one of the fastest cruisers in the US Navy, as it raced across the waves toward the rendezvous coordinates that he'd given to Darkdoom a few hours earlier.

"Still nothing on radar or sonar, sir," one of the sailors working the bridge stations reported.

"Looks like your friends are late," the captain said, scanning the horizon.

"Oh, I doubt it," Otto said.

"Surface breach!" one of the sailors standing on the starboard side of the bridge shouted in alarm. Three hundred feet away from the naval vessel a huge plume of spray was thrown into the air as the *Megalodon* burst from the surface of the ocean, easily matching the ship's speed.

"What the hell?" the captain yelled. "How did they get that close?"

"No idea, sir," the sailor replied, looking bewildered. "Still nothing on radar or sonar."

227

"That's impossible," the captain snapped.

"No, that's my friends," Otto said with a grin.

The captain hurried out onto the deck, staring at the huge vessel cruising along beside them. It dwarfed his warship and was, by an order of magnitude, the largest submarine he had ever seen.

"We're being hailed," a sailor reported, and the captain hurried back inside, giving a quick nod to the sailor running the communications station.

"Go ahead, unknown vessel," the sailor said.

"We're ready to commence cargo and personnel transfer," the voice on the speaker answered.

"Understood," the captain replied, turning to the helmsman. "Full stop, Mr. Davis."

A few minutes later, both vessels were stationary and a gangway slid out from the *Megalodon*'s hull, coming to rest on the *Independence*'s deck.

Darkdoom walked across the gangway and shook the captain's hand.

"A pleasure to meet you, Captain," Darkdoom said. "You have a fine ship."

"As do you, Mr. . . ."

"Call me John," Darkdoom said with a smile as Otto walked across the deck toward him. "John Doe."

"Of course . . . A pleasure to meet you, Mr. Doe." The captain nodded.

"Hello, Otto," Diabolus said as Otto approached. "I'm

228

glad to see you in one piece; after the unfortunate events in Italy, I feared the worst."

"I'm okay." Otto nodded. "We need to get that cargo on board." He gestured to a stack of crates on the deck of the *Independence*.

"With your permission, Captain?" Darkdoom asked. The captain nodded and several men began to cross the gangway from the *Megalodon* and carry the half dozen crates from the *Independence*'s deck back to the submarine. In a few minutes, the deck was clear and they were ready to depart.

"Thank you, Captain," Otto said, shaking the man's hand. "I know this might sound ridiculous, but you might just have helped to save the world."

"Not as ridiculous as you might think," the captain said. "Not every day I get a direct order from the president. Good luck with whatever it is you have to do."

Otto gave a quick nod and then followed Darkdoom back across the gangway to the *Megalodon*.

"Things may get a little weird . . . ," the captain said to himself as he watched the *Megalodon* sink back below the waves. "You can say that again, Mr. President."

"Hello, Max," Furan said as she walked into her old cell. Nero sat securely cuffed to a metal chair that had been bolted to the floor of the spartan room. "I do hope you're enjoying my old quarters as much as I did." She walked

229

behind him. "We wouldn't want you to be uncomfortable now, would we."

"I don't have time for your games, Anastasia," Nero said. "Just get this over with."

"A quick death?" Furan asked. "After everything we've been through together. Wouldn't that be rather anticlimactic? No, I have something much more enjoyable in mind. Natalya!"

Raven walked into the room, her face an expressionless mask, carrying a small table with a roll of black cloth resting on it. Raven placed the table on the far side of the room and Furan walked over to it.

"I'm afraid I've had to improvise, but your technical and medical departments had pretty much everything I needed."

She unrolled the bundle on the table to reveal an array of vicious-looking tools and surgical instruments.

"I was going to do this myself," she said with an evil smile. "But why have a Raven and caw yourself?"

She handed Raven a scalpel.

"Natalya, no permanent damage. Not yet, anyway. Just make him scream the way I taught you. . . ."

Miss Leon stuck her head around the corner of the gloomy corridor, checking for any sign of Anna's murderous robots.

"Coast looks clear," she said quietly, trotting down the

corridor with Wing and Penny just behind. As they proceeded, Miss Leon scanned the numbers on each of the corridor's identical doors.

"This one," she said, stopping in front of a specific door. "Miss Lancaster, if you please."

Wing stood watching as Penny set to work on the access panel next to the door, crossing various wires until there was a click from the door.

"What is this place?" Penny asked as they walked into the room and the lights flickered on. They were surrounded by all sorts of cardboard boxes, storage crates, and cabinets.

"This is my personal storage space," Miss Leon said. "Every staff member has one. There's only so much space in our personal quarters."

"What are we looking for?" Wing asked.

"That cabinet there, the one with the black diamond on the door," Miss Leon said, and Wing walked toward it.

"Whoa." Penny pulled a dust sheet off a glowing, six-foot-tall cylinder. Inside was the motionless body of a woman with long, dark hair, wearing a loose-fitting white gown. "What the hell?"

"Please put that sheet back," Miss Leon said, suddenly sounding angry.

"Who is she?" Penny asked, looking confused.

"Me," Miss Leon replied. "That's me."

"I don't understand," Penny said. "What do you mean, that's you?"

"Well, technically speaking, that's my cat, Kali," Miss Leon said.

"Not any less confused," Penny said.

"I am what I am because Professor Pike accidentally transferred my consciousness into this body while trying to give me the stealth and agility of my cat, Kali, during one of his experiments. Once the professor realized that it wasn't yet possible to reverse the procedure, he placed my body in that stasis chamber. Originally it was stored in the Science and Technology department, but that particular area of the school is notoriously prone to exploding unexpectedly, so I had it moved down here where I knew it would be safer," Miss Leon explained. "Now, would you mind covering it up again. I really don't like to look at her."

"Of course, sorry," Penny said, draping the dust sheet over the stasis chamber again.

"I'm sorry, which drawer is the right one?" Wing asked as he opened the doors of the cabinet.

"Fourth drawer down," Miss Leon said. "There should be a black velvet pouch."

Wing reached into the drawer, pulling out the pouch and opening it. Inside was a rectangle of black metal with a skull inlaid in its surface.

"What is it?" Wing asked.

"That, Mr. Fanchu, is a little project that the professor and I were working on before my . . . accident. It's called the Skeleton Key. It's a device that can bypass any of the electronic locks in the school. The aim ultimately was to create a universal digital lockpick. We used the school's locks as a proof of concept."

"I'm surprised that Dr. Nero would allow such a thing," Wing said with a frown.

"He didn't," Miss Leon said. "In fact he ordered it destroyed the moment he found out about it. I thought that was wasteful given how much time we'd spent on developing it, so it . . . erm . . . found its way down here. It is also our ticket out of here."

"What do you mean?" Wing asked.

"I can use that to get into Nero's office," Miss Leon said, "and then to trigger the evacuation system."

"There's an evacuation system?" Penny asked. "That might have been handy to know before now."

"Anna's attack was too quick for it to be activated," Miss Leon said. "And Dr. Nero is, perhaps understandably, not keen to publicize its existence. Not everyone is so willing to stay at H.I.V.E., are they, Mr. Fanchu?"

"That was our first year," Wing replied, slightly sheepishly. "Mistakes were made."

"It's not going to be easy getting up there," Penny said.

"I've got you this far, haven't—" Miss Leon stopped mid-sentence, her ears twitching. "Quickly, hide!"

A moment later, Wing and Penny heard the sound of mechanical footsteps from the corridor outside. They both ran for cover in the darkened corners of the room as the footsteps stopped outside the door. Miss Leon vanished behind the stasis tube as the door opened and two of the assassin androids entered the room, their clawed metal feet tapping on the concrete floor as they began to methodically search the space. As Miss Leon watched from the shadows, the robots began to move toward Penny's hiding place.

Miss Leon crept under the dust sheet and silently pressed a paw to a control on its base. The robots spun around as jets of white gas shot out from the frame of the stasis chamber, blowing off the dust cover as Miss Leon sprinted for cover. The stasis chamber lid slid open and a very confused, very frightened and, most importantly, very angry cat trapped in the body of an Olympic-level gymnast launched herself at the androids with a hiss.

Miss Leon hit the first android square in the chest, knocking it off its feet and clawing at the sensor array on its face. The doomed android flailed wildly as Kali ripped its chest plate open and attacked its delicate components with her teeth, ripping bundles of cables free as the robot sparked and twitched. At the same instant, Wing charged into the back of the other robot, hitting it like a freight train and sending it staggering. The robot fought to regain its balance, but Wing delivered a lightning kick to its knee joint, bending it out of shape and sending the machine toppling to the ground. Wing leapt on top of the android, blocking the lightning-fast blows from its thrashing arms and raining hammerlike blows down on its chest, buckling the armored casing and drawing blood from his knuckles. Kali leapt from the twitching remains of the robot she had butchered and moved, incredibly fast on all fours, across the floor toward Wing and the other android. She grabbed the android's head as Wing leapt backward away from her, ripping it straight off the robot's shoulders and throwing it across the room, continuing to tear at the robot with her bloodied hands until it lay still. The she crawled across the floor toward Wing, still hissing, her face twisted into an animal snarl.

"Kali! No!" Miss Leon said as she ran across the room and put herself between Wing and the advancing woman. Kali's face immediately softened as she saw Miss Leon and she dropped low, rubbing her face against Miss Leon's. She gave a plaintive mewing sound and then hissed again at Penny as she crept out of the shadows.

"Come toward me, very slowly," Miss Leon said calmly.

"Now I want you both to stroke her very gently behind the ears."

"What?" Penny asked, looking bewildered.

"Miss Lancaster, when the experiment failed and Kali got loose last time, she put seven H.I.V.E. security guards in the sick bay. As a result, one of them will never have children. I suggest you do as I ask."

Penny stepped forward as Kali let out a low growl.

"Slowly," Miss Leon repeated as Penny gingerly raised her hand toward Kali's ear and gave it a scratch, just as she would have done with a cat. Kali seemed to calm slightly as Penny took a step back. When Wing did the same thing, Kali closed her eyes and pushed her head into his hand.

"Is she purring?" Penny asked.

"Yes, I think she likes you, Mr. Fanchu," Miss Leon said.

"I won't lie," Wing said, swallowing slightly nervously. "This is deeply disturbing."

"Think about it from my perspective," Miss Leon said with a sigh. "Come on, we need to move—there's no way that didn't get the attention of the rest of these things. Let's go."

"Otto!" Laura shouted, running down the corridor and wrapping him in an enormous hug. "Thank God you're okay."

"Can't kill me," Otto said with a grin as she kissed him.

"Doesn't stop people from trying, though, does it," Shelby said, coming to join them.

"After Darkdoom told us what happened to you and Nero, we thought . . ." Laura shook her head.

"Thought you were toasted marshmallows," Shelby said. "Great. Now I've just made myself hungry."

"I'm a little singed around the edges, but I'm okay, which is more than I can say for Nero and everyone back at H.I.V.E. right now."

"Trying not to think about that," Shelby said. "Hope you've got a plan, big brain."

"I've always got a plan," Otto said with a grin.

"Oh, don't talk rubbish," Laura said, digging him in the ribs. "You're just making this up as you go along, and you know it."

"Nothing wrong with a bit of improvisation," Otto said. "Darkdoom wants us in the situation room, we'd better get going."

The three of them made their way toward the bow of the *Megalodon* and walked into the situation room, which was already buzzing with activity. Screens on the wall were displaying all sorts of schematics and diagrams: from technical designs for Cypher's robots to network architecture maps. The huge table display in the middle of the room was displaying cutaway elevations of H.I.V.E., with several areas boxed out and magnified. Darkdoom, Professor Pike, and Nathaniel Nero stood around the display in deep discussion, occasionally pointing out specific details on the schematics.

"Mr. Malpense," a familiar voice said behind Otto, and he turned to see the Queen enter the room. "I had a feeling you would manage to slip the Disciples' net."

"I'm glad to see that you managed to escape, too," Otto replied. "I'm sorry that we brought this war to your door."

"Wars have a tendency to arrive as uninvited guests. That is their nature. I would have had to choose a side sooner or later. Recent events have merely forced my hand."

"Who's the old Goth?" Shelby whispered to Laura.

"The old Goth, young lady, is *La Regina Delle Ombre*," the Queen said, her hearing obviously rather better than Shelby had been expecting. "Matriarch of House Sinistre; last of my line. And, *you really should try to be more polite*."

"I really am most terribly sorry, your majesty, I humbly beg your forgiveness for my appalling manners," Shelby said with a low curtsy. "I am your faithful servant."

"Please don't do that," Otto said to the Queen.

"Why not?" she said. "I think it's a definite improvement."

"I would agree, Your Majesty," Shelby added. "In

truth, my behavior to this point has not been acceptable. In the future I shall speak only when spoken to."

"Please," Otto said. "Let her go."

"Oh, very well." The Queen turned to Shelby. *"Ignore my last command."*

Shelby shook her head, looking slightly confused, as the Queen walked to the far side of the room and took a seat in the opposite corner, watching the activity around her with an air of detached amusement.

"What just happened? Did she just de-snark me?" Shelby asked in disbelief. "That was horrible."

"So wish I'd had a video camera," Laura said. "Even if it was just for the curtsy."

"Let's never speak of this again, Brand," Shelby said, glancing nervously at the Queen.

"Otto," Nigel said happily as he and Franz entered the room. "I was so glad to hear you were okay."

"*Ja*, me also," Franz replied. "I am hoping that now there will be some kicking of the ass."

"I hope so." Otto smiled. "Though that's usually more Wing's department, to be honest."

"I suppose so," Franz said. "You are actually normally the kickee, yes?"

"That's definitely not a word," Laura said, shaking her head.

"Which reminds me," Shelby said, pulling a tablet

display from her pocket and calling something up on-screen. "Here, look, dictionary dot com: 'pregnable: capable of being taken or won by force . . .'"

"Did I miss something?" Otto asked, looking slightly confused.

"No," Laura sighed. "You really didn't."

"Who's the big brain now, Brand, huh?" Shelby said triumphantly.

"Ladies and gentlemen," Darkdoom interrupted loudly. "If I could have your attention, please. I'd like to get this briefing underway."

They all moved to gather around the table display.

"I'm not going to lie to you," Darkdoom said. "There's a hard target and then there's this place." He gestured toward the schematic of H.I.V.E. on the display. "We have a very narrow window of opportunity here, and our success will largely hinge on the assistance offered by *La Regina del Ombre*." He looked to the Queen and Otto.

"I believe I can protect you and Diabolus's men against the effects of the girl's mind control," the Queen said. "But the rest, I'm afraid, is very much up to you."

"I think I've worked out how to stop Anna," Otto said. "I just have to get close to her."

"Would you care to expand on your plan?" Darkdoom asked.

"No, I wouldn't," Otto said. "It's to do with the things

inside our heads. It'd be hard to explain even if I tried."

"Freaky-deaky cyber-brain stuff. Got it," Shelby replied.

"You're confident it will work?" Darkdoom asked with a slight frown.

"Yes, confident enough to ask you all to risk your lives," Otto said. "Trust me."

"Okay." Darkdoom nodded. "So the tactical goal here is to put Otto and Anna in the same room somehow. To do that we've just got to get past an army of robot killers and God knows how many brainwashed members of staff and students. We'll attack in two stages—first the infiltration team will make their entrance and then the main assault team will follow behind."

"The infiltration team will be taking this route," Nathaniel Nero said, pointing out a flashing red path that seemed to pass through the very bowels of the school. "It's dangerous, but Diabolus assures me that he has vehicles that can survive the journey."

"I've also been working for the past few hours to fabricate ISIS suits for the insertion team. They'll be lined with the new electromagnetic shielding material that the Americans have so kindly provided," Professor Pike explained. "Which should protect them from Anna's abilities."

"Once we're in," Otto said, "we'll deactivate the

external defenses so that the second wave can attack."

"What's the signal?" one of Diabolus's squad leaders asked.

"We'll launch a flare from the crater," Otto said.

"Once we see the signal, the *Megalodon* will surface and launch the Shroud that will drop the assault teams straight into the crater," Darkdoom said.

"What are the rules of engagement in there?" another one of his men asked. "It could be hard to tell friendlies from hostiles."

"Nonlethal rounds for anything with a pulse," Darkdoom replied.

"I've modified the Sandman rifles to fire an electromagnetic discharge round," the professor said. "It should allow you to take down mechanical and organic targets without killing the latter."

"You sure they're effective?" Darkdoom's man asked.

"Yes, but feel free to use brute force against the androids, too," the professor said.

"Mr. Malpense, myself and three of my men will make up the infiltration team," Darkdoom said.

"Like hell they will," Shelby said.

"I don't remember asking your opinion, Miss Trinity?" Darkdoom frowned.

"No one knows that place as well as we do," Laura said. "It's not like it's the first hardened facility that we've gone up against."

"More like the sixth," Otto murmured.

"*Ja*, we are ready to fight," Franz said. "We are senior students now!"

"We're all going," Nigel said. "That's the deal."

"I'm afraid I rather think they're right." The professor looked at Darkdoom. "Nero could have sent a G.L.O.V.E. kill team into the Glasshouse, but he didn't, he sent this lot. They have a unique set of complementary skills, it's how they were trained. Honestly, there probably aren't many more skilled special-operations teams that we could assemble, especially at short notice."

Darkdoom paused for a moment, looking down at the mazelike corridors of H.I.V.E., then sighed.

"Very well, we're three hours from the launch point," he told them. "I need everyone who's going on the mission in the gym so that the Queen here can perform her magic. After that, I need you suited, booted, and ready to roll. Dismissed."

The situation room began to clear, and Darkdoom grabbed Nigel's shoulder as he walked past.

"Nigel, a word please," Darkdoom said, holding him back as the room cleared. He waited as Otto left, with a glance over his shoulder at his frowning friend, and then closed the door.

"You're not going," Darkdoom said, now that they were alone.

"What?" Nigel said angrily. "Why not?"

"Because you're my son, I love you, and it's too dangerous," Darkdoom said firmly.

"Yes, I know I'm your bloody son!" Nigel shouted. "And do you know how sick I am of hearing that? Do you know what it's like to be constantly reminded of the legacy you have to live up to? No, because you're the great Diabolus Darkdoom, hero of G.L.O.V.E., so you don't have to worry about people sniggering behind your back about the fact that you're nothing like your father."

"Nigel, I—"

"No," Nigel snapped, interrupting him. "I've had the same training as the others, I'm just as ready as they are, and you're not going to stop me from helping my friends just because I'm your son and you're worried about what might happen to me. How dare you?"

Darkdoom stared at Nigel for several seconds and then put his hand on his shoulder.

"You're absolutely right," he said. "I'm sorry. Of course I'm frightened of what might happen to you, but you are your own man now. The decision is yours."

"Thank you." Nigel took a deep breath. "Now, I need to go and get ready with the others."

"Of course," his father replied.

Nigel walked toward the door.

"Nigel."

"Yes?"

"Please be careful."

Nigel gave a quick nod and walked out of the room.

"Because if anything happens to you, your mother will hunt me down and kill me," Darkdoom said quietly to himself.

chapter ten

"Is it just me, or does this feel a bit like an assembly at H.I.V.E.?" Laura whispered as they lined up next to the other men and women who would make up Darkdoom's assault force in the *Megalodon*'s gym.

"I think this might be a slightly weirder experience," Otto said.

"What, even weirder than that time Francisco gave us the lecture on proper footcare?" Shelby asked.

"Well, maybe not *that* weird," Otto replied. "But close."

The Queen of Shadows walked onto the raised platform at one end of the room and the gym fell silent.

"Ladies and gentlemen, some of you may find this unpleasant," she said. "But, please believe me, this is the only way to ensure you do not fall under the control of our enemy."

Some of the troops in the room looked at each other nervously.

"Please try to stay as calm and relaxed as possible," the Queen continued, and sinister whispers started to twist between her words. *"You hear my voice. You hear only my voice. You will ignore the commands of any other with this voice. Their words will not control you. You will hear only my voice."*

A couple of people around the room shook their heads, as if trying to dislodge a bad memory; others just looked uneasy as the Queen's words slipped inside their heads.

"That's it?" Shelby asked. "I don't feel any different."

"I think that's sort of the point," Otto said, hoping that the Queen's confidence in her own powers was not misplaced.

"Well, let's just hope it worked," Nigel said.

"We better hope it did," Otto said, smiling grimly, "or this is going to be the shortest rescue mission in history."

"Hello, Joseph." Anna's face appeared on the main monitor in the Absalom lab. "Is it done?"

"Yes," he replied. "The nano-sequencers have completed their work making Furan's modifications. Your brothers and sisters will be fully mature in less than forty-eight hours. The rest of the process is fully automated."

"Excellent, I would like to thank you all for your help," Anna said. "You have, unfortunately . . . now, how did Anastasia put it earlier . . . *outworn your usefulness.* She does have such a lovely turn of phrase sometimes. Goodbye."

She vanished from the screen and instantly thick, yellow gas began to pour into the room from vents near the ceiling. Wright clutched at his throat before dropping to his knees, foaming at the mouth. All around him the Absalom scientists were suffering the same terrible fate.

A minute later, ventilation fans kicked in, clearing the gas from the corpse-littered room, and the only sound then was the regular beep of the timer on the main display.

TIME TO FULL MATURITY—FORTY-SIX HOURS, THIRTY-THREE MINUTES, AND NINE SECONDS

"Which way?" Penny asked as they ran toward a T-junction at the end of the corridor.

"Left," Miss Leon said.

Kali ran along beside them, somehow able to move just as fast as the rest of them despite her weird crouching run. They could hear the sounds of multiple robots pursuing them not far behind, and knew it was only a matter of time before they were trapped. H.I.V.E.mind was controlling them and no one knew the school better than he did.

"Back the other way," Wing yelled as more of the android assassins rounded the corner at the far end of the corridor and started sprinting toward them. They turned back, but it was too late; the other group of pursuing robots were already flooding into the passageway behind them, and they were caught between the two packs.

"There's too many," Wing said as the robots advanced slowly toward them from both directions, knowing their prey was trapped. Kali hissed at the robots, a low growl forming in her throat, as Wing suddenly saw a figure step out into the corridor behind one of the packs.

"Down on the ground!" Colonel Francisco yelled.

Wing pushed Penny and Kali to the ground as the huge multibarreled Gatling gun the colonel was carrying spun up. A second later, the corridor was filled with high-velocity tracer rounds that simply ripped the robots in the corridor to shreds, scattering shattered components and shards of metal in all directions. Wing held the struggling Kali down as the earsplitting roar filled the corridor for at least thirty seconds, until the backpack of ammunition the colonel was wearing ran dry. Suddenly, the only sound was the spinning of the weapons' red-hot barrels, and the sparking of the dozens of shattered machines that now filled the corridor on either side of the cowering group of nonmechanical survivors.

"I think you got them," Miss Leon said, surveying the scene of carnage.

The colonel dropped the massive machine gun and shed the empty ammo pack before walking down the corridor toward them, picking his way through the debris, checking that there was no movement from any of the demolished machines.

"Is that . . . ?" Francisco said as he saw Kali.

"Yes, I'll explain later," Miss Leon said.

Kali hissed at Francisco as he approached.

"You have to scratch her behind the ear," Penny said.

"Yeah, that's not going to happen," Francisco replied with a frown. "We need to keep moving, more will be on the way."

"Where did you get that thing?" Miss Leon said as they ran past the huge discarded weapon.

"You're not the only one with a personal storage unit," Francisco said with a grim smile. "This way."

"So this . . . What did you call it, again?" Shelby asked.

"Faraday weave," Otto replied.

"This Faraday weave that they lined our suits with," she said. "Did they deliberately make it annoyingly itchy or is it a natural characteristic of the material?"

"You're right," Otto said as he unpacked his own suit. "It'd be much better if Anna could just overheat and set fire to your suit with you inside it."

"Boil-in-the-bag Shelby, mmmm," Laura said with a grin.

"Actually, it'd probably be more like microwave popcorn," Otto said. "Except . . . well . . . burstier."

"Pop goes the Shelby!" Franz sang happily.

"Remind me why we're doing this again?" Nigel looked at his ISIS suit with a hint of suspicion.

"Gotta go save the big guy," Shelby said. "And everyone else, of course . . . but mainly my boyfriend."

"He's probably sitting there right now in the accommodation block, doing his concerned face," Otto said.

"Which, by a strange coincidence, is also most people's constipated face," Laura said.

"Hey, that's my baby bear you're talking about," Shelby said. "Little more respect please."

"Baby bear?" Otto said.

"Really?" Laura added.

"And I'm his Goldilocks," Shelby said with a grin, tossing her long blond hair.

"On that note, I've got to go and use the facilities before I put this thing on," Otto said, heading for the bathroom.

He walked into one of the cubicles and sat down on the closed toilet lid. He pulled up the leg of his jeans and took out the thin metal tube that he'd had tucked in his sock since disembarking the USS *Independence*. He held the cigar-sized tube in his hand, feeling its weight.

"Better to have it and not need it, Otto," he said to himself before palming it and heading back outside. Then, while the others were distracted, he slid the cylinder into one of the equipment pouches on the waist of his suit and quickly got changed. Shelby had been annoyingly right about the itchiness of the Faraday weave, he realized.

"I am thinking it must be made from the horsehair, yes," Franz said, shifting uncomfortably inside his suit.

"A horse with fleas maybe," Nigel said.

"Popcorn," Otto reminded them and they both stopped moaning.

The five of them headed for the bow of the *Megalodon*, finding their way to the torpedo room, where technicians were busy making final adjustments to the slim pods that sat on the loading rigs.

"You won't have to do anything to guide these things," the professor said. "They're fully autonomous."

"No controls at all?" Laura asked. "What if the guidance system malfunctions?"

"Well, you'll sink and either drown or be crushed by deep ocean pressures," the professor replied.

"Autonomously," Otto added helpfully.

"That's deeply reassuring," Laura said.

"See what you did there," Shelby added.

"If we're quite finished with the banter, we're nearly ready for your departure," the professor said. "Five minutes."

Otto sat down on an equipment box nearby and took a deep breath.

"You look nervous." Laura sat down beside him. "That's not like you."

"I don't think we've faced anything quite like this before," he said. "We can't afford to mess this up."

"Oh, come on," Laura said. "We're always up against the end of the world. How is this any different?"

"You don't know what Anna's capable of, Laura."

"So, Big Bad wants to destroy the world, what more is there to understand?" Laura shrugged.

"I'm not sure she wants to *destroy* the world," he said. "I think she wants to *enslave* it."

"Why?"

"Because that's what I'd do, if I was her," Otto said quietly, looking Laura in the eye. "I don't want to, obviously, but if I did, I probably could."

"The key words there are 'don't want to,' Otto," Laura said. "We're all capable of doing terrible things, but we choose not to. That's what Nero's been trying to teach us, surely? You don't have to play by the rules, obey the law, even be a good person, but you have to keep things in balance. Sure you're capable of inflicting a lot more chaos on the world than most people, but did it ever occur to you that might be why we were all recruited by Nero? Identify the people who could unleash genuine mindless, destructive havoc on the world and then show them that they shouldn't."

Otto sat in silence for a moment, before turning to her.

"I love you," he said. "I just need you to know that. You make me more human."

"Otto," Laura replied softly. "It doesn't matter what's been done to you, where you come from, the plans other people had for you, you're the most human person I know."

"Thanks." Otto sounded suddenly sad. "That means more to me than you probably realize."

"Hey," she said, putting her hand on his thigh. "This is going to be okay, you know. We'll stop her."

"I know," Otto said, the cloud vanishing from his face. "We're Nero's ass-kickers after all."

"Now, that's a team name I can live with." She grinned, before giving him a quick peck on the cheek. "For luck."

"Don't think I can't still spot a *Star Wars* reference, Brand, you hopeless geek," Otto said with a chuckle. They both stood up and walked over to where the others were standing.

"Okay, we're ready," Professor Pike announced as

Darkdoom walked into the room. "Helmets on, everyone."

"The Queen will be joining the crater-assault team to help with any staff or pupils who may be under Anna's control, so we can get them off the island if necessary."

"Make sure that your men understand how dangerous Anna is," Otto said. "There's no margin for error here."

"You just get that crater open, Mr. Malpense," Darkdoom replied. "They'll get you to Anna, don't worry."

"Time to go," the professor said as Otto and the others completed final cross-checks on each other's gear, ensuring that their suit seals were good and that their rebreather systems were fully operational. They each walked to their assigned launch-pods and climbed inside, the displays in the nose of each pod lighting up as they lay down in the padded interiors.

"Systems check complete," a technician reported. "We're good to go."

The hatches on each of the five pods began to whirr closed and the lights of the launch bay disappeared inside the pods, replaced by the glow from the systems-information panel.

"*Beginning loading sequence,*" a voice said in Otto's ear, and he felt the pod lurch as the large robotic loading arm picked up his vehicle and loaded it into one of the *Megalodon*'s launch tubes.

"*Closing inner hatches,*" the voice went on. "*Flooding*

tubes." Otto heard the sound of high-pressure water flooding the tube outside. *"External hatches open. Three . . . two . . . one . . . launching!"*

Otto held firmly to the handholds on either side of the screen as he felt a sudden rush of acceleration. The infiltration pods raced away from the *Megalodon*, their magnetic impulsion units leaving barely any detectable trail as they rocketed through the deep. He was surprised by how quiet it was, just a steady humming whine from the impellers as they pushed the pods through the water at incredible speed. He watched the screen as it displayed a three-dimensional rendering of the seabed below, heading for the vast, volcanic mountain that had been his home for the last few years.

The pods dived deeper, seeking the cover of valleys in the sea floor; they were almost impossible to detect with any sonar system, but there was no point taking any chances, their approach should still be as stealthy as possible. As the flanks of the volcano rose above the pods, Otto watched as all five turned in perfect unison, heading toward an opening near the base of the mountain. It was one of the seawater intakes for the geothermal system that powered H.I.V.E. Seawater was sucked in through the intake and then turned into steam, which in turn drove the massive turbines that satisfied the school's huge demand for off-grid electricity.

"Coming up on the intake," Otto said. "Hang on, guys. This is where it could get a little rough."

He braced himself as the pod shot into the circular opening, the hum from the impellers decreasing as the current caught the pods and they were effectively sucked into the pipe. The ride suddenly got a lot bumpier as the fast-moving water shook the pod, the display indicating that they were now less than a minute from their destination. Otto studied the schematics, spotting the section of pipe that passed through the underground cavern ahead. As the pods entered the target area, the impellers started to whine as they fought the current, slowing the pods and bringing them closer to the metal walls of the pipe. Magnetic clamps engaged and the pods attached firmly to the inner wall of the pipe, laser cutters slicing through the thick metal once a perfect seal was confirmed. A minute later, the hatch of the pod opened again and the night-vision system in Otto's helmet lit up the interior of the small cavern that the intake pipe had passed through. He dropped down to the cavern floor as more sections of the pipe fell to the floor and his friends joined him in the pitch-black cavern.

"Confirming all seals are good," Otto said. "We're in, and I'm not seeing any pressure drop in the system. So far so good."

"Roger that," Darkdoom replied.

"Engaging thermoptic camo," Otto said, touching the control panel on the forearm of his armor. He watched as his friends followed suit, the surface of their ISIS suits flickering for an instant as they vanished from view. Otto could still clearly see his friends thanks to the suits' onboard computer systems, but they would be near invisible to anyone else.

They quickly moved through the cavern, their Sandman rifles raised as they scanned for any sign of hostiles. They moved in silence toward the metal staircase at the other end leading up to a solid-looking metal door.

"Okay, Shel, you're up," Otto said, and Shelby quickly moved to the access panel next to the door and pulled her roll of tools from an equipment pouch.

"Thirty seconds," she said as she pulled a probe from the kit and set to work on the panel. She was done in twenty, the door sliding aside with a hiss.

They moved inside, finding themselves in one of H.I.V.E.'s countless machine tunnels, filled with the pipes and thick bundles of armored cables that were the school's life-support system. They fanned out into the corridor, checking the dimly lit passageway in both directions.

"Clear," Franz reported.

"Move up," Otto said, letting Franz take point as they moved down the corridor in a tight tactical formation.

Just a couple of minutes later, they were approaching the school's power plant and as they walked into the giant turbine hall, Franz slowed, holding up a single closed fist.

"Contact," he whispered over comms.

The others stopped immediately, dropping to a knee and raising their rifles. Ahead, they could see two of Anna's robots patrolling the walkway above the turbine room.

"Franz, Shelby, drop them on my mark," Otto said. "Three, two, one, mark."

Their Sandman rifles fired in perfect unison, the two assassin androids dropping to the floor with a clatter as the electromagnetic rounds struck them and instantly fried their internal systems.

"Okay, we need to pick up the pace," Otto said. "I have no idea whether Anna will have noticed that. Let's go."

The five of them moved quickly through the power plant, passing through the geothermal core, where massive heat exchangers plunged into the lake of lava far below them. It was the heart of the school's power system and the reason that Nero had originally chosen that location. Limitless off-grid power. A minute later, they were stepping back out into the familiar corridors of H.I.V.E. They had only been gone for a few days, but the place already seemed to have changed. The once-bustling corridors were empty, and the general hum of activity that they usually felt within the walls of the school was gone.

"Gives me the creeps like this," Nigel said as they moved through the abandoned corridors.

"Know what you mean," Laura replied. "It's a bit spooky. I thought there'd be more guards."

"Yeah, well. Guess they didn't count on H.I.V.E. being quite so *pregnable*," Shelby said.

"Oh, shush," Laura shot back.

"Okay, let's head for the crater," Otto said. "Franz, Nigel, take the south corridor. Laura, Shelby, and I will take the north. Get to the hangar control room. If I can't open the hangar from the launch bay, it'll be down to you guys, okay?" Franz and Nigel both gave a quick nod. "Okay, let's go."

They split into two groups, moving quickly in opposite directions, circling around to the hangar bay. Otto, Laura, and Shelby jogged through the empty corridors, finally reaching the blast doors that sealed off the hangar.

"Okay, this one's going to be a little tougher," Shelby said, looking down at the high-level security panel that secured the door. "You ready, Brand?"

"Aye," Laura replied, pulling a wire from the control panel on her left forearm. "Just need an access port."

"On it," Shelby said, beginning to work carefully at the side of the panel with her own tools. Otto stood guard, scanning the corridor in both directions for threats as they tried to open the doors.

"Okay," Laura said. "See that matrix there." She pointed to a cluster of components inside the panel. "I need you to bypass that the moment I say."

"Say when," Shelby said, a pair of probes ready.

"Wait for it . . ." Laura tapped at the display on her arm. "Wait for it . . . Okay, NOW!"

Shelby pushed the probes into the panel, and a moment later the hangar doors began to rumble open.

"Yes, we are the pregnators . . . No, wait . . . that doesn't sound right," Shelby said.

"Come on," Otto said, hurrying into the darkened hangar. They could just make out the shadowy shapes of the pair of Shrouds that were left in the hangar as they ran across the cavern.

"Okay, they're definitely going to know we're here once I do this," Otto said. "Be ready."

Laura and Shelby took defensive positions covering the hangar door, as Otto reached out with his abilities and connected to the giant motors far above him that moved the crater doors. There was a moment's delay and then the giant steel shutters began to open far above him, the stars in the night sky becoming visible through the ever-widening gap. Otto pulled the flare from the pouch on his waist and pointed it toward the sky, pulling the trigger cord and sending the bright-red signal shooting up and out of the crater.

"Oh God, no," Otto said. As the flare rocketed out of the crater, its bright red light reflected off the black-metal armored skin of the countless robots that were swarming the previously darkened crater walls above him. "It's a trap!"

"Thermoptic camouflage system offline," a calm voice reported in his ear.

He watched in horror as both Laura and Shelby flickered back into view and his own suit's cloak disengaged.

"Of course it's a trap," Anna said, walking into the hangar, surrounded by dozens more of the assassin droids, with several of the lumbering Behemoth units just behind them. Raven stood beside her, swords drawn. "Honestly, what did you expect?"

Shelby and Laura both opened fire as the assassin droids poured into the room, dropping several of the killer androids as they sprinted toward them, but they were both quickly overwhelmed. Otto raised his rifle and aimed it at Anna. An instant later, the gun exploded in a shower of sparks, damaged beyond repair. Otto threw the useless weapon to the ground and reached out with his abilities, trying to connect to one of the Behemoth units behind her.

That's not going to work.

Otto felt a searing pain as he heard Anna's words inside his head. He suddenly realized just how badly he'd underestimated the limits of her abilities. He felt a moment of despair as he heard the sound of the approaching Shroud from the *Megalodon*, summoned by his flare.

"Oh, how nice. You've brought me some more toys," Anna said with an evil smile. The Shroud began to descend into the crater, but then its engines roared, trying to ascend again as the scene unfolding in the crater below became clear to those on board. Anna reached out and effortlessly hijacked the dropship's flight controls and brought it down into the crater, finally bringing it to rest on the landing pad in the center of the cavern. The loading ramp at the rear of the Shroud opened and Darkdoom's men poured out with their weapons raised. Anna tipped her head to one side and the men instantaneously fell to the ground, unconscious or dead, Otto couldn't tell.

"You can come out," Anna said. "I can feel you in there, you old witch."

The Queen walked down the ramp. If she felt any fear, there was no trace of it in her expression.

"Many of my ancestors were called witches," she said, walking across the crater toward Anna. "We consider it a badge of honor. And you, young lady, need to be taught a lesson."

"Oh, really?" Anna said. "And who exactly will be delivering that lesson?"

"*You will submit to me,*" the Queen hissed, her voice

twisting in and out of her words, forcing compliance.

"No, I won't," Anna replied calmly.

Kneel.

The Queen's mouth dropped open as she heard Anna's voice inside her head and she slowly dropped to one knee, bowing her head before her.

Your reign is over, old woman. Now sleep.

The Queen toppled over, unconscious.

Now, far too late, Otto understood what the combination of his own abilities and the Voice meant. Anna could control people's will without even speaking. She could project the Voice straight into their heads. In that instant he knew that there was no way they could stop her, not like this.

"Raven, take the Queen to Anastasia. Apparently, she has some use for her," Anna said as two of her robots lifted the unconscious old woman from the ground and handed her to Raven. "It's probably some nefarious plot to stop me, but to be honest, I'm rather keen to see what she's got planned. I like a challenge."

Raven walked out of the room behind the robots carrying the Queen's limp body, as Anna made her way over to Otto. Two of her androids seized him by the upper arms and pulled off his helmet.

"Hello, brother," she said, stroking his cheek. "It's going to be so nice to spend some quality time with you at last."

"I'm NOT your brother," Otto spat. "You're just a second-rate copy."

"No, Otto," Anna said, "I'm the next generation and you know it."

He gasped, feeling another wave of agony inside his skull as Anna lit up his brain's pain centers.

"I could just tell you to obey me," Anna said. "But I think I'd rather break you. Much more amusing that way."

"Leave him alone!" Laura screamed as Otto cried out in pain.

"And you must be Laura," Anna said. "Nero kept detailed files on all of you. I understand that you and Otto have grown quite . . . attached to one another. Perhaps I'll make him torture you before he kills you. Wouldn't that be romantic? I really am so excited about all the fun we're going to have together."

"Get away from her, you white-haired cow," Shelby said, struggling against the iron grip of the robots holding her.

"Or, maybe, I'll just have you two kill each other in front of him? Decisions, decisions, decisions." Anna smiled nastily at Shelby. "Take these two to the detention area," she ordered two of the robots, who dragged the struggling Shelby and Laura toward the door. Then she turned to Otto.

"You're coming with me."

chapter eleven

"This is being very, very bad," Franz said, peering down from the control room, halfway up the cavern wall, to the hangar below. He saw Anna walk out of the hangar, with two of the killer androids half dragging a stumbling Otto behind them.

"That's your detailed tactical analysis, is it?" Nigel asked, crouched beside him.

"I am thinking we need the reinforcements, *ja?*"

"Wasn't that what they were supposed to be?" Nigel said, looking down at the fallen bodies of his father's men.

"No, I am meaning like the proper army," Franz said, "with tanks and bombers and things."

"You'd just be giving her an army of her own, or condemning them all to death," Nigel said. "You saw what she did down there."

"So, what do we do?" Franz looked at Nigel.

"I don't know," Nigel said, trying desperately to come up with a plan. Suddenly, an idea popped into his head. "Anna's using H.I.V.E.mind to control the school, right?"

"*Ja*, that is being my understanding."

"Well, without power, no H.I.V.E.mind, right?"

"So, you are suggesting that we stop the volcano?" Franz asked, sounding confused.

"No, but remember when Cypher attacked the school?"

"Yes, of course. All the robots are being giving me the flashbacks," Franz replied with a frown.

"Yeah, well, remember the room where we found the bomb that Francisco had planted when the Contessa was controlling him?" Nigel said. "That was the geothermal-power control room. If we can get back in there and, I don't know, stop the reactors or something, that might shut down H.I.V.E.mind and weaken Anna."

"I suppose it is being worth a try," Franz said with a nod. "I will not be having to fight Colonel Francisco again, will I?"

"Let's hope not," Nigel said. "Let's really, really hope not."

Laura and Shelby were half dragged in silence toward the detention area, the robots flanking them holding them in a viselike grip. They had nearly reached the entrance to the cell block when Miss Leon came trotting around the corner. The robots stopped, scanning the advancing cat, as if slightly unsure what to do.

"Is that . . . ?" Shelby said, just as Miss Leon let out a growling hiss at the robots.

A moment later, a screeching, hissing madwoman with long, dark hair and wearing white pajamas came racing around the same corner, galloping toward them in a bizarre, crouching run before launching herself at one of the androids holding Laura. The robot was knocked flat on its back as the woman, yowling like an incredibly angry cat, began ripping it, quite literally, limb from limb. At the far end of the corridor Colonel Francisco stepped into view, raising an antique elephant gun that was nearly as long as he was tall, and the other robot's head exploded in a shower of sparks, releasing its grip on Laura.

"Shelby, duck," a familiar voice barked behind her, and she crouched down as a massive four-foot-long blade whistled through the air just above her and cleanly sliced the heads off the two robots holding her; they toppled to the ground, sparks shooting from their severed necks. Shelby spun around to see Wing holding an enormous two-handed claymore sword and she launched herself at him, throwing her arms around his neck and hugging him tight.

"Oh my God, you're okay," she gasped, feeling a sudden flood of overwhelming relief that brought tears to her eyes.

"Are you okay?" Wing asked, gently placing his hand on her cheek.

"I am now," Shelby replied, resting her head on his chest.

"Are the others with you?" he asked.

"Yes," Laura cut in. "But the rescue mission didn't go quite as well we hoped." She gestured to the fallen robots. "Anna's got Otto."

"What about Nero?" Miss Leon asked as Kali crouched down beside her.

"Anna has him, too, but we've not seen him," Shelby said. "She captured him a couple of days ago. We're assuming she brought him here."

"This situation is spinning out of control," Francisco said. "We need to trigger the evacuation and get word to G.L.O.V.E. that they must send a full assault force to retake the island."

"That's not a good idea," Laura said. "Anna's much more powerful than we realized. She wiped out Darkdoom's assault force on her own, without so much as raising a finger. Brute force isn't going to work."

"All the more reason to evacuate," Penny said as she walked down the corridor toward them.

"Hi," Laura said. "Glad to see you're okay."

"Save it, Brand," Penny snapped dismissively. "I just want to get out of here."

"Hey—" Shelby said, about to snap back at her, but Laura put a hand on her arm.

"Fair enough." She nodded at Penny. "I think that's a sound plan. We can't fight Anna as it stands, so let's just concentrate on getting as many people as possible a safe distance away from her."

"How did you get back to H.I.V.E.?" Francisco asked.

"The *Megalodon* is just outside the school's defensive perimeter," Shelby replied. "We launched this epic fail of a rescue mission from there."

"Okay, the students are locked down in the accommodation blocks," Miss Leon said. "If we can trigger the evacuation protocol, we can at least try to get some of them out of harm's way."

"How are we going to do that while Anna has control of H.I.V.E.mind?" Laura asked with a frown.

"The evacuation system isn't under H.I.V.E.mind's control," Miss Leon pointed out. "Never forget that Nero is a paranoid, tactical genius. He always assumes that the worst-case scenario will happen and plans accordingly. If we can get to his office, we already have a device that will get us inside. Then I should be able to evacuate the school."

"Assuming we don't bump into Raven, of course," Shelby said.

"Let me worry about that." Francisco patted the large pistol in the holster on his hip.

"She is under Anna's control," Wing said with a frown. "She is a victim here, too."

"I understand that, Mr. Fanchu," the colonel replied. "But she may not leave us any choice. We all know what she's capable of."

"Let's hope it doesn't come to that," Laura said. "We'd better get moving."

They set off down the corridor, following Francisco and Miss Leon, heading for Nero's office.

"Okay, so who's the crazy cat lady?" Shelby quietly asked Wing as they jogged down the corridor.

"I'll explain later," he replied. "But, even then, I doubt you'll believe me. . . ."

"What the hell is going on in there?" Darkdoom demanded, looking at the large table display in the *Megalodon*'s situation room. It had been several minutes since he'd watched in horror as the vitals of the entire squad he'd sent into the crater had flatlined, and now the location trackers in the ISIS suits that the H.I.V.E. students had been wearing were showing three different groups in separate locations, none of which fitted in any way with the original plan.

"It's impossible to say without sending another squad in, sir," one of his men reported.

"There's no way I'm sending more of my operatives in there without knowing what happened to the first group," Darkdoom said.

"Sir, we're intercepting flash traffic from Langley—the orbital-launch platforms that they lost control of are commencing their launch prep cycles. They'll be ready to fire in less than twenty minutes," his comms officer reported.

"This is not going well, Diabolus," Nathaniel Nero said. "Perhaps we should prepare to carry out the backup plan."

"My son is in there," Darkdoom said. "As is yours, along with hundreds of students."

"I'm well aware of that." Nathaniel frowned. "And you know as well as I do that they would both say the same thing, under the circumstances. Need I remind you that there are hundreds of millions of innocent people in the cities those satellites are targeting."

"Still nothing from any of the operatives inside the school, sir," the comms officer reported.

"Reluctant as I am to admit it, Diabolus, Nathaniel is right," Professor Pike said. "We should at least prepare for the eventuality that the mission has not been successful."

Diabolus looked at the two old men in front of him and suddenly felt just as old himself.

"Fire control, prep launch tube one," he ordered.

"Loadout, sir?" the fire control officer asked.

"Bunker buster nuclear warhead."

• • •

"How are we going to get in there?" Shelby asked as they approached Nero's office door. "I mean, that lock is literally uncrackable . . . Or, so I've heard."

"Mr. Fanchu, you have the key?" Miss Leon said as they reached the door. Wing reached into his pocket and pulled out the Skeleton Key.

"What's that?" Shelby asked, curiously, as she saw the black tablet.

"Something that you will never, ever get your hands on, Miss Trinity," Miss Leon said.

Wing held the Skeleton Key up to the lock panel, and the tablet snapped out of his hand and attached to the panel. The skull design on its surface began to flash rhythmically, getting faster and faster until there was a soft beep and a click and the door slid open.

"Whoa," Shelby said. "Now I know what I want for Christmas."

"I dunno," Penny said. "Sort of takes the fun out of it, doesn't it?"

They hurried inside and Laura walked over to Nero's desk, tapping at the display mounted in the surface to wake it. Francisco and Wing took position keeping watch at the door for any sign of Anna's robot guards.

"Okay, what am I looking for?" Laura asked, scanning the display. "I don't see anything here about evacuation of the school."

"Look for references to the word 'exeunt,'" Miss Leon said.

"Okay, I've got a hidden command protocol with that name," Laura said after thirty seconds, tapping at the screen. "It's quantum encrypted."

"Of course it is," Miss Leon said. "Any way around the encryption?"

"Maybe, with a week's uninterrupted access to H.I.V.E.mind, but as it stands, no," Laura replied, shaking her head. She tried simply running the protocol and was completely unsurprised to see two words pop up on the screen.

ENTER PASSWORD

Laura typed in the word "password."

INCORRECT PASSWORD. TWO ATTEMPTS REMAINING BEFORE SYSTEM LOCKDOWN.

"Seriously? The best hacker in the school and that's the best you can do?" Shelby muttered.

"Always worth a try," Laura said with a shrug.

"Come on, Brand," Shelby said. "Work your magic."

"What part of being good with computers means that I'm going to be good at guessing someone's password?" Laura asked.

"Well, can't you just hack it or something?" Penny asked.

"How? There's no data port or systems unit, it's just

a display connected to H.I.V.E.mind, and I may be good at this stuff, but I couldn't hack Big Blue when he wasn't under the control of a creepy Otto clone. So, what exactly do you suggest?"

"One, two, three, four, five . . . ?" Shelby offered.

"Not helpful," Laura sighed.

Miss Leon stared at the portrait above the cold, dead fireplace. She'd once asked Nero who it was and he'd said, rather cryptically, that it was the most valuable thing he'd ever had stolen from him. She glanced down at the small brass plate, mounted on the bottom edge of the frame.

"Try . . . 'Elena,'" she said to Laura.

Laura typed it in.

ACCESS GRANTED

"How did you —?" Laura asked.

"Feline intuition," Miss Leon replied.

A second later, the portrait slid aside to reveal a smooth black panel.

"I need the key again," Miss Leon said.

Wing walked over to the fireplace and placed the Skeleton Key against the panel. In an instant, the entire fireplace rotated to reveal a large mechanical lever behind a sheet of glass.

"Please break the glass and pull the lever, Mr. Fanchu," Miss Leon said. "Then I think we'd better be ready to fight our way out of here."

"Why?"

"Because all hell is going to break loose," she said. "And they're going to know exactly where we are."

Wing smashed the glass and pulled the lever.

"*Emergency evacuation protocol activated. All students report to personal quarters immediately. Evacuation in T-minus two minutes. All staff report to designated evacuation areas. Evacuation in T-minus two minutes,*" a calm prerecorded female voice announced.

"Well, that's going to put me amongst the pigeons," Miss Leon said. "We need to secure the hangar bay so we've got a way off this rock, too. Let's go!"

"*Emergency evacuation protocol activated. All students report to personal quarters immediately. Evacuation in T-minus two minutes. All staff report to designated evacuation areas. Evacuation in T-minus two minutes.*"

"Why do I fink this has something to do with Otto," Block said.

"Cos it always does," Tackle said. "Come on, better do what the voice lady says."

The pair of them jogged down the landing to their room, passing the other students from the block who were all running to their own quarters.

"They gonna come and get us from our rooms?" Block asked as they entered their room.

"Spose so," Tackle said.

The display next to the door in their room lit up and a video began to play.

"*Please, lie on your beds and cross your arms over your chest,*" the smiling, computer-generated woman on the screen said. "*There is no reason to be alarmed.*"

"Better do what she asks," Block said, lying down on his bed and crossing his arms in the way the animated diagram on the screen was demonstrating.

"Yeah," Tackle said, lying down on his bed.

"*Thank you for your cooperation,*" the woman on the screen said. An instant later, restraining clamps shot out from the sides of both of their beds, securely pinning them down. "*There is no reason to be alarmed.*"

"I don't care what she says, I'm definitely alarmed," Block wailed from his bed.

"Yeah, me too," Tackle said, struggling pointlessly against his restraints.

"*Initiating pod launch in five . . . four . . . three . . . two . . . one . . . Launch.*"

The two boys felt sudden, massive acceleration, like the wildest white-knuckle ride they'd ever ridden, their faces twisted into unnatural grimaces by the massive g-forces they were being subjected to.

"*There is no reason to be alarmed.*"

"Aaaaaaaaaaah!"

• • •

On board the *Megalodon*, Darkdoom watched the monitors in the situation room anxiously, desperate for some good news.

"Well, that's unexpected," Professor Pike said, pointing to a small display that was showing the periscope's live feed of the exterior of H.I.V.E. Darkdoom's eyes widened.

"Put that full-screen," he yelled at the nearest crew member.

The main screen filled with an image of the island, and they watched in astonishment as hundreds of concealed hatches all over the rocky flanks of the volcano began to slide open.

"They're evacuating," the professor said, his eyes wide.

A few seconds later, pods the size of small shipping containers began to shoot out of the hatches, compact rocket-powered booster engines flaring, sending the boxy objects hurtling away from the island in all directions trailing plumes of white smoke. Some of the pods sailed over the *Megalodon* as they rocketed away from the island before arcing toward the ocean. Parachutes began to deploy from each pod, and large flotation bags explosively deployed from their bases. The pods slowly drifted down toward the sea, before splashing down gently and coming to a rest, bobbing on the surface.

Darkdoom and the rest of his crew watched in amazement as the pods continued to shoot from the island.

"Something tells me that things are not going well in there," Nathaniel Nero said.

"Really, Professor," Darkdoom replied quietly, his eyes fixed on the screen. "Whatever makes you say that?"

As Furan walked back into her old cell, Nero lifted his battered face with a defiant expression, despite the numerous, savage wounds that now covered his body.

"Hello, Max," Furan said with a smile. "I see that Natalya's been having fun with you. She really is very good at this sort of thing."

"She should be," Nero said, his voice hoarse from screaming in pain. "You trained her."

"Flattery will get you nowhere, Nero." Furan's smile was cruel. "Natalya has only inflicted a tiny fraction of the pain you have caused me and my family."

"YOU murdered Elena and our child," Nero snapped. "You took everything from me. You may not have taken the shot, but you ordered it."

"That bullet was meant for you!" Furan hissed back. "If you'd just stayed away from her . . ."

"I loved her, she was the only woman I've ever loved and you took her and my future from me," Nero growled. "You set us on this path. You could have just left us in peace."

"Peace! After everything G.L.O.V.E. did to my family?" Furan said. "Don't be so naïve. I warned you. I told you what the consequences would be, and you ignored the risks. *That* was what cost Elena her life. Your arrogance!"

"Just get this over with, Anastasia. You can't hurt me more than you already have," Nero said.

"I wouldn't be so sure about that, Nero," Furan replied, looking down at him. "You took my sister from me, and now I'm going to take something precious from you." She paused for a moment. "Or perhaps it would be more accurate to say: I'm going to give you something back."

She turned to the cell door.

"Natalya, please bring in our guest," she said.

Raven pushed the Queen of Shadows into the room in a wheelchair, her wrists cuffed to the arms.

"You know Francesca, of course," Furan said. "We all know the Sinistre witches in our little world. You think you know what they're capable of, but trust me, you don't. They can do things to your mind that you would not believe. Tell me, Nero, have you ever wondered why the Voice has no effect on you?"

"Maria once told me that it was a question of how strong a person's will is," Nero replied.

"Oh, that's nonsense, isn't it, Francesca?" Furan scoffed. "There's only two ways that you can become immune to the effects of the Voice. The first way is that you can have them use it to negate itself, effectively instructing you to forever ignore its effects in the future. That's what I had Francesca do to me and Pietor a long time ago; it was the only way I could ensure she would not double-cross me. But there is another way, isn't there, Francesca?"

"Don't do this, Anastasia," the Queen said quietly. "I beg you."

"You see, you can also be rendered immune to its effects if the Voice is used to manipulate you in such a fundamental way that you can never be affected by it again. Say, for example, if you wanted to change someone's memories of an event, permanently and irrevocably."

She took a bloodied knife from the nearby table and walked behind the Queen, placing a hand on her shoulder.

"In fact, if the Voice is used in such a terrible way, there is only one way to remove its effects, isn't that right, Francesca?" Furan leaned close to the Queen's ear. "Shall we let Max in on our little secret?"

She plunged the knife into the Queen's back, whose head tipped backward as she let out an unearthly howl, filled with countless different voices, before she slumped forward, dead.

Nero screamed in agony, feeling pain like he'd never felt before; as if red-hot needles were being forced into his brain. Then a flood of memories filled his head, memories that he knew with a sudden, terrible clarity were completely real, replacing the awful, breathtaking lie that he had unwittingly carried around inside his head for so many long years. Memories of . . .

Thirty years ago

Nero sat in the corridor outside the operating room, feeling like his world was collapsing around him. The voices of the people who walked past him seemed to be coming from far away as he sat, powerless to do anything, while surgeons fought to save Elena and his child.

An exhausted-looking doctor walked toward him, and Nero felt his blood run cold when he saw the look on the man's face.

"You are the next of kin for Miss Furan?" the doctor asked. Nero nodded, feeling the world start to spin around him. "I'm so sorry, there was nothing we could do. Miss Furan was too badly injured, but we were able to save your child. You have a daughter."

As Nero reeled from this information, a nurse walked out from the room behind the surgeon carrying a newborn baby wrapped in a blanket.

"I'm so sorry for your loss," she said as Nero rose and walked to her in a daze. She handed him the tiny bundle and he looked down at the face of his daughter, knowing that his life had just changed forever. She looked back at him with the same inquisitive, beautiful blue eyes as her mother.

"There is some paperwork that needs your signature, relating to Miss Furan," the nurse said quietly. "If you want, I can take the baby and clean her while you deal with it?"

"Thank you, yes I . . . ," Nero said, handing his daughter back to the nurse. Then he suddenly burst into tears, not knowing whether it was grief or joy. "I'm sorry," he said. "Can you give me a minute?"

"Of course." The nurse gestured to a nearby door. "I'll be just in here when you're ready."

Nero walked in a daze to the bathroom just down the corridor, then over to the sinks lining one wall. He ran the tap, splashing cold water on his face, before looking up at his reflection in the mirror.

He was a father.

"Hello, Max."

Nero turned, steeling himself for a fight, but he was too slow. Pietor Furan stabbed the hypodermic syringe into his neck and Nero staggered backward, already feeling his knees giving way beneath him. The room spun around him and then he collapsed to the floor, and the darkness claimed him.

Present day

"No, no, no, no," Nero said, shaking his head, as if to try and dislodge the memory that he knew now, with an awful clarity, was the truth of what had happened on that terrible day. "What did you do? What did you do?"

"You took something from me," Furan said, looking down at him with an evil smile. "So I took something from you."

"Where is she?" Nero yelled, feeling a rage burning in his chest unlike anything he'd ever felt before. "What did you do with her? Where is my daughter!"

"Oh, I had no interest in raising a child. Especially not when she would be a constant reminder of the grief you had inflicted on my family," Furan said. "We returned to Russia and put her into an orphanage under a false name. I already knew what I was going to do. I was going to keep tabs on her and then when she was old enough, I was going to take her from the orphanage and train her at the Glasshouse. Unfortunately, she had rather too much of her father's spirit and she ran from the orphanage when she was nine years old, disappearing into the Moscow underworld. It took me and Pietor more than a year to find her, but she was already demonstrating enormous potential. It took me some time to break her, but when I did, she became something magnificent, a killer like none I had ever trained before. All of this, so I could send her to kill her own father without him ever knowing. The perfect revenge. But things did not go as planned, did they, Natalya?"

Nero felt the room spin around him. He wanted to believe it was lie, but as he stared at Raven, he suddenly knew it was true. From the moment he had seen Natalya, he had felt a connection to her, something he had never quite been able to put his finger on, but now he knew what it had always been.

"I'm going to kill you, Anastasia," Nero said, a cold determination to his voice.

"No, Nero. Finally, after all this time, your own daughter's going to kill *you*," Furan said, placing a hand on Raven's shoulder. "I should thank you, really. If you had done what I would have done, and killed me when you captured me, I would have been denied the pleasure of this moment. Isn't it funny how the universe has a way of finding a balance? After all these years, finally my revenge will be complete. For Elena, for Pietor, for this." She gestured at her own hideously scarred face.

She turned to Raven.

"Natalya, kill him."

chapter twelve

"So, now what?" Franz asked, peeking round the corner at the Behemoth mech that was standing outside the geothermal-power control room.

"I'm thinking," Nigel said.

"Have you thought yet?" Franz asked after a few seconds.

"Not helping," Nigel replied. He peered around the corner again and studied the giant robot. "Okay, I've got a plan."

"Okay, what is it?"

"When you see its back, shoot it a lot," Nigel said, handing Franz his rifle as well.

"That is being a plan?" Franz asked.

"Best I've got," Nigel said. With that, he sprinted around the corner screaming like a banshee. The Behemoth turned toward him and opened its massive arms wide as Nigel dived between its legs, its battering-ram fists swinging through the air just inches above his head. Nigel sprang to his feet and set off running, still screaming as the Behemoth lumbered after him with an alarming speed that belied its size. Nigel reached the dead end at the far end of the corridor and turned around, his battle cry turning into a more terrified scream as the giant machine stomped toward him, much faster than he had been expecting.

Behind the Behemoth, Franz leapt out from behind the corner, a Sandman rifle in each hand, also scream-ing, as he let rip on full auto, spraying the Behemoth's weaker rear armor with fire. The Behemoth staggered as the electromagnetic rounds fried its systems. It half turned back toward Franz and then toppled over on top of Nigel.

"Nigel!" Franz yelled, running down the corridor toward the fallen mech. "No, no, no."

He reached the pile of sparking wreckage and found Nigel struggling to pull himself out of a tiny gap between the massive collapsed robot and the wall.

"Little help here?" Nigel asked, trying to lift the mech's limp arm off his leg.

"Oh, Nigel, I was thinking you were being the pan-cake," Franz said as he helped him out from under the wreckage.

"Wow," Nigel said. "That was quite a lot of scream-ing."

"Yes, but it was seeming appropriate at the time," Franz replied.

"Yes, yes it was," Nigel agreed. "Come on."

They both ran back down the corridor and through the door into the geothermal-power control room. A wave of heat hit them as they entered, the walls around them lit with a reflected red glow from the lake of lava far below.

"Up there," Nigel said, pointing at the observation windows set into the cavern wall. He ran up the staircase to the control room, taking the steps three at a time, with Franz close behind. Nigel ran into the room and felt his heart sink slightly. The control panels that lined the walls were bewilderingly complex, covered in an array of switches, dials, and flashing lights.

"Where's Laura when you need her," Nigel said quietly.

"Erm . . . this is looking . . . complicated," Franz said with a frown.

"Yes, it is," Nigel said with a sigh, moving to the main control panel. He didn't know where to start.

"Nigel, I am not wanting to put any extra pressure on you, but we have company," Franz said, looking down toward the entrance where at least a dozen of Anna's robots were marching into the room.

"I'm working on it," Nigel said, still trying to make any sense of the bewildering array of controls.

"Working on it quickly, *ja?*" Franz said as the robots looked up at the control room.

"Franz!" Nigel snapped.

"Sorry, it's just that our little trick with the big robot has used nearly all my ammo," Franz said.

"Okay, okay, okay." Nigel frantically began pushing random big red buttons in the hope that one would do the sort of thing that big red buttons generally did. It was no good. Though a couple of new lights started flashing, nothing seemed to be happening. Franz looked at the ammo counter on the side of his rifle and then at the androids that were now charging up the stairs toward them.

"Here goes something," Franz said quietly to himself. "Nigel! Get out of the way!"

Nigel turned to see Franz leveling his gun at the control panel and dived out of the way. Franz opened fire. The electromagnetic rounds blew the controls to pieces, sparking components flying in all directions as the panel exploded.

Then the lights went out. A few seconds later, the room was bathed in red light.

"*Emergency systems online,*" a recorded voice sounded in the hangar. "*Switching to secondary reactors in two minutes.*"

"What did you do?" Nigel said, looking at the ruined control panel.

"I am saving us from the robots," Franz said, pointing at the collapsed robots that now littered the stairs leading up to the control room. "Perhaps we should be going before they are waking up again?"

"That sounds like a very good idea," Nigel said.

They both ran down the stairs and out of the cavern, sprinting down the corridor outside.

"Fall back!" Francisco yelled as more of the assassin droids poured down the corridor toward the hangar bay doors, with several of the hulking Behemoth units stomping forward just behind them. "We can't hold them!"

He, Wing, Shelby, Laura, and Penny slowly backed up, maintaining their firing line and picking their shots as they used the Sandman rifles from Darkdoom's fallen men to drop as many of the advancing androids as they could.

"We have to hold the hangar," Laura yelled. "We can't leave without the others."

"We may not have a choice, Miss Brand," Miss Leon said over the high-pitched whine of the electromagnetic rounds. "Kali, no!"

Kali took a step toward the robots, but then stopped and hissed at the advancing wall of killer machines.

"Fall back to the bay and seal the doors," Francisco ordered. "They won't hold them forever, but it'll buy us some time."

They did as he instructed, falling back inside the hangar as he slapped the door controls. Nothing happened. He slapped the control again, still nothing.

"Okay, that's bad," Shelby said, turning and firing into the advancing horde again.

"Get back to the Shroud," Francisco yelled. He knew that there was next to no chance of them getting off the ground before they were overwhelmed, but some chance was better than no chance at all. He sprinted up the landing ramp and headed for the flight deck, hauling the body of Darkdoom's pilot out of the flight seat and stabbing at the controls to spin the engines up. Dozens of assassin robots were now pouring through the door and dashing across the hangar floor toward the others. Wing dropped his rifle and pulled the claymore from the long scabbard on his back. He ran toward the approaching droids with a terrifying battle cry, swinging the massive blade. The sword cut through the first few droids like a scythe, sending severed limbs and components flying in all directions as Wing became a destructive whirlwind. Kali sprinted forward and leapt into the melee beside him, scratching and tearing for all she was worth, while Laura, Shelby, and Penny continued to blast away with their rifles. Miss Leon ran into the Shroud and up to the flight deck.

"Are we ready to launch?" she snapped.

"Thirty seconds," Francisco replied. "They'd locked this thing down, I'm having to bring the engines back online."

Miss Leon looked out the window at the advancing horde as Wing and Kali began to be overwhelmed by the sheer number of attackers.

"We're not going to make it," she said quietly, glancing up at Francisco.

"I know," he murmured, his expression grim.

Outside, Wing grunted in pain as an assassin droid's claw raked his chest and another grabbed one of his arms, pinning it. He felt the sword being twisted from his grip as Kali yowled from somewhere off to his right.

"Wing!" Shelby screamed as she saw him fall. "No!"

Then the lights went out.

The robots that had been seconds from ripping them all limb from limb fell to the ground with a loud clattering sound, as red emergency lighting flickered on around the hangar.

"*Emergency systems online,*" a recorded voice sounded in the hangar. "*Switching to secondary reactors in two minutes.*"

Shelby ran toward Wing as he began to climb out

from under the pile of fallen machines with a pained groan. She helped him to his feet as Penny and Laura pushed more fallen machines off Kali, who was still breathing but badly wounded.

"Get her on board the Shroud," Laura said to Penny. "I'm going after Otto."

"As am I," Wing said as Shelby helped him to his feet.

"And me," Shelby said.

"Are you all mad?" Penny asked. "Those things could be back on their feet in a minute."

"Then leave without us," Wing said. "We will find another way out. I am not leaving my friend behind."

"What the big guy said," Shelby replied.

"Aye," Laura said with a determined nod. "I think I know where Anna will have taken him."

"How are you going to stop her?" Penny asked, looking at them as if they were insane. "You saw what she can do."

"We'll think of something," Laura said as the three of them turned and walked back into the school. "We always do."

Otto struggled fruitlessly against the iron grip of the robots dragging him down the corridor toward H.I.V.E.mind's data core. He had tried several times to use his abilities to assert control over them, but it had been pointless; Anna's abilities were too powerful. All he could do was wait and hope that an opportunity would present itself for him to put his backup plan into action.

The doors to the data core rumbled apart and they walked inside. Otto looked at the white pedestal in the middle of the room and saw H.I.V.E.mind's head hovering above it. His usual blue color had been replaced with the same deep red that Otto had seen when Anna had first remotely attacked the school. He also noticed that H.I.V.E.mind's head was now bowed, as if he was showing his obedience to Anna, quite different from how his friend normally looked.

"H.I.V.E.mind," Anna said as she walked up to the central pedestal. "How long till all of the satellites have firing resolution?"

"Seventeen minutes," H.I.V.E.mind replied. "I will notify you as soon as all targets are acquired." His voice was flat and lacking in any of the more recognizable characteristics that Otto had grown used to. H.I.V.E.mind had changed so much over the years Otto had known him, become so much more *human*, that seeing him like this was heartbreaking.

"What's the point of taking over the world if it's just a scorched radioactive cinder?" Otto asked as Anna turned back toward him.

"Oh, Otto, you do continue to underestimate me, don't you?" she said with a smile. "I'm not going to destroy the world, just a few bits of it. The areas that might put up any kind of resistance to what comes next."

"What do you mean, what comes next?" Otto asked with a frown.

"In just a few days, our siblings will be fully grown. And when they are, I will have prepared the way for them," Anna answered. "The world will be in total chaos, the centers of authority destroyed, and we will step into the breach and lead them out of the darkness."

"No one's going to follow you, you're insane," Otto said, shaking his head.

"What makes you think they'll have a choice?"

"You may be powerful Anna, but you can't enslave the whole planet," Otto said.

"Not on my own, no," she agreed. "But you don't understand yet what my siblings are capable of. Our powers don't just add to each other, they increase geometrically with each new brother or sister that is born. The first twelve of us will be enough to control the minds of millions at once—another generation or two, and we will be able to control billions. A true H.I.V.E.mind, not just an amusing pun."

Otto suddenly realized why she was so dangerous. He had met more than his fair share of megalomaniacs, but they were usually delusional. Anna had a concrete plan for quite literally taking over the world, and at this point there was no one who could stop her.

"Why do this?" Otto asked. "Why not try to use your abilities to improve the world?"

"What do you think I'm doing?" Anna asked, walking toward him. "Look at the world out there, Otto. Eight billion people, all driven by greed and self-interest. Left to their own devices, they won't need the weapons of mass destruction they've built to destroy themselves. I may be launching a handful of nuclear weapons in a few minutes' time, but that is nothing compared to the devastation they have already unleashed on their own planet. Very soon, perhaps even already, the damage they have done to the environment will be irreversible. As catastrophic feedback loops start in the planet's environment, humans will not be equipped intellectually or behaviorally to deal with them. They won't just wipe themselves out, they'll wipe out all life on the planet and leave it a boiling, sulfurous rock. We will save them from that."

"Or, you could try to help them help themselves," Otto said. "They're so much better than you believe them to be."

"*They*, Otto?" Anna asked. "Not *we*? You see, you're already halfway there. Join me and your brothers and sisters. You may have some human frailties now, but we can fix that. You can be part of our new world, a leader, a true savior."

"And if I do?" Otto asked. "What happens to my friends, the people I love?"

"They'll live in peace and contentment in a world that is finally run for the collective good rather than just to make a tiny percentage at the top of society richer and more powerful. Look at Furan, she's pathetic, a power-hungry fool. She's like a dog chasing a car, she'll never catch it and she wouldn't know what to do with it if she did."

"You can't judge the whole of humanity by its worst examples," Otto said, shaking his head. "Nero's spent his whole life trying to keep a lid on the chaos. That's what this place is actually all about, it always has been. He understands that humanity has to be nudged onto the right path, not brainwashed into following it."

"Too little, too late, Otto," Anna said. "They've got less than twenty years to turn things around. Tell me, honestly, do you really believe they will?"

"No," Otto said. "Not as it stands, but that doesn't mean they can't."

"You have more faith than I do," Anna said. "I refuse to sit by and watch. I will save this planet, one way or another. Will you help me?"

"Never," Otto said quietly.

"Why not?"

"Because someone once told me that there always has to be a choice—and they died fighting someone just as deranged and power hungry as you. I'll fight you to my last breath."

"Very well," she said. "You know you're far too dangerous for me to let you live. So why don't you just go ahead and *take that last breath right now.*"

Otto felt his free will slip away and his breath catch in his throat, as it closed up involuntarily. He struggled pointlessly against the robots holding him, feeling his lungs freeze.

Then the lights went out.

Otto felt the robots holding him loosen their grip as they toppled to the ground with a clatter on either side of him. In the darkness he reached for the pouch on his belt and pulled out the metal cylinder he'd concealed there earlier. He twisted the tube and pulled out the syringe inside.

"*Emergency systems online,*" a recorded voice sounded in the data core. "*Switching to secondary reactors in two minutes.*"

The room was suddenly bathed in red glow as the emergency lighting kicked in and Otto moved toward Anna.

"Oh, I don't think so," she said, and Otto fell to his knees in pain, his head filled with agony. She glanced at the seething black liquid in the syringe he was holding and grinned. "That was your master plan for stopping me? Poison? Pathetic."

"It's not meant for you," he said through gritted teeth, before jamming the needle into his own neck and depressing the plunger. "It's for me."

The Animus surged within him and felt like it was the most natural thing in the world, boosting his abilities to undreamt-of levels as he gave in to its power. Anna watched, her eyes wide as Otto rose to his feet, the veins in his face turning dark as his eyes filled with inky blackness. He didn't try to fight the Animus as he had in the past, he abandoned himself to it, feeling it integrating with the organic computer in his skull as if, finally, he had been made complete. Anna used her abilities, transmitting another wave of pain toward him, but it seemed to have no effect on him. He just calmly walked toward her.

"What have you done?" she gasped. She tried to use her abilities again, but Otto simply gave her a wry smile.

"I've upgraded," he said, feeling a strength like nothing he had ever felt before.

He reached out with his own abilities and started to interface with the computer in Anna's skull that was identical to his own. He showed no mercy as he twisted the psychic knife in just the same way as she had done to him, sending Anna to her knees gasping in agony.

"It's time someone taught you a lesson in the real use of power," Otto said. "Now, just *shut up and die*."

She screamed, staggering across the room clutching her head and falling against one of the white monoliths, reaching up and placing her hand on the white slab.

"This is not over," she growled at Otto. "I won't let you stop me."

The monolith began to pulse with fierce red light as Anna began to convulse, foaming at the mouth before her limp body dropped to the ground.

Otto ran to the monolith and placed his own hand on its cool surface. He reached out with his abilities, feeling Anna in the data core, as she tried to flee through the network to safety. Using every last drop of his remaining power, he dragged her digital spirit back into the core and then erected a series of powerful firewalls around it, trapping her inside. Now he could feel her hammering against the walls of her virtual cell, screaming at him to release her.

He dropped to his knees, feeling the power began to drain, and then slumped back against the pedestal in the center of the room.

"Otto," a familiar voice said. "What have you done?"

He looked up at the hovering blue head of

H.I.V.E.mind floating in the air above the pedestal.

"What I had to," he said weakly. "She's trapped in there." He nodded toward the monolith with Anna's body lying at its base. "She thought she could escape into the network, but I'm keeping her restrained within that data core."

"That's not what I meant," H.I.V.E.mind said. "You know that."

The doors to the room rumbled open, and Laura, Wing, and Shelby ran inside.

"Otto!" Laura shouted, seeing his blackened eyes and the dark veins running across his face. She felt a chill run down her spine. The last time she had seen him look like that, he had been possessed by Overlord. She held up a hand, telling Shelby and Wing to get no closer.

"Otto," she said cautiously, frowning. "Is that you?"

"Don't worry, I'm not a rampant, megalomaniacal AI," Otto said with a tired laugh. "Not today anyway."

Laura ran up and hugged him as he slowly got back to his feet.

"What did you do to yourself?" she asked, glancing at Anna's fallen body and then stroking the blackened veins on his face.

"Animus," Otto said. "Don't worry, I can still purge it from my system later."

"I thought it was all destroyed," Laura said.

"It is now," Otto said. "I just used the last of it."

"I am so glad to see you alive, my friend." Wing stepped forward and gave him a bear hug.

"I could say the same thing, big guy," Otto said with a smile.

"Knew you'd come up with something, byte brain." Shelby grinned.

"Don't I always?" Otto smiled back at her. "Get back to the Shroud and wait for me there. We need to return to the *Megalodon* and go and destroy the lab she was made in. I just need to make sure that all traces of her hack have been erased from old blue eyes here." He nodded toward H.I.V.E.mind's hovering head. "I'll be right behind you."

"Raven, kill him."

Then the lights went out.

Nero struggled against his bonds, but it was no good, he couldn't break free. A moment later, the cell was bathed in red emergency lighting.

"Emergency systems online," a recorded voice sounded in the hallway outside. *"Switching to secondary reactors in two minutes."*

Raven took a step toward Nero, drawing one of her swords.

"Wait," Furan said. "Not too quick. I want to enjoy this."

Raven gave a nod and walked over to the table with the various torture tools that she had recently used on

Nero, selecting a scalpel and turning back toward him.

"Take his eyelids first," Furan demanded.

Raven got closer to Nero and raised the scalpel toward his eye. But then she stopped, looking confused for a moment, and Nero saw the monstrous zombie who had tortured him disappear, replaced by the eyes he had known for so long.

"Anna's dead," he said calmly.

"What are you talking about?" Furan demanded. "How do you know?"

"Natalya," Nero said. "Explain it to her."

Raven whirled around, drawing the glowing purple sword from her back and driving it through Furan's heart in one fluid move. Furan gasped, her eyes wide with sudden shock.

"Die like your brother, you piece of dirt," Raven spat at her, her face just inches from Furan's, pulling the blade from her chest. Anastasia's hideously scarred face slackened, and she fell to the floor, dead.

Raven walked over and took the keys to Nero's manacles from the table, releasing him and letting him get to his feet. He rubbed his wrists as she began to walk away from him.

"What do you remember?" he asked quietly.

Raven stopped, then turned back to him.

"Everything," she said, and there were tears in her eyes. "Oh God, Max. I'm so sorry."

"It wasn't you," he said, coming to her, reaching up and stroking a tear from her cheek. "It was her, it was always her. She took everything from us. She took your mother and she took you from me, but it's over now, she can't hurt us anymore."

"I can't believe . . . all this time . . . we were . . ." Raven struggled to find the words to express the torrent of emotions she was feeling.

"I think in some way I always knew," he said, looking into the eyes that suddenly reminded him so much of Elena's. "It may have been buried by her witchcraft." He gestured to the slumped body of the Queen in the nearby wheelchair. "But you can only bury something like that so deep."

"We've lost so much time," Raven said.

"No, we haven't," Nero replied. "I've known you nearly your whole life and I could not be prouder of what you became after what she did to you. The fact that you're my daughter doesn't change any of that, it never will."

Raven hugged him tight, and he suddenly felt as if a weight he'd been carrying for thirty years had dropped from his shoulders.

"Come on. We need to work out how on earth we're going to put this school back together after all this," he said with a smile as Raven released him. He picked up his shirt from the floor, quickly slipping it on.

They both walked out of the cell and along the walkway. Nero was halfway across it when he stopped and walked back into the cell, seizing hold of and dragging Furan's body to the edge of the walkway, where he used his foot to roll her over and down into the boiling lava below.

"Burn in hell," he said quietly, and then walked away.

Franz and Nigel walked up the rear loading ramp as Nero and Raven strode quickly across the hangar toward the waiting Shroud.

"It's good to see you, sir," Francisco said as Nero walked on board. "We're just waiting for Mr. Malpense and then we can get back to the *Megalodon* and regroup."

"We seem to have several hundred pupils floating in the ocean," Nero said, raising an eyebrow. "I don't suppose any of you know how that might have happened?"

"It seemed like a good idea at the time," Shelby said.

"Hmm," Wing said, looking sheepish.

"One wonders how that would be possible without forcing entry to my office and breaking into my personal computer system," Nero said. "Perhaps you could enlighten me, Miss Brand? Miss Trinity?"

"I'm afraid it was my idea, sir," Miss Leon said. "It seemed the safest course of action."

"Indeed, I would probably have done the same thing myself." He looked down at the injured woman sitting next to Miss Leon, who was eyeing him suspiciously. "And this must be Kali," he said.

Kali hissed at him.

"You have to . . . ," Penny began.

Nero reached out and scratched Kali behind the ear, drawing an immediate, warm purr from the wounded woman-cat.

"I am quite aware how to make a cat happy, thank you," he replied.

"Yes," Miss Leon said quietly to herself. "You give her a pay raise. . . ."

Suddenly, the loading ramp at the rear of the Shroud began to whirr closed, and a moment later the aircraft's engines began to roar and it slowly rose from the pad.

"What the hell?" Francisco said, running toward the flight deck with Raven close behind. He slipped into the pilot's seat and killed the throttle, grabbing the stick, trying to bring the Shroud back down.

"The controls aren't responding," he said as the Shroud tipped its nose toward the sky and rocketed up and out of the crater, everyone on board grabbing for something to hang on to as the engines maxed out, afterburners roaring, sending them on a course to rendezvous with the distant *Megalodon*.

"What's happening?" Laura yelled. "We have to go back and get Otto."

"I have no idea," Francisco yelled. "I have no control."

Suddenly the screen on the flight deck and in the passenger compartment lit up. On them both was Otto's tired-looking, dark-veined face, his eyes still jet-black.

"Anna's not dead," he said, his voice weak. "She's trapped in H.I.V.E.mind's data core, but the moment I lose concentration, she'll break free again. There's only one way to stop her from launching the missiles at the cities she's targeted."

"Otto," Laura said, fear in her voice. "What are you saying?"

"I'm dying," he said. "I lied to you about the Animus. The sample was found in the ruins of the Advanced Weapons Project by the Americans, but the nuclear strike that destroyed the facility had made it highly radioactive. I can't . . . purge it, and it wouldn't do any good if I could, it's too . . . late. Knew it was probably a one-way trip . . . but . . ." He paused for a moment as if trying to find the strength to continue speaking. "But . . . I knew you wouldn't let me . . . do what had to . . . be done. I'm sorry for . . . lying . . ."

"No, no, no, Otto . . . Oh God . . . please don't . . ."

Laura sobbed, tears rolling down her face. "Bring us back to the school, let us help you!"

"Nothing . . . you . . . could do," he said. "Love you, Laura, love you all."

The screen went black.

Otto severed the video feed and slumped back against the central pillar in the data core. His whole body felt like it was burning, but there was one more thing he had to do.

"H.I.V.E.mind . . . open a . . . connection to the Absalom lab servers," he croaked.

He felt the data connection open and he effortlessly smashed through the supposedly impregnable firewalls surrounding it. His virtual self was stronger than ever, even as his human body died.

He issued a single command to the automated incubation systems.

TANK 1 . . . PURGED
TANK 2 . . . PURGED
TANK 3 . . . PURGED
TANK 4 . . . PURGED

He could feel Anna's rage as she thrashed against the confines of her digital cage; he made sure she could see what he was doing, it was no more than she deserved.

TANK 5 . . . PURGED

TANK 6 . . . PURGED
TANK 7 . . . PURGED
TANK 8 . . . PURGED

Anna's digital howl of rage echoed in his skull, any vestige of sanity she may have once possessed slipping away.

TANK 9 . . . VACANT
TANK 10 . . . PURGED
TANK 11 . . . PURGED
TANK 12 . . . PURGED

That was it. It was over. There was just one more thing to do. He connected to H.I.V.E.mind one last time, enabling the school's self-destruct protocols.

"Is . . . everyone at . . . minimum safe distance?" he asked, his voice now just a rasping whisper.

"Affirmative, all escape pods are clear of the perimeter, as is the *Megalodon*."

Otto felt the Shroud that he had hijacked touch down on the pad of the giant submarine and he relinquished his control over it, knowing that his friends were safe.

"I'm sorry . . . old friend," he said to the hovering blue wireframe head. "There's no . . . other way . . . to be sure."

"I agree," H.I.V.E.mind said calmly. "Otto, you have made me more human than I ever dared to dream possible and you have been the best of friends to me. I will miss that."

"So will . . . I . . . ," Otto said, feeling incredibly tired.

"Otto," H.I.V.E.mind said. "I am sorry, too."

"For what?"

"For this . . . ," H.I.V.E.mind replied.

Otto felt excruciating agony, his head filling with unimaginable pain, as though his whole consciousness was being torn apart.

"What . . . are . . . you . . . doing to me?" he screamed, writhing in agony.

"What has to be done."

As Otto slumped to the floor dead, H.I.V.E.mind triggered the small tactical nuclear bomb at the very heart of the volcano's magma chamber far below.

The Shroud touched down on the *Megalodon*'s landing pad, and Nero sprinted down the landing ramp. Darkdoom was already running across the deck toward him.

"Take us back to H.I.V.E.," Nero said. "We don't have much ti—"

He stopped in mid-sentence as the early dawn sky was lit up by a bright flash from the direction of the island. He turned, shielding his eyes as the volcano detonated in a cataclysmic explosion, huge chunks of rock and ash scattering across the ocean in all directions. A few seconds later, the shockwave hit them, sending everyone on deck staggering.

"No," Nero said softly.

Laura fell to her knees, a wail of grief escaping her, as Wing and Shelby dropped down beside her, wrapping her in an embrace; all three of them watched in horror as the remains of the school continued to tumble into the ocean, rivers of lava flowing from its shattered shell and into the sea.

H.I.V.E. was gone.

In a darkened chamber, a long way away, an empty tank with the number nine on it began to slowly fill with pink liquid.

Meanwhile, servers hummed, absorbing and analyzing the massive data transmission they had just received from an unknown source.

A minute later, the display at the bottom of the tank flared into life.

NEW PROGRAM.
SEQUENCING COMPLETE.
PERSONALITY ENGRAM STORED.
COMMENCING ACCELERATED MATURATION.
PROJECT 0110

299 Days 23 Hours 59 Minutes 59 seconds to completion.

299 Days 23 Hours 59 Minutes 58 seconds to completion.

299 Days 23 Hours 59 Minutes 57 seconds to completion.

chapter thirteen

One year later

"What is this, Natalya?" Nero said, looking at the object he was holding as if it might explode.

"That is a Father's Day card," Raven said with a grin.

"I can see what it is." Nero placed the card on the table next to the scattered blueprints. "But I would hardly describe myself as . . ." He picked the card up again and read the message printed on the front. "'The world's greatest Pops.'"

"Don't you like it?" she teased.

"I've killed people for less," he said. "Well, strictly speaking, *you've* killed them for me, but my point stands."

"Someone's grumpy today," she said, sitting down on the crate beside the table. They were currently based in Darkdoom's construction facility, which was serving as a temporary home for the school while designs for the new facility were being finalized.

"It's just these designs," Nero said, gesturing at the blueprints. My father and the professor have been working nonstop for the past week to make sure that they're ready for the start of construction, but I still feel they're missing a certain *je ne sais quoi*."

"Not enough secret passageways?" Raven asked, looking down at the plans.

"Indeed, one can never have too many secret passageways, my dear," Nathaniel Nero said as he approached. "It's simply not possible. How's my favorite granddaughter today?"

"Hello, Nathaniel," Raven said with a smile. "I'm fine, thank you."

"When did you get back from the Philippines?"

"Yesterday."

"Successful trip?" he asked.

"Well, they're going to need a new president, so . . ."

"So, yes, very successful," Nero said. "Now, about these latest plans . . ."

On the other side of the huge chamber, Franz was taking some first-years through basic weapon-stripping training.

"So, you see, the easiest way to prevent a jam like this is being to make sure that these parts are well oiled . . ."

"Mr. Argentblum!" One of the students raised their hand.

"Yes, Martin," said Franz.

"Is it true that you knew Otto Malpense?" the boy asked.

"Yes, Martin, I did," Franz said proudly. "He was one of my best friends."

"What was he like?" another student, a girl, asked.

"He was very clever and very brave and he saved the whole world on at least six occasions," Franz said. He was used to fielding these questions from the younger students, Otto having assumed something of a mythological status within the school after his death.

"Really?" the girl asked. "That sounds like it's made up."

"It does, doesn't it?" Franz said with a smile.

There was a sudden bustle of activity on the other side of the chamber, and the huge sea doors at the far end of the dock rumbled open. The *Megalodon* slowly slid through the opening, coming to rest at the dock as Darkdoom's men prepared supplies to be loaded on board.

"That's enough for now," Franz said, glancing over at the giant submarine. "Class dismissed."

The first-years gathered their notes and books as Colonel Francisco walked over to join Franz.

"So, how is my newest Tactical tutor getting on?" Francisco asked.

"Good, thank you," Franz said. "Though I think that Mr. Lewis might be trouble."

"They're all trouble, Franz," the colonel said with a smile. "That is, after all, sort of the point."

"*Ja*, I suppose so," Franz said. "Would you mind excusing me, sir? I haven't seen Nigel for a few months and I wanted to go and say hello."

"Of course, Franz, tell him I said welcome home," the colonel said.

Franz walked over to the gangplank that had extended out from the *Megalodon*'s hull to the dock and gave a wave to Nigel as he walked ashore.

"How was the trip?" Franz asked.

"Long, boring, but successful," Nigel said. "We think we've found a deep-sea trench that would make a perfect spot for the new school."

"Indeed we have," Diabolus Darkdoom said, striding down the boarding ramp and clapping Franz on the shoulder. "Good to see you again, Franz, how's teaching treating you?"

"What, you mean apart from half the final-year students having a crush on him?" Nigel said.

"You can't help being popular with the ladies, can you, Franz?" Diabolus said. "It is a cross I, too, have had to bear for many years."

"It's not just the ladies," Nigel said quietly.

"Teaching is highly rewarding," Franz said, blushing slightly. "Though it would be nice to have some slightly better facilities."

"We're working on it." Nero approached with Nathaniel. "Hello, Diabolus, how was the voyage?"

"Excellent. Nigel's found you a perfect spot for the new facility," Diabolus replied. "Man-eating sharks and everything."

"Hopefully, construction won't disturb the local eco-system too badly," Nigel said. "We're going to need more deep-sea construction vehicles, though."

"Have you seen the construction budget recently?" Nero said with a sigh.

"We should be able to break ground next month," Nathaniel said, shaking Darkdoom warmly by the hand. "Although I suppose technically it's break seabed, in this case. A fully submersible facility, it's going to be magnificent."

"It's going to be expensive," Nero said with a sigh.

"Natalya!" Diabolus said as Raven joined them. "How's my favorite Nero?"

Nero thought back to the moment when he'd told his oldest friend the truth that Natalya was his daughter. Darkdoom's response, after a moment's surprise, had been quite simple. "But of course she is."

"Very well, thank you, Diabolus. And thank you for

the pair of Tantos, they're beautiful," she said.

"I'm glad you liked them," Diabolus said with a smile.

"To be honest, it was just good of you to remember my birthday," Raven replied.

"Oh, I'm never going to be allowed to forget that, am I?" Nero said, rolling his eyes.

"Hello, Diabolus," a female voice said behind him.

"Tabitha!" Darkdoom said. Miss Leon walked toward him holding Kali in her arms, both of them looking much happier to be back in their old bodies. "I see the professor was as good as his word. I must say it's a *definite* improvement," he said, taking her hand and kissing it.

"He really is quite incorrigible, isn't he?" Raven said quietly to Nero.

"Yes, yes he is." Nero sighed.

Wing sat in silence, legs crossed, and eyes shut.

"It's boring, Mr. Wing," a child's voice said, interrupting his meditation.

"It is supposed to be boring, Carlos," Wing said, not opening his eyes. "One must find peace through inner tranquility."

"Can we start hitting people soon?" another voice asked.

"No, Maria, first we must find peace," Wing replied,

his eyes still closed. "Remember that violence is only ever a path to peace. Violence without purpose only begets more violence."

He heard a familiar snigger from somewhere behind him.

"Okay, children," he said, opening his eyes. "That's enough for today, open your eyes."

The assorted children in front of him, none older than ten years old, did as they were instructed.

"Shelby!" the children shouted as Wing stood up and turned to her with a smile. His students swarmed around her, hugging her and bombarding her with excited questions.

"Did you have an adventure?"

"Have you brought us presents?"

"Can we do more of your lessons?"

"Why do we have to do meditation?"

"Okay, okay!" Shelby yelled. "I am very glad to be home, but I'm stinky from the journey and I need a shower or Mr. Wing won't want to kiss me."

"I wouldn't be so sure of that," Wing said, picking his way through the excited children and embracing her. "Though, yes, you are just *a little* stinky."

"Don't push it, big guy," she said with a grin, and kissed him. "Missed you. How've you all got on?"

"It has been a long week," Wing said with a sigh. "But fun, yeah, children?"

"Meditation's boring," one little boy said. "I thought Mr. Wing would be doing 'hitting people' this week, but it's just been sitting with our eyes closed a lot."

"Which is really dull," another young girl said.

"It is, isn't it?" Shelby said. "Tell you what, tomorrow we'll have a whole day of Shelby lessons, how's that sound?" The suggestion was met with much cheering and excitement. "Right, you lot, wash up before dinner. Come on, scoot."

She ushered them all out of the wooden dojo that Wing had recently built.

"Violence without purpose only begets more violence?" she said with a snort as the last one of the children ran out the door. "I so wish I could show them some of Mr. Wing's old school videos. . . ."

"A world I have left behind," Wing said. "As have you. Did you have a good trip?"

"Yes. It was lovely to see her," Shelby said, walking out of the hut with Wing and into the dusty sun-baked playground outside.

"How is she?" he asked with a slight frown.

"Okay. Still sad, sometimes, but better than she was." Shelby sighed. "You know what it's like with the big brains, they think too much. She misses him."

"We all do," Wing said, looking up at the hand-painted sign above the door to the main building on the other side of the playground.

"I should come with you next time," Wing said. "It's been too long since I saw Laura."

"I know, big guy," she said. "Give it some time, though. I think it's hard for her to see us—we bring back a lot of bad memories."

"That, I understand," he said with a nod, a sudden sadness in his eyes.

"Come on, I'll show you what I found on my shopping trip." Shelby smiled.

"Shopping trip?"

"Well, I had a stopover in London and there are all these really beautiful, not terribly secure, jewelry stores."

"Shelby . . ."

"What? This place isn't cheap to run, you know." Shelby gave him another smile as a jeep pulled up just inside the main gate in a cloud of dust. "Looks like we've got visitors. You want to go deal with them?"

"Of course," Wing said with a nod.

He walked over to where two men in tatty old military uniforms were getting out of their jeep.

"Can I help you, gentlemen?" Wing asked as they approached him with rifles slung over their shoulders.

"I don't know," the first soldier said. "You in charge of this place?"

"I'm one of its owners, yes," Wing replied. "Why?"

"Because I want to know why you're not paying for

321

protection like everyone else in town," the soldier said. "What makes you so special?"

"Nothing," Wing replied calmly. "I simply do not believe in giving in to extortion."

"Oh yeah?" the other soldier asked. "Well, maybe we should show you why you need protection, especially with such a pretty girlfriend." He threw a sucker punch straight at Wing's jaw.

Up on the veranda, Shelby watched the events of the next twenty seconds with mild amusement. She felt a small hand tug on the leg of her trousers, and she looked down to see one of the children who was also watching the unfolding scene below.

"Miss Shelby," the little girl asked. "Is Mr. Wing finding inner tranquility?"

"Yes, Lisa, that's exactly what he's doing."

"Dougie, no," Laura said, taking the envelope that the toddler was busy chewing out of his mouth. She put it down by another on the table and sighed.

"Come on, Brand, make your mind up," she said, looking at the two envelopes in front of her. "Oxford or MIT."

"Are you sure I can't post it on social media?" Mary Brand asked her daughter as she walked into the room. "Just a wee brag to make the other moms jealous."

"No, Mom, you can't," Laura said. "You shouldn't be

using social media anyway. I told you, it's poison."

"Aye, but funny, gossipy poison," her mom replied with a smile. "What's the point of your daughter getting unconditionally accepted into the two best computer-science courses in the world if you can't tell everyone?"

"And let's not forget what the letter from MIT said." Laura's dad sat down next to her. "What was it again? 'One of the most exciting candidates that the interviewers had met in years.' You can't help it—you get your brains from your father."

"If you believe that, you'll believe anything," Mary said, picking Dougie up and dumping him in her husband's lap. "At least you didn't get his looks."

"Aye, well, she may be a genius, but that doesn't get her out of doing the drying up," he said. "Even Einstein had to do chores."

"I'll make a decision tomorrow," Laura said. "There's no rush."

She got up from the sofa and walked into the kitchen, picking up a glass and drying it with a tea towel, star-ing absently out across the back garden to the Scottish Highlands beyond. These days she was much happier thinking about her future than the past. The past was still too raw a wound.

The front doorbell ringing brought her out of her thoughts.

"I'll get it!" she said, walking out into the hall, still holding the glass.

The next thing Mary Brand heard was the front door opening, then the sound of shattering glass.

"Laura! Are you alright, love?" Mary asked, but there was no reply. She got up with a slightly worried frown and walked into the hallway.

"What on earth—"

Laura was standing on the doorstep, hugging a boy like he'd disappear if she let go of him. A boy with snow-white hair . . .